T0060808

'As affecting as it is intellectually agile, *Diego Garcia* achieves what few novels even aim at—it opens up fresh ways of reading both history and fiction.'

— Pankaj Mishra, author of *Run and Hide*

'In reading Diego Garcia, we transcend the 'I' of the singular, towards the 'we' of the collective: of nation, homeland and of a people displaced. Through the intricately woven histories and the corresponding fictions within fictions, the compassion expressed in Diego Garcia highlights the absence of it in those who, forsaking their obligations towards other human beings, exiled the Chagossians from their home, and in doing so impressed upon themselves a kind of exile of the spirit, a penetrating sadness witnessed through the melancholy characters of this story and the society that looms as their backdrop. Written in a language at once distant and interior, dazzling, we see that until the Chagossian people are home, nobody is home.'

— Vanessa Onwuemezi, author of *Dark Neighbourhood*

'Focusing on the ongoing atrocity of the Anglo-American occupation of the Chagos Islands and displacement of their native people, *Diego Garcia* is a subtle contemplation of the uses of fiction and narrative (for good and bad) and how, where and why individual and collective narratives meet. Taking in artists from Kader Attia to Sophie Podolski, as well as depictions of the Chagossians in poetry, documentaries and essay films, it is a moving study of friendship, allyship and creative forms of political struggle.'

— Juliet Jacques, author of *Trans: A Memoir*

'*Diego Garcia* is an important and highly original work, incredibly well-researched and thought-through.'
— Philippe Sands, author of *The Last Colony*

'Listless and urgent, dulled by sadness and yet dancing with anger, moments of unexpected beauty and strange, bright comedy—in *Diego Garcia*, these tensions are held together by the energy of a singular collaboration, where the interplay between fundamental separation and common cause is staged even at the level of page layout, the writing of the sentences themselves. It is a novel of shared and unshared experience that is wholly unapologetic about not knowing how such a thing is to be written, but risking it nevertheless. The result is compelling, challenging, unprecedented, essential.'
— Kate Briggs, author of *This Little Art*

'*Diego Garcia* is a beautiful, poignant, anarchic experiment in collaboration and collectivity. This novel does wonderful, innovative things to form and to politics—to style, to voice, to creolisation, to propaganda and power and archipelic thinking—and especially to the denials inbuilt to British novels and British politics. Somehow it finds a way of exposing Britain's ongoing shameful occupation of the Chagos Islands while also being a document of literary resistance and originality. It offers models for future thinking.'
— Adam Thirlwell, author of *Lurid & Cute: A Novel*

'This thought-provoking, brilliant book sends a hypersensitive probe into the subduction zone between solidarity and exploitation.'
— Nell Zink, author of *Avalon*

Published by Semiotext(e)
PO BOX 629, South Pasadena, CA 91031
www.semiotexte.com

Cover design: Lauren Mackler
Design: Hedi El Kholti

ISBN: 978-1-63590-162-7

Distributed by The MIT Press, Cambridge, Mass. and London, England
Printed in the United States of America

Natasha Soobramanien
and
Luke Williams

Diego Garcia

a novel

semiotext(e)

At the heart of this novel are two real events. One is a personal tragedy. The other is historical, though its impact continues to devastate people's lives today: the expulsion of the Chagossian people from their homeland, the Chagos Archipelago in the Indian Ocean, by the British government between 1968-1973, so that the largest of the islands, Diego Garcia, could be leased to the US government for the construction of a military base.

It is this event we wish to highlight here: the facts of it, and their foundation on a fiction.

The facts are these: in 1965, at the behest of the US government who had expressed an interest in the island of Diego Garcia as a site for a strategic military base, Britain coerced Mauritius, then a British colony, into ceding part of its territory, the Chagos Archipelago, as a condition for independence. Not only was this strategy of partial decolonization a breach of international law but the British government created from the ceded territory a new colony, British Indian Ocean Territory (BIOT), at a time when the international community had committed to a global process of decolonization.

In 1968, the year of Mauritian independence, the forced exile of the Chagossian people to Seychelles and Mauritius began. They were coerced into abandoning their homes, communities and stable employment for a hostile environment, and lives of extreme precarity and misery, with families broken up across two countries lying over 1,000 miles apart. Those who did not survive are deemed by their community and those who support their struggle to have died from a condition called sagren.

At the time of writing, the Chagossians continue to fight for reparations and the right to return to their homeland. Meanwhile the base at Diego Garcia is still operational, and remains one of the US government's largest bases on foreign soil. The Chagos Archipelago is now recognized by the United Nations as Mauritian sovereign territory. Britain's continuing control of the territory allows it to pursue geopolitical ambitions in the Indo-Pacific region, namely inclusion in AUKUS, the strategic military pact with the governments of Australia and the US announced in 2021.

In our novel we have referenced, through the testimony and research of others, the facts of these events, identifying some of the Chagossian people who suffered as a result, but who nevertheless resist the injustices that continue to be perpetrated against them and their descendants by the British government. For example, in echoes of the ongoing Windrush scandal, the continued breaking up of families through systematic deportations of younger members of the Chagossian community who do not share the status of British citizenship granted to their elders under the current law.

In highlighting the *facts* of this event we must also highlight its foundational *fiction*: the one collaboratively authored by the British and US governments in 1965 In making the false claim to the United Nations assembly that the Chagos Islands had no settled population, we ask readers to note that the UK and US governments claimed by implication that the Chagossians' status as a people was a *fiction*.

— Natasha Soobramanien and Luke Williams
November 2021

In memory of Saul Daniel Williams
and for all those who have died of sagren

"Rann Nu Diego!"
— Chagos protest chant

"The coalition emerges out of your recognition that it's fucked up for you, in the same way that we've already recognized that it's fucked up for us. I don't need your help. I just need you to recognize that this shit is killing you, too, however much more softly, you stupid motherfucker, you know?"
— Fred Moten

DANIEL & DIEGO

I. DEBT

This is the story of a book we are still writing.

* * *

Edinburgh, July 2014. The sluggishness of early afternoon. The sky clouding over, a slight chill in the air. The same *uninterrupted sadness*, a kind of listlessness that went with everything we did. We'd made it to the Meadows. It had taken us a while to get out of the flat, him offering to buy us a coffee from the Swedish café and one of those cardamom buns we liked so much if she would come to the library. We noticed how people passing noticed us. She noticed how much thinner he was than in London, joggers slipping down on his hips, constantly tugging at the waistband. We slowed our pace. We were still talking about the morning as if something out of the ordinary had happened, when really we'd spent it the way we spent every morning, him coming to her room with coffee, her accusing him of switching the heating off, him denying this. He'd told her, We really must get up earlier. It won't help to stay in bed. This because we sometimes spent entire days in bed. In the kitchen she lit a tube, picked the raisins out of his cereal, milk still unpoured, put them with the other raisins extracted from other breakfasts. *Currency* she said, They'll see us through The Emergency. He ate. We stared at his opened screen. We argued about whether to cycle to the library. But the sky seemed unsettled and unusually close from up here, on the sixth floor. We decided to walk. The billboard above ScotMid still read 'Straight Talking Money. Wonga'.

In the Meadows, some kind of fair. Tabletop stalls and food tents. Let's mill she said. He began to look for something—a set of *Encyclopaedia Britannica* 1911—he was *always* looking for a set of *Encyclopaedia Britannica* 1911. By the time we met again the rain was falling. She took him to a stall and said, I'm buying this dress. Is that a dress? Yes she said. She paid then disappeared with the dress, made of material with some kind of special effect, like oil on water. When she came back she had it on over her jeans and rain-coat. Just imagine there are whole loads of famous people who were never photographed she said. He thought about this. She thought: He looks like a young Nosferatu. Max Schreck. He would not know which screen star to liken me to because he's ignorant about these things.

A fine rain. Dim light through the cherry trees. We walked away from the fair not speaking and when we reached the part of the Meadows that opens onto the tennis courts, just before the university library, we turned up onto Middle Meadow Walk. Ignoring the unbroken row of posters—comedy acts appearing next month at the Festival—not ready to stop—not ready for a coffee or a bun or the library—we took flight at the traffic lights and cut through Bristo Square, after that letting ourselves be carried by chance. And *the sadness opened out.*

* * *

The city is built on several hills. There are valleys and there are bridges and there are stairwells that connect the two. In those days we would stop on one or another of the bridges and lean over to observe the streets. Sometimes we watched the gardens but never the rail tracks. It was frightening and thrilling to come upon these sudden and dramatic views, which made us think of the postcards sold everywhere on the Royal Mile and all over the city for that matter. 'The Old Town and the Grassmarket', 'Cowgate at Night', 'Princess Street Gardens', 'Princess Street Looking West'. We would stand there looking down but she didn't say what she would have said before: We're too fuckin scared to jump.

Because, when we walked, we failed to take in our surroundings, and because when we stopped walking we usually stopped on one of the bridges and looked down, we always had the sense of living above the city, of looking down—dizzy—on its many faces. We watched people flowing past as though caught in a flood. Knowing the city this way, from above, having arrived only recently, we didn't feel part of it, though it had once been part of him, the city of his student years. We were nervous and irritable. This seemed to increase our togetherness. It gave us—only us together, not individually, never alone—a place in the world that we had not had before. We wandered the streets, unwelcome, leaning miserably into the wind or drinking ourselves stupid in a pub. All of this under the ugly haar-obscured sky that we didn't realize we'd invented ourselves.

* * *

The first time she saw him was in a photograph on a website for a magazine. She thought he looked odd and his story sounded odd. She couldn't find the story anywhere but found his email address. He could not send her his story because he had bought all the remaining copies he could find of that particular issue of the magazine and had shredded them at the vulgar, pseudo-political, faux-Dada readings he had given for a while at various art schools and gonzo bookshops—though he didn't tell her any of this. The first time we met she said, I hope you've brought money and he said, I have. She showed him a photo of V. S. Naipaul and said, This is my dad, we don't speak. He pointed out a figure in the audience and said, That's my brother, he rarely speaks. Or else he never stops. Later when we went for a meal, Daniel came too and he and Daniel ate like rats let loose in a grain-store, even finishing the leftovers on a nearby plate, and it was sad but in the end it didn't matter all that much. The second time we met it was at a party in a library. The party was honouring a famous English writer—one of those realists who writes like a politician—whom she approached saying, Do you want my autograph? The second party we went to together was a few months after that. We happened to be in Edinburgh at the same time. We found ourselves in a basement bar. We talked *beautifully* about Can Xue, Dambudzo Marechera, Elfriede Jelinek, all the while drinking ourselves stupid. At one point he came back from the bar with two shots of vodka spiced with hot chillies, we chimed the glasses and she said, To the Mauritian Greats, Devi, Pyamootoo, Appanah, Patel. I am indebted! We drank the vodka down and he said, Hang on! He ran downstairs to the toilet and boaked into the bowl. Meanwhile she'd gone and got talking to a dangerous-looking character who could not look or step or speak without a sparking flow of words conveying his stupid thoughts spilling into the smoky room. By the time he returned from the toilet she and the character were on their way out. She said, Come on come on, we're going to a party. We left the bar and hailed a taxi. We drove through town. We looked out the windows at the passers-by, many were dressed as police, or perhaps they were police dressed in uniform, and many others were dressed in kilts, and we burst out laughing because we remembered it was New Year. The party was at Restalrig then it wasn't so we drove on further out of town.

Our character was subterranean, his style of conversation mineral, the way the headlights of the passing cars slanted across her face seemed to dazzle him. London she said when the character asked. He handed round the tubes. She said, Can we? and the character said, This is Scotland and opened his mouth wide to catch the tube and lit it while his sparking words continued to flow. Can I have some of your water she said. Without stemming the sparking he reached into his jacket pocket. With his left hand he passed her the water, with his right an Apple Mac, she drank it down, eyes expanding like cameras chasing mirages in a desert. Would you mind not talking so much he said to the character. Jesus, OK. But the sparking…

We heard the party before we saw it. Felt the speakers in our chests. It was in a field somewhere up the coast, on a small promontory. Red 2 playing as we got out the cab. The character threw his head back and yelled, grabbed her hand, pulled her to the stage. He found them pressed up against the wall of speakers. The character reached out to encircle her with his arms (she didn't move away) while the sparking flowed into her ear. She stood still, shivering slightly. Then the sparking was in his ear and he moved away, back through the crowd, he saw one of Daniel's friends who told him Daniel was here, he went to look for him then needed to boak, and then there was Daniel, dancing & she started to dance thinking: Where is he I want to talk to him. She took another Apple Mac and the sparking.

When we came together again it was among a group sitting on the edge of the promontory. From there we could see the black and white sea, the moon, the character gone. Two women were building up the fire. A guy was pissing off the promontory. There were seagulls we heard above the noise of the music and the sound of the waves. Where is she I want to talk to her? Then we were next to each other and Daniel was there and Daniel was trying to tell us something. What? Do you know. What? we said. Do you know the German word for. What? we said. The German for. What? The German for promontory is *half-island*.

* * *

Standing on North Bridge, the station roof like a hothouse roof. The rain gone, the afternoon swelling with warmth. She took off her raincoat. *The sadness*—amplified by something with an edge that felt like hunger. Some kids were throwing bottles onto the mess of broken panes. Now is a dumb lie. Her screen flashed, 'Unknown number'. She didn't answer. Since coming to Scotland she almost always kept her screen powered down. She was afraid that RBS, with their clever moves to try to recover the substantial sum she owed them, would find out she was in Edinburgh, right under their noses. She was also afraid but defiant of the nefarious tactics of DCA Mappots, the debt collection agency EDF had sold her less onerous but not insignificant debt on to after two years of failing to recover it themselves. He said, Why don't you just answer? She said, Why don't you stop giving advice? He had given his screen away a few months previously, straight off the train from London, numb and crazed, to a teenager who'd asked us for change. Now he didn't have a screen of his own. He wasn't on Facebook, Instagram, Twitter, etc. for the same reason: The Emergency. She respected his viewpoint and listened with grave concern to his theories concerning asset bubbles, derivatives, guns and whisky and hollowed-out Bibles, total surveillance, TEOTWAWKI, the precariat, Charles Ponzi, the distribution of pornographic images and images of abuse, the totally administered society, the Pharmacopornographic era, structural adjustment, Bitcoin, gold, hunger, debt—personal, civic, regional, national, federal, continental, intercontinental, transnational, global, universal, dark pools of—but she could not rouse herself to respond in any particular focussed way. Even so, she did not want them watching him. He did not want them watching her. He did not want them watching us. We did not want them watching us. She did not mind them watching her because she didn't believe in them, not really, not when it came down to it.

The kids smashed another pane on the station roof, all of the panes dazzling in the sun, now the broken bottle too. She took off the dress from the fair and threw it onto the roof and we watched it being dragged here and there by the wind, which wasn't so much wind as a kind of constant agitation of *stuff*, the kind that collects around those sites of perpetual transition such as railway stations, docks, border crossings, motorway service stations, etc. She put her raincoat in our bag. She leant her elbows on the bridge, rested her chin in her hands. He took a deep breath, feeling really shit. Allowing *the sadness* to overwhelm him, he closed his eyes and rested his head on her shoulder. She smoked a tube. He started to doze. Her/his shoulder/neck felt warm against his/her neck/shoulder. We stayed there resting on top of the bridge while she, not taking her eyes off the station roof, tried to remember a dream she only now realized that she'd had. It had left her feeling lost. She was trying to find her way back into the memory of it, to the almost pleasurable sadness it had left her with, searching for the point where it had begun. But then her ringing screen pulled her back, and his needling about her not answering. He had been in the dream too. A dream about that day in London, the time they tried to find Daniel. The blue honey of the Mediterranean, that's what Fitzgerald said he'd said.

It was the kind of thing he would say, the quoting of a writer. At least it was the kind of thing he *used to* say. Since we'd come to Scotland she could not remember him doing it once, this previously constant quoting thing. Unlike most white men who liked to quote writers he would quote as many Black and brown writers as he did white. Dambudzo Marechera:

> Whatever insects of thought buzzed about inside the tin can of one's head as one squatted astride the pit-latrine of it, the sun still climbed as swiftly as ever and darkness fell upon the land as quickly as in the years that had gone.

But all men. Always, always men. She had had to teach him to read women, and now he read mostly women, and no longer quoted.

She shook him and without knowing she was going to say it, said, I'm hungry. Do we have any cash? He lifted his head off her shoulder—feeling really shit, almost violent—saying, Yes, but we should go to the library. I need spaghetti vongole she said, they have it at Marcella's. Not wanting to feel violent. She took out a tube and lit it to take the edge off her hunger. I don't think they have it at Marcella's he said. We stood in silence while she smoked, looking down at the station roof. The dress was still there. Why did I throw the dress away? The kids had gone, leaving smashed panes and the dazzling. When she'd nearly finished her tube she said, Let's ea then go to the library. OK he said, but I'm not hungry. You can't share mine she said. She took a fresh tube from the pack and lit it with the still live butt of the first.

It was at the moment of ignition that we first laid eyes on Diego.

* * *

He was standing on the opposite side of the road, visible in flashes between passing cars, bent over a heap of bags. He seemed to be looking for somewhere to sit down. Why didn't he just sit down on his bags? Maybe he didn't want to. We watched him thrust his hands into the pockets of his jeans then pull out a small black notebook. He squatted down, unzipped the side pocket of one of his bags and took out a pen. He balanced the notebook on his knee and wrote in it. When he stood up again, he looked around, nervously. No—more than nervous he seemed afraid—his fear telegraphed by every jerky and deliberate movement and by his body which he held as if about to break off down the street, away from the heap of bags.

What was he writing? He said, Do you think he's OK? He thought: *Daniel.* The neon numbers above Argos showed 14:10. He felt his face break out in a sweat. Then she said, He looks like he's waiting for someone. No he doesn't. Let's go she said. We started walking along the bridge, in the direction of Marcella's. The noise of the trains, the electric sound of the track, the roof shaking in the sunshine. He stopped. We could be friendly he said. What do you mean? Show him around or something. Does he look like a tourist? He has bags. Too many she said, anyway I'm hungry. It would give us something to do he said. I thought you wanted to go to the library. We carried on walking along the bridge toward the High Street. Every now and then we turned to look back at the man. A bus with an ad for Wonga—'Tired of waiting? Money in your account in 15 minutes. Wonga'—stopped, blocking the man from our view. We waited for it to move. Some school kids got off, they were carrying screens playing a song, the same song at different times. The bus drove off and he said, I'm going to speak to him. He lit a tube and darted back & she thought: There's something in the way he's holding his tube down by his thigh there's something about the way his back suddenly looks a bit less collapsed & as he got closer to the man he examined his face, about his own age, early 30s maybe & she watched how he—back straighter still—gesticulated, tube in air, then tossed it to the ground, stamped on it carelessly. The man seemed wary at first but then smiled taking out his own pack of tubes, patting his pockets, saying, Wait a minute, I don't have my lighter, saying it in an accent he recognized from her family! Always a surprise to her and so to him to encounter a Mauritian accent in people not personally known to her. She thought: When he frowns he looks older and when he smiles he looks younger. But there was something else, what was it? My friend has a lighter he said, and jogged across the road to her, saying, Can I have our lighter? I'm going to give it to that man. You want to give our lighter away? Yes he said. Arsehole she said handing him the lighter. He said, I think he's Mauritian! I recognize the accent. He turned and faced the traffic, almost bounding across the road.

* * *

She asked him what they'd talked about but he didn't say, just that when he heard Diego's voice he was sure he was Mauritian. Did you ask? No he said. I should have gone over and spoken to him she said, but I'm too hungry. You can do that later, we're meeting him for a drink.

On our way to Marcella's we passed Till's. He wanted to go in. She didn't. In this mood she could not be persuaded to do anything unless it involved food or the promise of food, so he offered to pay for lunch. Spaghetti vongole she said. Till's sold mostly novels. Some of the novels were old and some were new and written in a slightly different style from the old which now read exactly like the new. We browsed the novels then went to the back room where the shelves were labelled History, Social Science, Philosophy, Literary Biography, Botany, Psychology, Science, Popular Science, Reference—a set of *Encyclopaedia Britannica* 1933 (incomplete)—and Film. We hung around by the Philosophy section where there was an armchair. She sat down. He happened to pick up *Minima Moralia* by Theodor W. Adorno. He happened to sit down on the arm of her chair and flick through it and stop on page 42. The section was called 'Articles may not be exchanged'. Honest giving is impossible in these inhuman times, Adorno wrote. We read:

> Instead we have charity, administered beneficence, the planned plastering-over of society's visible sores. In its organized operations there is no longer room for human impulses, indeed, the gift is necessarily accompanied by humiliation through its distribution, its just allocation, in short treatment of the recipient as an object. Even private giving of presents has degenerated to a social function exercised with rational bad grace, careful adherence to the prescribed budget, sceptical appraisal of the other and the least possible effort. Real giving had its joy in imagining the joy of the receiver. It means choosing, expending time, going out of one's way, thinking of the other as a subject: the opposite of distraction.

He folded the corner of the page. This made her angry. She reached across to unfold it, scolding him because it wasn't our block. Also because the corner folding suggested he was getting interested and might stay to read on and she was hungry. Let's go she said. He didn't answer. It was hard to concentrate especially when she was looming over his shoulder like she was and he could hear her breathing and even see the page lifting slightly from her breath, but he thought he'd understood the gist of Adorno's argument. Moment of lightness.

It was hard to concentrate when she felt as hungry as she did but she'd been moved by what she thought was the gist of the argument, despite her hunger and its present insatiability. She thought: blocks blocks blocks and not a fuckin thing to eat. Ten minutes you said she said. Don't you think this is amazing? he said. She was too hungry to understand and this was making her angry. The point about object and subject was clear enough. What was hard to grasp was the last bit. What does Adorno mean by distraction? What about my spaghetti vongole? He said, Let's finish this paragraph, then we'll go, I promise. Which made her even angrier. Which made her even hungrier, that dangerous spiral known as *hanger*. He began to read aloud:

Beside the greater abundance of goods within reach even of the poor, the decline of present-giving might seem immaterial, reflection on it sentimental. However, even if amidst superfluity the gift were superfluous people who no longer gave would still be in need of giving. In them wither the irreplaceable faculties which cannot flourish in the isolated cell of pure inwardness, but only in live contact with the warmth of things. A chill descends on all they do, the kind word that remains unspoken, the consideration unexercised. This chill finally recoils on those from whom it emanates. Every undistorted relationship, perhaps indeed the conciliation that is part of organic life itself, is a gift. He who through consequential logic becomes incapable of it, makes himself a thing and freezes.

He thought this was one of the most brilliant things he had ever read. She thought it might be brilliant but her hanger was preventing her having any kind of nuanced understanding. Each word evaporated before she'd fully registered its meaning. Soon her hanger would prevent her not only from understanding this or any other argument in *Minima Moralia* but pretty much anything at all— whether philosophical argument, moral argument, negative dialectics, the workings of chance, questions from tourists, how DCA Mappots had got her number, why the green person was never green when we came to the lights—the condition of *hanger* being something like debt during The Emergency in that its growth factor is exponential, the greater one's hanger the more difficult and specific its assuagement becomes, which meant at this moment—as we left the shop and headed at pace across the Meadows—it was no longer enough just to eat spaghetti vongole from Marcella's, the spaghetti vongole from Marcella's had to satisfy a particular set of requirements which became increasingly precise as her hanger raged unchecked, e.g. it was important that the dish be *hot enough* when served, without being *so hot* that she could not immediately eat a mouthful and begin to arrest the hanger. We passed the fair. It was busy. He said, We're nearly there. He thought: It's almost 3 and we're still not at the library. She said, I want a Coke with my spaghetti vongole. She thought: can you move please can you move please can you just fuckin move THANK YOU. He said, OK (conceiving of forms of giving which might be possible when The Emergency is over). We reached the edge of the Meadows and spotted Marcella's. He thought: Emergency, the rule and mode of existence hence never over. He tried to say something about giving and The Emergency. Don't talk to me she said. It was no longer enough that the spaghetti vongole be *hot enough* without being *too hot*, now it had to have the correct ratio of sauce to pasta and vongole to sauce, fresh not dried parsley, and if the sauce appeared with the tell-tale bubbles of microwave convection—

but there was no spaghetti vongole.

In Marcella's she swore at him. She tried to swipe the napkin holder off the counter but he removed it in time. As we left she was almost in tears saying, Fuck this let's just get a pie. Back across the Meadows. The sun hot. Tourists and students in our way. Progress slow, the people, peopling paths, the grass, everywhere, moving in all directions. She waited outside while he bought a chicken pie, a cup of tomato soup and a can of Coke. We took her lunch to Greyfriars Kirkyard, pushed through the tourists. Our usual bench near the entrance, near that long list of buried bodies. She sat down and ripped open the bag, tearing off pieces of pie with her teeth, muttering to him—now sat down next to her—with a mouthful of pie, Don't talk to me. *Distorted relationship*. Suddenly she stood up half-sobbing and flung the pie across the yard. It hit a gravestone, disintegrated. Lumps of white sauce on the stone, chunks of white meat sliding. He said, Drink your Coke, please? He walked over to the gravestone. Bent to wipe it with his napkin and pick up the bits of pie, then turned back. You hit Greyfriars Bobby. She shrugged. Greyfriars Bobby, the dog he said. I know who he is. I'm sorry. My pie was cold. She started to cry. It's OK he said. Dogs love pies. Right she said, dogs *are* greedy bastards.

* * *

They is the THEY. That's what Marechera said she said.

* * *

(30)

A bench outside the pub we always went to, though it was not our favourite pub. The sky clear and bright and the sun hot but not too hot. *The sadness* as always but the listlessness abated just a bit. He'd bought a new lighter, a pack of tubes, two pints and now we were sitting and smoking. The pub was dead inside, through the window yellow with dust and reflections we could see the barperson with their mongrel who was sleeping. The picnic bench where we were sitting was dry. None of the slats was missing like on some benches outside pubs sometimes and it was stable on its legs too. She helped herself to a third tube—she normally chain-smoked while drinking—and he did not object. He was too excited to care. Nose like a beak poking in his bag, a mumbling coming from the bag which could have been *Leave me alone* or *I feel great*. He reemerged. Flexed his shoulders. Then he took two tubes and tossed one to her. She lit it and held it between her knuckles then lay her arms flat on the table and leant forward, resting her cheek on one arm and letting the tube just burn. She said, What's wrong with you? He said, I'm thinking. About what? I don't know he said. Yes you do. You're thinking about Adorno. No, I'm not thinking about anything. She lifted her head and took a drag of her tube, looked at him directly. I demand you tell me what you're thinking about. Then when he didn't answer she said, You're not looking yourself these days.

A motorbike drove by noisily. A sort of tearing sound. Once, we walked through Regent's Park with Daniel in the early morning, passing the zoo, hearing a tiger roar—a tree being torn up. She lifted her head from her hands and said, Look at me. Do this with your mouth. As the noise of the motorbike receded we looked at one another, she opened her mouth wide as if she were afraid—he didn't move his mouth—she smiled with her teeth showing, she closed her lips and furrowed her brow. We continued to look at one another but he didn't move his mouth or change his expression in any way. You know what? she said, It's those stupid glasses. Why do you mend them with Sugru? He reached inside his bag and took out *Minima Moralia* and began to read. Did you buy that? It was a present. He said this without looking up from the page. Who from? He didn't say anything but carried on reading for several minutes. All clear now but not like he'd thought. The argument about giving and capital. She leaned her arms on the table and rested her cheek on one arm. After a minute he looked up from *Minima Moralia*. He said, It was stupid of me to give Diego your lighter. She didn't move or say anything, just let the tube burn itself out. He looked at her hand then returned to the page. Her tube burned completely out and she sat up and threw it under the table. She said, That was Scottish giving. What? He looked up from *Minima Moralia*. Scottish giving. It's when you give something away that belongs to someone else. Huh? You know, like 'Indian giving'. Meaning someone gives you something then takes it back: you know, white settler-colonialists murdering Native Americans and calling it trade? *You* are being a *Scottish* giver—being Scottish. But I gave you that lighter in the first place he said, and I took it to give it to someone else— someone who needed it. *Needed?* We stopped talking and sipped our pints. He put *Minima Moralia* on the table and thought about The Emergency, then he looked at her, at her beady eyes, and he thought about how clever her eyes looked, especially with her green raincoat. Hey and what about the block? she said, That's a kind of giving. You're right. The shop gave me the block. I suppose but I was thinking more about the writing of the block. Didn't Adorno write it for his friend's birthday? German giving she said: a gift that places a burden of reciprocation on the receiver. After a while, smiling at her, he said, Mauritian giving: when you give something with a flourish in a show of great generosity when it's something you owe anyway. Like the Chagos Islands she said, That's what the *British* would say. Britain says Mauritius *gave* the Chagos Islands to them… That Mauritius *owed* them to Britain, in exchange for independence. The US thinks it *owes* Diego Garcia to the British but really the British owe the Chagos Islands to Mauritius, who owe it to the Chagossians. The pub was in a courtyard, overlooked by antique buildings. Our voices resonated. She said, Mauritian giving is when you give something great to someone who doesn't really deserve it. Well, Scottish giving is when the gift is so much greater than the recipient deserves that it dignifies the receiver. Sounds like Adorno she said. Not exactly he said, Adorno says—I was *kidding*, you arsehole! Then, No, sorry, tell me, I want to hear. He thought for a moment. I don't want to talk about it right now.

She finished her pint. She stretched her arms out in a curious way then rubbed the back of her neck. He lit a tube and said, So what about American giving? Oh that's when you give something with a huge flourish and lots of pomp but the gift is shit. Or lethal. He finished his pint and went inside to order more from the barperson who was trying to attract the attention of the decrepit pub dog. He left the barperson pouring the pints and took a piss then splashed water on his face & she picked up *Minima Moralia* and read the page he'd been reading, a section called 'Doctor, that is kind of you' which she thought very good & he made a murmuring noise in front of the bathroom mirror and closed his eyes tightly like he'd been staring at a bright light & she put *Minima Moralia* down and examined the composition of the rubbish below the table, empty packets of Walkers, Snickers, an empty bottle—green glass with the label peeled off, some tube stubs, all the same brand, the wrapping of a Subway sandwich, a till receipt from Starbucks & he thought of the comics whose faces lined the Meadows and how unfunny or even tragic they looked collectively & she thought about Diego and wondered if all of those bags had meant he had arrived from somewhere or if he had nowhere to go & he dried his face continuing to look into the mirror his eyelids now stinging, wide open and the water still cold on his skin and he decided he knew nothing & she thought about whether it was bad or good his habit of stealing bad blocks from chains to leave in shops that sold good blocks so he could steal good blocks of equivalent *financial* value from them, the five finger discount she thought, and then she thought about how 'discount' can mean 'not to consider' & he moved his eyes slowly from the bathroom mirror to the bathroom window because he'd seen a group of tourists, he could see them now looking up towards the top of a building, and he could see that they were laughing, and their guide was laughing, and fuck it the sky was laughing too, and so were the open windows of the building and he tried to think how he could tell her this & she thought that she should have brought a block or bought one from the shop but she couldn't bring herself to read another one after the one she'd just abandoned, *Women as Lovers* by Elfriede Jelinek, whose Nobel Prize lecture-performance remained her favourite of Jelinek's works & he thought it wasn't OK but then he remembered *Minima Moralia* and how everything had become clear to him earlier, suddenly, but not the way he expected; his hatred of capitalism, it being the very thing preventing him from doing anything whatsoever—not having to just hate but love it too, the two at the same time, & she thought about an idea for a story or maybe not maybe an essay but more fictional and why not a kind of fictive criticism? or maybe it was just a good title, 'Factory girls', an essay comparing Bolaño's dead girls from the *maquiladoras* and Jelinek's poor bitches in the bra factory, and she thought about the job she had had in the turkey processing plant one summer when she could never rid herself of the smell of fat and became vegetarian for five weeks though treacherously she could not remember the first bite of meat that had hooked her back & he thought how it was a double bind but anyway that was better than this fuckin... this *massive* amount of hatred blinding him so that its effects had been a done deal & she wondered if she would give him the German gift of a block she had written just for him—he always mocked her for dedicating her first and only published novel to her parents, while she mocked him for dedicating his first and only novel to her—and she thought about the block she once bought him for Christmas, a 'celebration of writerly friendship' which he had taken back to the shop and exchanged for Knut Hamsun's *Hunger*, while his present to her had been a jumper with holes under each arm & deciding he'd better get back he turned from the mirror and walked out of the bathroom with a tenner in his hand to pay for the pints, but when he got to the bar he saw the barperson had fallen asleep on a stool with their head on the bar & and she thought what she would give him was music because unlike Daniel he didn't know jackshit about music in the most dumb and basic way and she remembered playing him 'Hallogallo' by Neu! and him nodding his head more birdlike than ever, as though he was pecking at the ground, saying it was good music to write to and writing to it as he said it, and she lit another tube and gagged which was a sign she had drunk too much too fast and smoked too many tubes and she thought maybe The VU, he only knows the obvious ones, the sweet tinselly ones, but she detected in him of late a taste for *Gelassenheit* and wondered if this was her influence which made her laugh out loud a honking sort of laugh to think how outrageous he'd find her & he turned from the barperson to the dog who was whining but louder now he was moving towards it & what is that noise she thought and wondered where he was & as he got close to the dog it began to tear at the webbing on the underside of the barperson's stool, but despite this the barperson didn't wake up, so he knelt down beside the dog and made a sucking sound with his teeth and rubbed his thumb and forefinger together until he got its full attention & it was true that he'd love 'The Murder Mystery', specifically the simultaneous recitations of competing lyrics and contrasting choruses, he'd find it very *contemporary* she thought & then it occurred to him that the mongrel had the wiry long hair of a lurcher but the flabby flanks of an ageing lab & she thought of the very first time that she knowingly heard The VU which was also the very first time she had tasted espresso which was in the bedsit of a busker ten years older than her who she'd followed home, a beautiful long-haired woman with a broken smile who had looked at her sad then proud when describing how, inspired by The VU, she had once been a heroin addict and how some months later when she had forgotten all about her, this woman had rung her up from a phone box asking for help and how she had made an excuse for why she could not see her thinking, What does she want from me, I'm only 16 and how that first song, the one that had prompted her to ask, What *is* this? was called 'The Gift' & he thought if Daniel had been a dog he would have been a lurcher, he had a peculiar love of dogs, not strange when you consider his vegetarianism, but perhaps strange when you consider what bitterness he had at times for all things living except perhaps for her. He stroked the dog's head until he'd calmed it and gently led it away from the bar and towards its bed, then he went to the bar, picked up the pints and returned outside to the bench.

We looked at one another as if all the strangeness of the day was not a new experience. After all we often got side-tracked from the library and not infrequently ended up at the pub. But the day *did* feel strange and, in being strange, felt surprising, an instance of insanity or hunger, insanity-hunger, what Marechera called the *House of Hunger where every morsel of sanity was snatched from you the way some kinds of bird snatch food from the very mouths of babes.* We picked our pints up and each lit a tube and after a short pause he looked at her and said, Tell me about English giving. It's when you give something to someone that really you want for yourself… *you* English-give all the time. What do you mean? Well for example every block you've ever given me you've wanted to read yourself. OK he said after a while, that's true. No! What about that, oh who was it by? It was the bad kind of autofiction you love to read. Remember? When we were in Brussels? I remember she said, but you didn't *give* that to me. You bought it for me because I didn't have any money. You never have any money he said, how come you never have any money? How come you always have money? We heard a scratching sound and looked up. The mongrel was trying to get out of the pub. Let the poor thing out she said. He got up, opened the door then returned to the bench. She reached out and gently stroked its temple. The dog followed then began sniffing at the rubbish below the table, sticking its muzzle into the bright packets and licking the sugary, salty stuff inside. Get outta here she said and nudged the dog gently with her knee. The dog moved off and lay down outside the door of the pub. We sipped our pints. What were we saying? I can't remember he said. There was a pause. Come on, you *do* know. What? I really don't! You don't? No! he said. You do, yes you do she said I want to know. He didn't say anything. Tell me! He pretended to rummage in his bag before finding the packet of tubes on the table then lighting another. She looked at his hand, thinking, the way his fingers move ever so slightly the way the smoke rises without it seeming to rise. She looked directly at him but he just looked at her as if confused and smoked his tube. She thought: *If pressed to say why I love him I'd reply, because it was him, because it was me.* OK she said, in that case I'll tell *you*. We were talking about how come you have money and I don't. It's because my credit rating is better than yours. That's not hard she said and slumped on the table. Then, after a while, I thought we were having a nice time. She took the screen from her pocket, turned it on. It flashed—*debtfuckersdontanswer.* He said, They'll never find you here. She turned the screen off and put it in her pocket. We put our elbows on the table and our heads in our hands our faces close together. If it makes you feel better he said, I have less money than you, I mean when you count how much I owe. Tell me, she said. Will it make you feel better? She nodded. He thought for a while. I don't know. I know *who* I owe money to though. I have an overdraft from HSBC and another one from Co-op, a handful of student loans, a bank loan I took out when we couldn't pay the rent last year, credit card debt I pass from one card to another whenever they send me an offer. What else? A bike-to-work scheme loan. But you lost your job and your bike got stolen! Yes he said, but I still owe the money. He drank down half his pint. So as well as what I already told you, let me see, I owe working tax credit because I signed the form too late, and there's money I owe T-Mobile because I didn't finish my contract before I chucked my screen. Arsehole she said. Then, What about Daniel? He must have left debt. Yes he said. He had a student loan, and he owed me, as well as the library at Goldsmiths. That is strange she said. What's strange? What else but money can you have less than none of? Wait, I owe even more he said, There's PayPal and the library, two libraries! Some of that debt was from blocks I borrowed for *you* and—wait—I haven't included the public debt I'm paying back, I mean all of us, every poor fucker. Ah yes she said, that billboard ticker thing in New York. The National Debt Clock. The numbers constantly ticking up, I can't remember how much it was when I saw it but it was a lot, it was… I don't know, it was fuckin… it was a massive amount of dollars, and then below the National Debt Clock there's another set of numbers also ticking up but more slowly and it said 'Your Family Share in Dollars'.

* * *

When we left London Daniel was dead, but at that time and for a long while after we had thought of him not as dead but *dying*. Not *dying* in the sense of a gradation, a shading from life to death, but stuck in a continuous present, an enduring, in the form of this gerund that was not-*living*. We thought of Daniel's *dying* as we had always thought of his *dancing*. Daniel was not always *dancing* but when he was *dancing* he seemed in a state beyond *living*—*living* being a state to be endured, while music for Daniel completed a circuit in his brain, animated him, *moved* him. Or moved *through* him: while Daniel was *dancing*, music was *living* through him, relieving him, in that moment, of the duty of *living*. And that is how Daniel's *dancing* made time overwrite itself, continuously, in precisely the same way that the thought of his *dying* did, for us.

* * *

Bankocracy consists in circulating debt to make money solely from money and time. The primary relationship between a creditor and a borrower is not important. Everything is arranged in order to multiply the number of people involved in the chain; debt must circulate to the point that the debtors no longer know to whom they owe money. A state that wants to offer reassurance regarding its solvency need only increase its penetrability. In reality, it is of little importance if it will be able to repay what it owes. The objective is not for debt to be settled but for it to circulate in order to produce profit. Strictly speaking, 'what one owes' is not to return the money but to continue playing the game. The imperative is less to keep a promise than to make the structural adjustments so that promises can multiply. What is important is not the initial promise but further surplus-promises, the game of simulacrum and its bluffs.

* * *

Diego was standing by his bags outside the library, blocking the pavement. We said hello and each picked up some bags, Diego took the rest and we walked to Sandy Bell's on Forrest Road. Inside it was hard to hear because there was a fiddler playing, but we talked anyway. We talked about the weather we talked about the city we talked about the independence vote. We talked about mountains and she and Diego talked about Mauritius. We talked about her name and Diego's: from a nineteenth-century popular novel and an island named for a Portuguese colonial explorer, though Diego told us that Diego was not his real name but the name he now chose to go by. We talked sometimes in English and sometimes in French and then she and Diego talked in Mauritian Kreol. We leaned back on the bench and exhaled. We watched our reflections in the window and drank our pints. We bought more pints and one for the barperson, who we wished was our friend. We talked about boats we talked about cancer. We exited to smoke tubes, first she and Diego with him guarding the bags, then him. When we started to talk about tubes Diego told us about the packs he'd brought over en route from Mauritius. They're called Horseman and they're strong and foul-smelling. His favourite brand is Sportsman. He has a load in his suitcase. Do we want to buy some? OK we say, we love the name but we don't know the brand. We decide to look it up on YouTube, on Diego's screen. We watch the best goals of the season we watch the National Debt Clock live we watch piglets being kicked across a pig farm in Kentucky we watch Stromae singing 'Formidable' and falling about in the street in Brussels right where we'd been the year before, but nothing is like the ad for Sportsman tubes. We love the song for the ad. We sing it. We buy more pints and we drink them. We watch our reflections in the brass trim of the bar. When we run out of money we sell several packs of Horseman to the fiddler and buy more pints. Diego points to his bags and tells us what's in each. Tubes. Shit plastic toys. Codeine. Saris. He talks for ten minutes about the fake Nike. Then he asks us what we do and when we tell him we're writers he says, Have I got a story for you. We ask about the notebook. What were you writing? Wandering lines he says. Can we see she says and Diego says no, some poems are not for you. We exit to smoke tubes. He says he wishes Arsène Wenger was his dad. Fuck Wenger says Diego, he lacks the killer instinct. We take codeine. He can no longer feel his feet. He doesn't know whether this is because of the codeine or his vegan shoes. Diego says to the fiddler, I'm watching you and we exit to smoke tubes. Where do you feel you are from? No one has ever put the question like that before she says then says London but not any more. And you? He is the only one who has not spoken these last minutes. He cannot stand straight. He goes to buy a Coke from the shop across the road and when he returns she and Diego are gone. Shit he says. He drinks the

Coke, thinks he should eat something, then goes to buy an iron bru. He feels like having sex with a stranger. He doesn't feel like but anyway contemplates jumping from a bridge. He explains to himself that really it is best if he goes home. He starts walking & she and Diego are holding hands in the toilet of Sandy Bell's. Let's get out of here she says and they stow the bags under their bench, then exit Sandy Bell's & he is walking off too, he can't feel his feet, the world is colourful, things go on and on & she's thinking that's what's so sad about anything and how he'd said nothing's worth anything in the end and how she'd said that's not true there's got to be something worth *something* and how he'd said do you have a point here at all? do you? do you?

II. INDIVIDUALISM

July 2014, Edinburgh. The brightness of the morning. Sky flat. No clouds. When he came into her room with coffee she was already awake. She didn't tell him to go away or chuck a pillow at him. She didn't swear at him or hide her face in the duvet or ask him to go fetch tubes from the kitchen only to block his return with a chair. She was sitting up in bed, eyes closed, her notebook on her lap, pen moving slowly across the page. Was she awake? She put the pen down and opened her eyes. He was wearing a thin cotton robe thing of hers. She said, You look really great, like that Guibert photo of Foucault. He put our mugs down then climbed up beside her. He was trying to decide whether he was upset about what had happened—her leaving him outside Sandy Bell's, her staying out with Diego. She said, You missed a *great night*. What happened? We mostly just talked. *He* talked. About what? Oh, lots. The man's a *storyteller*. And the way he puts things! *Some guy in a wig made my sister British.* What about Diego? He was born too late for a British passport. Is that what you're writing down he said, Things he said? Yes she said. Also things he made me think. She waved the book around. She was writing in it upside down. Is that *the* notebook? Yes she said, Daniel at one end, now Diego at the other. They might meet in the middle. Me and Diego met a submariner from Faslane! She told us about being on submarines. Under the sea for ninety days! Beds like coffins! Messages from home held back till you land! No daylight no fresh air no fresh food! And the *smell*! I never know where the fuck I am she said, they never tell you. Then Diego said, You could have been in Diego Garcia!

He handed her a mug, saying, Drink your coffee. I don't want coffee I want Lucozade she said. Then, without pausing, That's where they keep the torture cells. On ships in the lagoon. That's why they can say, *We Don't Torture Anyone ON Diego Garcia*. She lifted her jeans off the floor with her big toe, hooking it through a belt loop, tossing the jeans onto her bed. She pulled a crumpled pack of tubes from the pocket—Horseman—then we went to smoke out the window. The billboard above Scotmid still read 'Straight Talking Money. Wonga'. She said, Last night I remembered that when my dad first joined the RAF they sent him out to Gan. That's like 200 miles south of Diego Garcia! He didn't answer so she said, I'm sorry I left you last night, I'll never leave you again… It's just we wanted to talk in Kreol. He said nothing. You don't have to talk she said, I'm fuckin crawling with stories. Write them down he said, at the library. I don't know if I can she said, suddenly feeling tired and nauseous, The light hurts. Put your sunglasses on he said, I'll treat you like a star in rehab.

* * *

The branding of Horseman cigarettes is a rip-off of Sportsman. Instead of the profile of a horse's head there's a profile of a horse with a jockey on its back. The artwork is the same—a drawing in eighteenth-century realist style—and the packet is the same red as Sportsman. But instead of Sportsman (in lowercase) it says HORSEMAN. In 2007 British American Tobacco Kenya, makers of Sportsman, sued CUT Tobacco Kenya, makers of Horseman. The judge said: It has to be observed that the use of the colour red as the predominant colour in a packet of cigarettes is not the exclusive preserve of anybody including the plaintiff. The judge said: Having regard to all the above different characteristics of the get up and/or appearance in the two packets, particularly the principal colours thereof whereby one packet (Sportsman) has two major colours (red and white) while Horseman has one (red) it is my opinion that there is no way anyone who is able to see clearly could be deceived by the appearance of the two packets.

* * *

The Meadows. Buskers. Her walking on ahead, his hand on her shoulder. *The sadness* as always but today it was *funny*. How sad things were how shit we felt. We were ridiculous! She was feeling better. She felt a charge of happiness and broke into a run. He noticed that her check shirt was buttoned up wrong, the neck too open, jeans falling off her hips like a 14-year-old boy. He found her standing next to a busker who was playing the VU's 'Ride Into The Sun' (she recognized it, he didn't). The busker was not singing but she was: 'It's hard to live in the city / It's hard to live in the city, oh—oh—oh.' Come on star in rehab he said, taking her arm. She leaned over and whispered in the busker's ear. The busker nodded, started to play. Something sweet and broken like birdsong and then she began to sing and then he did too. She has a frail voice that cracks sometimes and his is maybe too low but we didn't mind. *Sunrise and love love love love ever lasting.* The bright sun, the dust off the path. Sun Ra. A tear, now tears rolling down her cheeks. Seeming sad but also joyful or comic because of her shades, which was odd, shades and tears, like celebrities at funerals, or stars in rehab. Her nose started to run and she wiped the snot with the back of her hand the way boxers in their gloves do. She ran off toward the Swedish café.

When he entered the Swedish café she was sitting at the table we liked to sit at, her mood changed. The light was hurting again, she was feeling the nausea, feeling awful. She said, Will you get a coffee? Can't you? No she said, I don't want to look at anyone. You're wearing sunglasses. I don't want anyone to look at *me*. He looked at her. The question is, she thought, How long can my skin hold me in? She said, Will you please just get a coffee please.

The thing about the Swedish café was that sometimes we liked it and sometimes we didn't. It depended on our mood, on whether we were taking things personally that day. Often we couldn't bear it, yet we stopped there most days on our way to the library. Even at the time we wondered why we kept going, despite the prices being steep despite the shelves being filled with desirable products we couldn't afford despite it forming an unexceptional part of the totally administered society. He might tell her that he liked it because the coffee was good and because it took credit cards and didn't have wifi. And she: because the cardamom buns were *delicious* and because the workers were friendly and looked so good in their grey-brown aprons. And he: if we were feeling stupid or insane when we were there our thoughts and sentences seemed less stupid and more sane. Yes she might have said, it could bring a sense of unhurried calm to the most agitated emotions. But the real reason we continued to go—although we did not articulate it at the time—was because of a fantasy. While we attributed *the sadness* to the systematic contradictions of life under The Emergency, there were times when this conviction faltered, and we'd dismiss the idea of The Emergency as just that, nothing more than an appealing totality. We'd attribute *the sadness* locally, to our own personal deficiencies, or else we'd feel so fragmented we'd say simply, *I feel shit* or *I'm losing it. It's nice to talk like everybody else, to say the sun rises when everybody knows it's only a manner of speaking.* It was then *the sadness* became a feeling we could no longer share. Sure, it was something we had in common, we both felt shit and/or mad more or less often. But its effects on us were so radically different—she: drinking herself stupid, over-social, spending whole days in bed, spiralling; he: ranting, not eating, researching emergency supplies, going over Daniel's final days, trying to work out what he could have done differently, looking quietly critically stupidly at the ground—that we forgot that our feelings resulted from the same phenomena. At such times, the only correspondence in *the sadness* was that s/he seemed bound to suffer it on her/his own. We failed to recognize it as something bound up with uncontrollable global abstractions; instead we'd turn for comfort to that *scene of community* offered by the Swedish café. The clean wooden décor, the smells of home baking and *delicious* coffee, its open-faced staff, its notice board advertising infant yoga classes, writing retreats in the Highlands.

He returned from the counter. Her arms were spread on the table, cheek on arms, head empty. He nudged an elbow aside and put down the coffee and bun. She felt very strongly that her head was close to breaking. He sat down and took a sip of the coffee which was *delicious*. He considered taking his screen out to look over his notes on *Minima Moralia* or one of the other blocks he was reading, or else to try to look again at one of the things he thought he ought to be writing. She thought: If I move my arms my head will fall apart. He thought: If I take my screen out something might happen. Then: Something *always* happens, my thoughts peter out, they wander off like *cats*. She thought: What's he doing I hope he doesn't drink all the coffee. And he: No, *rats*, the thoughts scurry away like rats. He looked up at the people in the café with their screens and their blocks. He looked down, her eyes were half-open, we looked at one another briefly. She thought: Can't see his eyes just the light on his glasses. She closed her eyes, thinking, If he gets me a straw I could drink some coffee without moving my head. She opened one eye and looked around. Scrubbed wood, yellow sun, reflections off the glass. He cracked his knuckles without realizing he was doing it, thinking, Every morning we look at the billboard opposite to see what's changed. He again: We were better off in London after all, at least we were writing then, at least we'd written blocks that were published and read… reviewed even, at least we managed to turn up to the library, to keep regular hours. Now we can't seem to write anything. *I* can't seem to write anything. As for her, she never stops! But she never finishes. She thought: I really could do with a fuckin straw. He: But then again we do get the odd teaching gig, and there is the not infrequent invitation to do *something* which is better than *nothing*

Straw!

Since nothing feels possible—and isn't this what Daniel thought

Straw!!

As if the point is to carry on writing whilst achieving nothing with the writing

STRAW!!

I need a fuckin *STRAW!!!*

He lowered his face to hers. If-you-get-me-a-straw she said—I-can-drink-some-of-this-coffee-and-I-will feel-better. He was impressed by her strategizing.

Once she'd drunk she removed the straw from her mouth and slowly, carefully, sat up. She felt a rush of feeling and looked at his face. She began to eat the cardamom bun, offered him some, he shook his head. I used to have to fight you off for these she said, you lost your taste for them? He said, Tell me more about Diego. Did he tell you more about his mum? About Diego Garcia and Chagos? She stood up and almost toppling the chair dashed to the bathroom where she boaked into the pristine wooden bowl that functioned as a sink.

When she returned she was feeling calm and her stomach was a bit calmer. We left the Swedish café. We could hear the busker. She was playing 'Rock & Roll' by the VU, which we like to play in the mornings if we're feeling *all right*.

* * *

On our way to the library. The day brighter still, light shifting on the paving slabs. Her screen flashed—*debtfuckersdontanswer*—and she threw it at the ground with all her force. He ran to collect the scattered parts, she carried on walking and we came together at the traffic lights, the sun on our faces, *the sadness opening out to something like joy*. He slid the screen together, handed it back to her. Did you go back to Diego's? You've got it all wrong she said. Last night was about the *stories*. And I've still got the post-traumatic sex disorder. Hetsex is so *fucked*. She took his arm. We crossed Lauriston

(49)

Place onto Forrest Road. She stopped to light a tube. Then she told him the following story.

* * *

Me and Diego were having a great night, we'd been to a few different places and were walking through the Meadows. This couple was passing and the bloke said something to us, or Diego *thought* he said something to us, something unacceptable. So Diego stopped, called after him, told him to come back, then when he didn't, ran at him and pushed him onto the grass. Then we saw that the bloke was really young and the woman with him was really young. She was wearing a cross around her neck, a gold one on this very fine chain, which she kept pulling at. And the bloke, as he picked himself up and moved quickly to hold his girlfriend, shouted at Diego, asking what the fuck he thought he was doing. Diego looked shocked, like *he* was in shock. But still there was this thing that had been said that the man said he had *not* said. But it felt to me like it was the *cross* that had shaken him. I gave Diego my arm and he took it, sort of stunned, and we walked away, him leaning on me. His stare—I was suddenly reminded of Daniel. It was then that Diego started telling me about himself. His mother had only been a kid when the British made them leave Diego Garcia. I knew about the Chagos Archipelago and how the British had forced the Chagos Islanders to leave because the Americans wanted to build a military base there, but to hear the story from someone who's lived it, whose life has been shaped by it... She'd been only a kid herself when she'd had his sister and then him. And younger than he was now when she'd died. His dad was Mauritian, a junkie, totally absent. So Diego and his sister Rose were raised by his dad's parents. They ended up with better prospects for it: good home, good education, even university if he'd wanted. But he'd lost all connection to Chagos he said. His mother's story. She was Catholic he said, but my dad's folks weren't. Not that she ever went to church he said. Too ashamed. And he started to cry. So I started telling him about my own parents, them coming from Mauritius to London, still pretty much kids when they'd had me, my sister. My mum's job washing bodies in the mortuary, my dad going into the RAF to give us all a future. How he always talked about the time he got posted to Gan. These crazy photos of unbelievable beaches and British soldiers in uniform on them, my dad one of them. The box of shells he brought back, that we played with as kids. How they came from the same sea.

* * *

With controversy still raging over Britain's treatment of the islanders of Diego Garcia when the atoll was handed over to the United States Navy ten years ago, Whitehall is negotiating compensation terms for another group of Indian Ocean islanders—the Maldivian and Pakistani inhabitants of Gan—which could prove just as politically explosive in another ten years.

This time there is no question of evacuation, except by the RAF, which is scheduled to pull out on 1 April next year. And nobody else has been invited to move in. On the contrary, the strategic object of the negotiations is to make sure of keeping the Soviet Navy out of what could be an exact counterpart of the base facilities the US Navy wants to provide for itself in Diego Garcia.

But the human problem of compensating local people for the arbitrary whims of imperialist policy—albeit in Britain's case a decidedly faded imperialism—is the same.

Gan is an airfield staging post on the military supply route linking the UK with Hong Kong. It also has a deep-water lagoon, ideal for naval refuelling. About 900 Maldivians and 100 Pakistanis are employed there, but not housed, they come over each morning from neighbouring islands in support of RAF personnel. Military flights will continue to call there until the end of the year after which the base will be rapidly run down.

* * *

There were things we liked about the city and things we disliked about the city. We liked the fact that our credit stretched further up here than in London. We disliked the office/lifestyle apartment buildings that were appearing around the Meadows. We liked the fact that the Sainsbury's on our way home from the library had a well-stocked 'reduced' section which we called the 'gourmet' section. We disliked the New Town, that unimaginative part of the city where the buildings seemed to have no insides. He liked that with her it felt like a new city, though he had lived there before. She liked that although she was new to the city it already felt familiar to her, the way a museum can make the past seem recent, even if it is not your past. We liked the tap water because it tasted different, fresher, and the light which made everything appear as if filtered. We disliked the wind but sometimes we liked it, though not when it made us cold and knocked us about. We liked the galleries, the national modern one and the long unspeaking waterside treks we'd take to get there. And the Portrait Gallery where the portraits seemed to have no faces at all, just paint. We liked that the city has a volcano in it, an extinct fake-looking one that looks down on a royal palace. We disliked the Royal Mile although she liked the sound of bagpipes but only live bagpipes. We liked the gruffness/gentleness of the people, and that we never knew which we'd get, or even, sometimes, which was which. We disliked those English boys and girls from Edinburgh University who wore pyjamas in the street, and the spectral whiteness of the city's centre. We liked not feeling part of the city, which didn't seem part of the world but like the absence of any kind of world.

Of his incarceration, Stiegler says: 'I no longer lived in the world, but rather in the absence of a world, which presented itself here not only as a default, but as that which is *always* in default, and as *a necessary default*—rather than as a lack.' Stiegler says: 'the milieu in which we live is, like water is for a fish, that which is most close and thus *structurally forgotten*; water is what the fish *always* sees; it is what it *never* sees.' Stiegler says: 'While incarcerated I considered the milieu while being able to extract myself from it, in the same way as a flying fish can leave the water: intermittently.'

Because the things we liked about the city outnumbered the things we disliked; or rather—since we could always find more things to like and dislike—because the quality of our appreciation for the things we liked outweighed the negative effect of those we didn't, we had the sense that that strange city, which we would not leave until it had set its mark on us, was a better place than the place we had left.

* * *

Greyfriars Kirkyard. Smell of dog shit mixed with two different kind of roses—honeyed, soapy. The sun brighter still. Having drunk a Coke she was excited, and she went to sit on our bench. A group of exchange students was staring over at us. Hostile boredom. He said,

Let's go and sit over there—pointing to a kind of bed-shaped mon-ument away from the students. Graves aren't meant to be *sat on* she said. What about him? he said. *That* guy? That waxy-looking guy in the Children in Need sweatshirt? I think it's the Great Ormond Street logo. Whatever, the junksick don't give a fuck. He hung his head, she stared back at the exchange students. Then she saw their guide, who was talking and laughing, pointing to things around the kirkyard. She said, He's *beautiful*. He thought: She loves the way the world looks. She was jabbing at him, saying, *Look at him!* Please he hissed, Let's just go and sit back there. No! She threw her sunglasses, they hit him on the chest then slipped down onto the ground. He let them lie where they fell. He got up and walked away from the bench, exhausted. A massive change, he thought, if you can have massive change in a place like this. He was feeling cold, despite the sun. She sat for a moment looking at the *beauti-ful* guide speaking to his exchange group. She started feeling awful again, really awful, nauseous, self-conscious, and she got off the bench and ran to him, taking his arm and dragging on it in an annoying way. We reached the grave/monument. The sky was clear, the rich colours of the city floated beyond the kirkyard walls. She said, What's wrong with you? He didn't say anything. She lit a tube and looked directly at him. Were you feeling a bit self-conscious? I mean in front of the exchange students? Like we were part of the tour? Huh? You know she said, the guide telling the kids about Burke and Hare and Greyfriars Bobby and all that: *And then over there on that grave under the chestnut tree you can see a rare species of Scottish urban wildlife, two stray, mongrel dogs...* He stood and began walking away, saying, You're not Scottish. And it's *not a grave*. She shouted, My gom's gom was Scottish... oh come back, please! He stopped, turned, walked back, *the sadness* mixed with anger, overwhelming him. He didn't know what he was going to say until, getting close, he said, Fuck off. She got up and walked away, leaving him standing there, leaving her soup, her pie, walking at pace through the kirkyard gate and out into the street thinking, Where you were born—why does this matter more than where you die?

* * *

She decided against the National Library and went instead to the Public Library opposite, climbing wide stone steps to the top, to the art section, to sit amid the potplants, well-lit under skylights, empty except for her and the librarian. Her desk facing into the room, the peaceful light, looking at the librarian who was busy with a stack of blocks and she thought of his *fuck you* and thought fuck HIM. Taking out her screen she opened it. Dear O., I have this line in my head from *The Piano Teacher*: 'Erika says that she, Erika, is an individualist. She claims she cannot submit to anyone or anything. She has a hard time just fitting in. Someone like Erika comes along only once, and then never again. If

In the kirkyard he picked up her pie and went to find another monument, one made of stone this time, out in the sun, because he was still feeling cold and he wanted to warm himself like a lizard, like a chameleon which he knew are soft to the touch, softer than one might imagine, and he found a monument with patches of moss on it, he lay back closing his eyes but he didn't feel any warmer, even in the direct sunlight he was feeling cold. Without knowing why, he laughed out loud. As soon as his laughter died down he felt cold again, even colder than before. He got up wanting to find her, wanting to tell her he was sorry. But when he got to the road he realized he something is especially irreplace-able, it is called Erika.' I think it's sick or funny/ odd though not funny/haha that Jelinek's transla-tors—into English— are all men. I include the director of the film of *The Piano Teacher*. But I think of Huppert, who plays the title role, as being a female translator of this novel, in effect. I would like to write the novel of the film of *The Piano Teacher*, in the first person, based on Huppert's performance. Though maybe I don't need to now I've had the idea. I am sorry I left you. I should not have left you. You should be here, with me. Do you remember the first time we met, we went to the library, or was it a party, or was it a party in a library, I don't know, I remember being with you in a library soon after we met, the reading room at the British Museum, before it closed, I remember going to sleep under the desk and you watching out for me. I wish you were here. And not just cos I need to sleep right now. *Really* need to sleep! Not just from last night but all this

didn't know where she was. The library? Maybe she'd gone back to the Swedish café or maybe she'd taken one of those buses she sometimes took for no other reason than the sound of the des-tination—Jewel, Hunter's Tryst. He checked the Swedish café then Sandy Bell's, then he went to the library but found himself unable to go inside, his need to find her somehow swept away by his ter-ror of entering the library. He turned away and let himself be carried by chance, but he didn't want to go too far from where he thought she might be (the library) and after a little while he found himself back at Sandy Bell's where he asked the barper-son if he could please use her screen to send a message and she said sure and something about bags that he didn't catch and after sending the message he leaned over the bar and said, Have you ever stroked a chameleon? They feel soft, not dry like you'd think, they feel like chamois leather, and the barperson said, No, I churning in my head from what just happened with you—need to crawl under the desk and crash but I can't—not when you're not here, I never can sleep in public unless you're beside me. I just looked online to see if they're ever going to reopen that reading room in the British Museum and on the website is a list of famous people who applied for tickets in its heyday, Karl Marx, Lenin, Bram Stoker, Conan Doyle. No Virginia Woolf, no mention of the research she did or failed to do there for *A Room of One's Own*. Did these famous people ever nap under the desks I wonder. No, perhaps not, but perhaps they sat next to many a hungover writer who napped, nameless, under their desks for decades then left the library as unknown as they'd entered it... She saw a message: *D it's me (on barperson's screen). In Sandy Bell's. Come.* She continued typing: I just got a summons from you. I will join you in a minute. It's not like I'm working well. I have just taken off my shoes and I can feel the carpet on my feet. I

have not stroked a chameleon, and a woman at the bar, listening, said, Do you keep them? And he said, I was just in the Meadows once with my brother when we were teenagers, smoking a joint, and a couple of girls came up to us to ask for a light, one of them had this lizard-thing crouching on her arm, it was a chameleon, she invited us to stroke it, and its eyes were what we found most amazing, orbs that swivelled 360 degrees in their sockets, and they have these grumpy, turned-down mouths. The girl told us she planned to breed chameleons in captivity and then release them into the wild. When he finished speaking he realized he felt cold. The barperson turned to another customer. He thought he ought to get warm, and left the pub. He went over to the charity shop across the road. She often went into charity shops while he never did, he always waited outside while she browsed the china and bric-a-brac section which she called 'heirloom corner' and the have the words to a song in my head: *And just like in a movie/Her hands became her feet.* That lyric reminds me of the way I pick things up with my feet, my feet are like hands. The lyric is by Lou Reed. After he went solo. Lou Reed was always solo, even when he was in the VU. And it's something I am starting to think about you. Do you know 'Perfect Day'? (Everyone knows it but you rarely know what everyone knows.) An account of a perfect day shared with someone. Written in the first person singular with reference to the second person singular and third person plural— one half of a couple singing to the other. Reed said it was about his then-wife Betty but some people reckon it's his love song to heroin, in which case the 'we' in the song is really 'I', not to mention the 'you'. The singer was really alone (heroin being an individualizing kind of drug). If 'Perfect Day' is about a drug experience then that's like Reed singing to/about an invisible friend. I mention this because sometimes, lately, I think, Have I

vinyl and the blocks. He stayed for a while, picking up one block then another. A zine slipped out from one and fell to the floor. Xeroxed on yellow paper. He picked it up and started flicking through its pages, stopped when he saw a name he recognized: Fred Moten. Daniel had talked about Fred Moten, had once told us he was a philosopher-poet, like Glissant. He read:

> a queer phenomenology of perception, a late phenome- nology of the feel, one slow enough to be able clearly to see the misty air, the mystery, to sense the blur, and not some normative individua- tion, as the field from which differences spring.

He folded the corner of the page, excited although he didn't com- pletely understand what Moten was saying. But the words! Strange and beautiful how they ran together. He read them aloud to himself, quietly. The normative made him (AKA you) up? Is it time to go our own ways? Is that what you mean with your 'fuck off'? Well then maybe I *will*. Ever since Brussels last year I've thought it was a city where I could live not so much alone but *without you*. So yes if you want me to, I'll fuck off. But I will always be your friend.

Damaris x

individuation of his telling her to fuck off. He thought: The blur of friendship, is this is our field? He glanced around, took *Minima Moralia* out of his bag, placed *Minima Moralia* on the shelf, put the zine into his pocket. Then he walked out of the shop and back to Sandy Bell's.

* * *

At the door of Sandy Bell's she spotted him sitting in the corner, near where the musicians sat. What *is* he wearing? She sat down next to him, we looked at one another in surprise. He pushed his pint over and she took a sip. Then he took out a paper bag saying, You forgot your pie… I'm sorry, I didn't mean… of course I didn't… he collapsed into tears. As he sobbed, she put an arm around him, pulled him into her, he did not resist, burying his face in her shoulder. His/her forehead/shoulder felt hot against her/his shoulder/forehead. We stayed that way while she watched our reflection in the brass trim of the bar. After several minutes he was still weeping so she lowered her lips to his ear. *Here you have an example of two mongrel scavengers, the first some kind of colli*e-sheltie cross, with a set-ter likely in the mix. The second a whippet-terrier cross—her voice soft, reverent. *Interaction between the collie cross and the whip-pet cross is a surprising phenomenon: the collie-cross is usually found in remote rural environments while the terrier cross is an urban breed and due to her high social drive and low boredom threshold is unable to keep regular company with any one mate.* His snort was muffled by her shoulder. *Members of these breeds rarely encounter one another due to their different habitats. And yet these two seem to have formed a freakish relationship, a symbiotic partnership. Look at how the terrier is overcoming her habitual disdain for all other breeds! Look at how she marvels at the collie, see how she puts her paw on his flank as he sits up, trembling!* He sat up, rubbing his face, and took the pie from the bag. *He's trembling with excitement as—look!—he starts to eat that basic staple of the urban terrier's diet: pie. Terriers prize pies of any kind, it doesn't matter what's in the pie, meat, veggies or mash, even macaroni, who cares, as long as it's sealed in a greasy crust.* Stop he said, making choking sounds. *You can see the collie, at first sniffing cautiously, is now snaffling the pie with great gusto, he's enjoying it so much that he's wagging his tail with joy as he chews.* Stop! Nudging her with an elbow. She went to the bar and ordered two pints. The barperson was saying something about bags. The warm voice, the cool face. Bags? The ones you left under the bench last night. Oh! she said, They're not mine. Someone needs to take them or my manager will hand them to the police.

We leave a note for Diego. It takes us three trips to get the bags out onto the street. What if the bags contain contraband? Street drugs! Explosives! Taxidermy! He goes off to fetch a shopping trolley and when he returns the bags are piled up and she's sitting on them. The red electric clock above the corner shop shows 17.24. She jumps off the bags and together we load the trolley. One of the wheels is fucked and the pile of bags is high so manoeuvring it requires both force and delicacy, also: concentration, coordination. We bicker in the road. How funny things are, how odd. *The sadness* comes and goes. Crossing over to the Meadows we blast through a red light and the brown nylon suitcase branded *Fashion!* topples off. At the top of Middle Meadow Walk the trolley picks up speed and the bags start to wobble. We pull back and turn off at Sainsbury's to check out the gourmet section. He waits outside, examines the composition of the pile. A wind picks up, the sun is weak through the trees. He's starting to feel cold again. When she emerges from Sainsbury's our bag is bulging. A number of packages all marked with yellow 'reduced price' stickers, including coriander. Tonight it is her turn to cook so she will make us lentilles rouges with satini brinzel and salad karot, his favourite. We move off, the trolley rattles down Middle Meadow Walk, the front left wheel snagging and squealing on the path. The trolley speeds up on the incline and he races to the front, bracing himself against it while she navigates past students in expensive boots that look like slippers, tourists and festival types. With one hand she dips into our bag, pulls out a box of éclairs, opens it with her teeth and shakes one out. The chocolate strip doesn't survive the operation, it's stuck to the inside of the box. She swears to herself, and when the éclair is gone she tries to retrieve the chocolate strip from the packaging which loosens her grip on the trolley: it shoots forward into his back, the dark green vinyl suitcase sliding, she grabs for it but the strap comes off in her hand

BOOM

The trolley has run aground on the grass verge. He's lying beside it, clutching his ankle. When she tries to get him to his feet he cries out in pain. She looks at the colour of his face. The codeine. Twenty minutes later, with the help of a woman dressed as the ghost of a Victorian undertaker, we manoeuvre the trolley downhill to the bottom of Middle Meadow Walk, over the confused intersection and onto North Meadow Walk, passing buskers, posters for the YES campaign and posters for the NO campaigne. Only now can he climb—with her help—onto the pile of bags, the codeine having kicked in, though was ever a kick so soft so dreamy so molten so creamy. He lies back on the bags, lips spread in a wide half-smile. *The sadness* mixed with a new curiosity and the stupid white light. She bending double against the trolley to get it over a rough patch. He saying, If you are a beast of burden then I am a burden. Her: You look like one of the bags. We're silent for a while. She tells him something she remembers from last night. Something Diego said. When the US soldiers arrived in 1973 to force everyone off Diego Garcia, the Chagossians were only allowed to take one suitcase.

What was left behind? Yes what was left behind? What about their animals? Pigs, chickens. Eaten or commandeered but not the dogs, do you want to know about the dogs? Yes he says, he wants to know but at the same time he's looking up at the trees seeing how the sun is low in the trees and the gathering of the trees and while he is thinking about the trees she is telling him the story of the dogs on Diego Garcia and how the British rounded them up, herded them into a copra processing shed and gassed them. Before they gassed the dogs they had tried poisoning them though this turned out to be inefficient, unhygienic. Diego remembered his dog going missing, then, playing on the beach one day, seeing what looked like a rock and his friend's dog circling it and howling and when they ran up there was Elvis, his stomach burst and maggots crawling out. Though that can't be right she says, Diego wasn't even born then. It's his mum's story. It's *someone's* story. *Sing! Sing! Sing!* goes the fucked wheel. He laughs. I can't sing. Will you sing? OK, but what? Sing to me in Kreol. I only know one song she says and she sings it, 'Roseda'. We exit the Meadows, crossing Home Street. And then Diego goes and leaves his bags he says. Maybe he feels lighter without them. Think about the effort of me pushing you she says, think about this journey home. But he says, But. We are home we are always home.

Edinburgh, September 2014. The horror of the sky. The air thick with rain to come. We no longer drank our first coffee of the day together. It had been weeks since he'd come with a mug in each hand to her bedroom door, nudging it open with his foot. He no longer climbed onto her bed and we no longer propped ourselves up, him tucking his feet under the duvet (if she let him). No more discussing the blocks we'd read before falling asleep, no more leaning out of the window to smoke the first tube of the day, looking to see if the billboard above ScotMid had changed, to read it for signs. Mornings in the flat were still filled with the smell of coffee, which he still made, but since we no longer drank it together we'd come to associate its smell with *the sadness*. She waking up to it now in bed, him breathing it in as he sat with his mug at the kitchen table, staring at Diego's bags, which were piled in the corner.

When she came into the kitchen she was already dressed, wearing that blue plaid shirt a lover had left behind. She put some post on the table, saying, Bulletins from the world of Emergency Supplies. He grabbed the pile not looking at her. Do they accept bitcoin? she said. Trading's not going so well he said. She turned away, poured herself a coffee. She opened the fridge, the cupboards, took out a box of muesli. She said, Nothing to eat but dusty raisins. *Currency…* Don't he said. Something in the way he wouldn't look at her, something in the way he held his coffee and rubbed his forehead with the tip of his thumb. A new tiredness and sadness.

She said, I'm going to eat one of the astronaut meals. This is how she referred to the freeze-dried food packs he ordered in bulk online and tried to hide from her. They're for The Emergency he said. This *is* an emergency! He glanced at Diego's bags. She put on her kindest face, laid a hand on his shoulder. Diego is *gone*, you know that. She raised the kitchen window, lit two tubes and held one out to him. We looked at the sky. Horizon crumbling away, plunging headlong into an abyss of fire. The billboard above ScotMid read *YES*: white caps, background of Saltire-blue. She said, If you're not making us any bitcoin then we should open Diego's bags, see if there is anything we can sell. We can't do that! Then I will eat an astronaut meal. We watched the swift grey clouds. He'll be back for those bags one day. Fuck the future she said, stubbing out her tube, ducking back into the kitchen—him still leaning out of the window—the billboard saying YES—but we had no vote we had no hope.

The Meadows. Same sky. Strange yellow light. People dragged about by the wind. The ends of his tracksuit bottoms frayed, trailing on the path. He was walking as fast as he could but his leg was still bad from his fall. She quickened our pace, he dragged on her arm, the wind was shaking the tops of the cherry trees. She was telling him we should get to the library because a storm was going to hit. He said, We *have* to find him. Then because she didn't answer he shouted into the wind, Diego! Diego! The rain came, pouring onto the grass, onto us, bouncing—high!—off the path. We joined hands and ran, turning up Middle Meadow Walk, passing posters for the YES campaign and posters for the NO campaign, *a nation strung out on fibre optic nerves.* Passing the Swedish café, Sainsbury's, Starbucks, slowing to a walk because we were soaked through, set on getting to the library—laughing now because rain gets no wetter in the end—set on getting down to our blocks and our screens because as much as we could not bear our blocks and our screens we had organized our lives around them and didn't experience this as a contradiction.

* * *

Ever since we'd taken Diego's bags home, we had been searching for him. Not knowing his real name, we couldn't find him online. So we went all over the city looking for him. We tried the hostels near the Grassmarket and behind Princes Street. We tried the pubs we tried the parks. We did not try the police. We asked again at Sandy Bell's but he'd not been back. We took the bus to Edinburgh Festival Campsite and picked our way among the tents, calling, Diego! Diego! We've got your bags! We called this out in English and then she called it out in Kreol. Next day she decided to speak only in Kreol. This did not lead to Diego and *it did not lead to any literature that we wrote.* We were disturbed by his failure to reappear, and this added strangeness to our unreal life: false sightings in the street, the confusion with Daniel. The days passed, no different than the rest. *The sadness* came and went. The same *sadness...* no, not the same, the vacancy and tedium the same but *the sadness* itself just what it is, always different but the same. One day her screen flashed— 'unknown number'—and he urged her to answer, saying, It might be *him.* Fuck Diego she said, He doesn't want to know us. This produced in us a feeling of shame we couldn't explain.

We stopped looking for Diego. We returned to the library. We sat among the stacks and read about Diego Garcia, the island where Diego's mother had been born, the same island soldiers had forced her to leave fourteen years later, to make way for the US military base. We made it to the library the next day, and the day after that.

On the fourth day he hissed, Have you seen the US Navy website? The history section of the Diego Garcia page? *Pure fuckin fiction.* That there had been people living on the islands prior to the base being built; that these people, the Chagossians, had been living there for many generations—no mention of them or their forced exile on the website. *Ghosted.*

We found the UK Chagos Support Association website, one of the groups formed to support the Chagos community in their fight to return to their islands. We read:

> The Chagos archipelago is a chain of 65 small coral islands in the Indian Ocean, about halfway between Africa and Indonesia, seven degrees south of the Equator. The largest island, Diego Garcia, covers only 17 square miles—the others are much smaller. The climate is hot and humid, and tempered by sea breezes. The soil is very fertile and the seas around the islands are rich in fish.
>
> The islands were known to Arab seafarers in early centuries, and the first Europeans to discover them were the Portuguese, in the 16th century. They did not settle the islands but they gave Diego Garcia the name it still holds.

We read:

> In 1776 a handful of French colonists were given permission by their government to develop coconut plantations in the Chagos islands on condition that they also establish a leper colony there. They brought in slaves from Madagascar, Mozambique and Senegal. Coconut palms and sugar cane flourished on the islands.

When British colonists took possession of the islands in 1835, after the Napoleonic Wars, one of them recorded that there was already a settled population when they arrived. The slaves were freed, became the plantation owners, and developed their own economy.

We read:

The Chagossian people evolved their own distinctive Creole language and their own culture. The social system was matriarchal—almost certainly a legacy of the leper colony, as women survive leprosy better than men.

We read:

In the late 1960s and early 1970s, this unique and peaceful way of life came to an abrupt end.

We read:

In the midst of the Cold War, the United States decided it wanted a military base in the Indian Ocean to keep the USSR and China from threatening the Arabian Gulf. Suddenly the Chagos archipelago was more than just an insignificant speck on the map.

We read:

In 1966 Britain secretly leased Diego Garcia to the US for 50 years, with the option of an extension. This was done in exchange for a discount of millions of dollars on Polaris nuclear submarines—a way of concealing the payment. The US pays rent of one dollar per year. The deal was not disclosed to the US Congress, the British Parliament, or the United Nations. Until this time the Chagos islands had been part of the British colony of Mauritius, but in order to lease Diego Garcia to the US, Britain had to avoid giving the islands back to Mauritius when that country became independent in 1968. So, in 1965 the 'British Indian Ocean Territory', as the archipelago is now officially known, was invented for the sole purpose of setting up the base. It is the only new British colony to be established since decolonisation.

* * *

Charity shop on Forrest Road. Wet through and dripping rainwater. She skipped straight to the *boutique* section to put together a new outfit for him. Do the same for me she said, cosy but edgy. We exchanged outfits. When we had changed we walked with inscrutable expressions to the counter. She feeling emboldened by her new outfit, him feeling shit but relieved somehow. Before paying she passed by heirloom corner picking up a pair of eggcups in duck-egg blue, also a block with the cover torn off, and the very last umbrella in the shop. Total: £11.75.

Ace Cleaning Centre. Gentle racket of the dryers. In the drum our old wet clothes. On us, the new old clothes that smelt like the grave. He: blue checked chef's trousers and a red-and-black flannel shirt, flecked oatmeal mountaineering socks. Her: batwing jumper in dark shimmery green, yellow flip-flops, brown fake suede skirt, bright pink anorak. The dryer came to a halt. She said, More change.

Yes he said, but how? *Coins* you arsehole! He dug into his pockets. We're running low, all that shit we bought from the charity shop. *Boutique* she said. He took out two 20ps which she fed into the dryer. He said, Why is it me who always pays? She took out her screen, showed him an animated gif of the national debt clock in New York with the numbers ticking up. It was true that she never had any money while he sometimes did. We often argued about it. This was *sad* but in the end it didn't matter all that much. It suited us both. She got to feel like a punk, he like we'd stick together—if not out of love then necessity—so that money was not for us just the ultimate abstraction but something to share between bodies. We sat on the bench opposite the row of dryers. He leaned his head on her shoulder. Rain pummelled the window. We watched our clothes turning, our trainers thudding against the drum. He said, Why did we buy those eggcups we never eat boiled eggs. She said, We never eat boiled eggs because we have no fuckin egg cups. We were silent for a while. Then he said, I don't think I'm going to make it to the library today. She said, I miss our coffees in the morning. He went outside and stood hunched in the doorway smoking a tube. When he returned he didn't look at her. She said, What's wrong with you? I don't know he said. Yes you do. You're thinking of leaving. No he said, I'm thinking we should go our separate ways. She said, Your plans are our plans. She paused. Except if I get that residency at Cove Park. If I get it then I'm going alone. You could visit on the weekends though. A washing machine shifted into spin cycle, the machines out of sync. He took a deep breath and said, I can't believe you bought a *Better Together* umbrella! You should have tried it out in the shop. It's bad luck to open umbrellas indoors she said. He said, You're so superstitious! It's only superstition to those who don't believe she said. My mum's grandmère *died* from the Evil Eye. I told you about her, the indentured labourer. Working the sugar cane fields. One night she had a fever, she cried out—*she's had the evil eye put on me!* then died. *Who* had the evil eye put on her? Supposedly the wife of the *blan* who managed the plantation. My great-grandfather. Anyway, would you call *her* superstitious? Remember *Caliban and The Witch*. She took her jumper off and folded it up. She put it on his shoulder and her neck on the jumper. We didn't speak for several minutes. His/her shoulder/neck was becoming numb. He said, But we are though, aren't we? Yes she said, You're Caliban and I'm the Witch. No! *Better together*. Fuck the union she said. Independence for Scotland, co-dependence for us. He turned his head and looked at the top of her head with his blue eyes.

We stayed sitting on the bench, quiet, unable to shift our gaze from the tumbling clothes, our trainers making that elliptical thud against the drum. The dry heat, the felted air. Outside, the trees thrashing their heads, roads running with water. A while later she lifted her head. We were right to come up here she said, England wanted us dead... no not England. *London*... not London. *The state*. The state doesn't want us dead he said, it just doesn't care if we are. Most of the time when the state speaks of sacrifice the state means THANK YOU FOR LETTING ME EAT YOU, that's what Ariana Reines said she said.

* * *

The battle against magic has always accompanied the development of capitalism, to this very day. Magic is premised on the belief that the world is animated, unpredictable, and that there is a force in all things: 'Water, trees, substances, words...'

* * *

Still Diego did not reappear. We continued to read about Diego Garcia. We found a book, *Island of Shame*, published in 2009 by the anthropologist David Vine who spent years living with people from the exiled Chagos community in Mauritius and the Seychelles. We read:

Marie Rita Elysée Bancoult is one of the people of the Chagos Archipelago.... Most live 1,200 miles away on the western Indian Ocean islands of Mauritius and the Seychelles.... Rita, or Aunt Rita as she is known, lives in one of the island's poorest neighborhoods, known for its industrial plants and brothels, in a small aging three-room house made of concrete block. Rita and other Chagossians cannot return to their homeland because between 1968 and 1973, in a plot carefully hidden from the world, the United States and Great Britain exiled all 1,500–2,000 islanders to create a major U.S. military base on the Chagossians' island Diego Garcia.

We read:

Initially, government agents told those like Rita who were away seeking medical treatment or vacationing in Mauritius that their islands had been closed and they could not go home. Next, British officials began restricting supplies to the islands and more Chagossians left as food and medicines dwindled. Finally, on the orders of the U.S. military, U.K. officials forced the remaining islanders to board overcrowded cargo ships and left them on the docks in Mauritius and the Seychelles. Just before the last deportations, British agents and U.S. troops on Diego Garcia herded the Chagossians' pet dogs into sealed

sheds and gassed and burned them in front of their trauma-
tized owners awaiting deportation.

We read:

> Over the past fifteen years, in litigation mainly in the U.K., the
> Chagossians have sought to establish their right to return to
> their homeland and to receive compensation for the damages
> they have suffered as a result of their expulsion and exile. As a
> result of this litigation, the Chagossians have won a court
> determination, accepted by the U.K. government, that their
> expulsion from their homeland was unlawful, but they have
> not yet succeeded in their efforts to win the right to return to
> Chagos and to obtain fair compensation for their wrongful
> dispossession and four-decade exile.

Reading the UK Chagos Support Association website, and then
David Vine's book, was like an event or a spell. We were struck by
the precision with which Diego Garcia's history and the story of the
Chagossian people's exile was set out, the tireless articulacy of the
writing, which felt like a kind of preparation, a roadmap for when
the base would be shut down. *Out of synch, but in time.*

We spent more and more time at the library, and in the
evenings we continued researching online. We found a text written
by the activist Rita Bancoult in 2011, 'An Open Letter to the British
High Commissioner in Mauritius':

> Do you know how it feels to be snatched from one's homeland
> and dumped in the wild? You are treated worse than an animal.
> You have no dignity. But worst of all, you have no identity.

We read:

> do not make the mistake of thinking that we are a harmless
> bunch. We may not have education and arms, but we have our
> faith in God and the will to fight injustice.
>
> Your government has taken us heartlessly and brutally
> from our heaven and dumped us here in hell.

We read:

> I want you today to know that I will stop fighting only when
> I breathe my last and lie down with my hands crossed over my
> chest... I will not surrender my dignity and I will show the
> British of what mettle I am made.

We read legal scholar Stewart Motha, who examines the series of
court rulings on the Chagos case in his book *Archiving Sovereignty*:

> the Anglophone common law is constituting the Indian Ocean
> as an archive of sovereign violence.... These offshore sites of
> sovereign violence become places where certain figures, peoples,
> individuals are beneath consideration. That is, they become a
> space in which individuals or peoples cannot be seen, heard, felt:
> and in which their insubstantiality comes to define the Indian
> Ocean and its islands as ghostly, haunted, unfathomable.

We read newspaper articles, court records, minutes of meetings. We
watched YouTube clips of coconut crabs on the beaches of Diego
Garcia, fighter jets landing on its runway, b&w footage of workers
picking coconuts. We read a report by Reprieve called 'Ghost

Detention on Diego Garcia' about the state of legal exception under which Diego Garcia operates: 'The Convention Against Torture does not apply to Diego Garcia.'

The sadness changed shape, a form we had no word for yet. What we talked about: the law as presentation and legitimation of arbitrary force. What we concluded: the world will always sustain the maximum of destruction possible; the worst possible thing happens always.

* * *

Leaning into the wind, warm in our dry clothes, crossing Forrest Road. Almost 12 she said, and we're still not at the library. Let's get a coffee first he said. We stopped outside the National Museum which had a café. The building like a fort, the café like a bank. At the counter she said to the barista, He'll pay. This made him instantly tired, so weary he could barely pass his card over. *Credit is silent.* We left the café and entered the Grand Gallery, passing displays of feathers, a skeleton of a big cat, the skull of some huge beast. She said, We can share the coffee. A sperm whale. It had died swimming the wrong way up the Firth of Forth. We walked on until we came to the atom smasher, that giant metal structure that always surprised us. Built like a sculpture but with a function. It looked like a huge prop, like something from the set of a 1950s sci-fi B movie. Silver and red, bulbous, set on legs like giant screw threads, it loomed high above the floor of the Grand Gallery. We read:

The Cockcroft-Walton generator was developed in the early 1930s to accomplish the first   artificial splitting of the atom. Particles were fired at high speeds through the tubes and made to collide with atoms. The resulting pieces from the collision were detected and analysed. The experiment can be likened to dropping a television from the top of Big Ben, then trying to determine its structure by examining the pieces.

She sipped the coffee, offered him the cup. He waved it away. She turned to him, saying, Look at me. He kept his eyes on the atom smasher. He was feeling shit again, quite violent. Without looking at her he said, Maybe we *should* go our separate ways. She stood in front of him. Look at me! He didn't look at her or change his expression in any way. Smile she said. He started to walk away and she ran to catch up. We stood facing one another, she put the coffee on the floor and placed her hands on his shoulders. OK, I tell you what, I'll count to eight and if by eight you haven't smiled, we'll go our separate ways. She looked into his eyes, One… two… you look very sad… three… OK then I will make you sad… four… five… my life will be great without you… five-and-a-half… I'll move back to London… six… I'll find Diego and we'll collaborate on his life story, why not… seven… I have a friend who has bright blue eyes… seven-and-a half… he sounds surprised when he laughs, I think he is clever and brave but such a pitiful fool… seven-and-three-quarters… and he's so, so sad… boo hoo hoo!… seven-and-six-eights…my name is Oliver Pablo and I'm so so sad!!! seven-and-nine-tenths… Waaaaaaarrrrggggghhhhhhhahaha!!!! I'm soooooooooooo saaaa… Ah, that's better.

* * *

Greyfriars Kirkyard. Smell of rain on metal, on stone, moss. Our favourite bench. She took off her raincoat and laid it down on the bench. Wind shaking the trees, raindrops shaking from the leaves onto our faces. She opened the umbrella, saying, Hold this. *Better Together?!* I'm not sitting under that thing, but he took it anyway. She thought: *His eyes are the brightest blue and change all the time.* We looked around the kirkyard. Couple of schoolkids on a bench staring at their screens. We sat in silence for a while. A blackbird in the tree overhead. He said, I'm going to chuck it away later. Can't we just fuck up the branding she said, Tape over 'Better'? He smiled and she smoked and we drank our coffee, enjoying the pattering of drops overhead. His arm felt stiff because he was holding the umbrella at an angle so that it covered only her. Here she said, taking the batwing jumper, laying it over his shoulders— it suits you. I'll have a tube now he said and she took one from the pack, lighting it with the still live butt of her own. It was then that we noticed a figure on a grave slab, watching us. She was shading her eyes to get a good look—at what? She was squinting, frowning, scowling. At *us*? She started to move… no, run *at us*— fuckin rhino. Get that thing out of here! the woman shouted. Fucking travesty! a FUCKING MOCKERY! Oh shit he said, it's the umbrella. He dropped his tube and moved to collapse it. She grabbed it, managed to flip the catch as the woman came running, him holding up his hands in defence/deference, I'm sorry, we totally agree, we don't even believe… The woman wrenched the umbrella from her and started to wave it around like the Queen of Hearts playing croquet. The schoolkids staring. We dodged the umbrella, which flapped uselessly, saw the schoolkids holding up their screens *filming?!?* We broke for the kirkyard gate, the woman behind, bellowing. With her extravagant manoeuvres she must have activated the umbrella's catch, which sprang open. Now we heard a scream, we looked back to see her standing, hands clamped over her one eye. For a second she went still; silent. Then a worse sound. She began to cry.

* * *

A&E. Pink walls like pink soup. Moulded plastic chairs on bolted-down metal frames. We'd brought Saoirse here on the bus. Does it hurt? we'd asked. No said Saoirse, surprised. Accent from a stately home. I cannot feel any pain. Sure, absent pain doesn't make itself felt. Since being poked in the eye Saoirse had been calm and gentle. No pain apparently but she could not see so we'd had to guide her off the bus, past the smokers with their tubes—smoking them, attached to them—to the hospital. The receptionist irritated because Saoirse failed to account for herself. *My name means Freedom.* Now Saoirse was with the doctor and we were waiting.

The place was packed, rows of people waiting to be seen, those who'd had an accident, who'd experienced—were experiencing—an emergency, emergencies happening at different speeds, the people accompanying them, everyone staring at screens. *The sadness* as always yet here we were having a nice time. A&E was warm, we were dry, *we had helped someone.* Our usual routine upset which was not unusual but this time for a Good Reason. Feeling a rush of love he went to get us a treat from the machine. He came back with a packet of salt and vinegar Hula Hoops and a Wispa. She was reading the block from the charity shop. *Voices from the Emergency—All India Anthology of Protest Poetry of the 1975–77* Emergency. Read me something he said. She unwrapped her Wispa, bit off a chunk, read:

After a day of tiring struggle
We only talked theory, argued, discussed

And watched the life we knew
Being wrapped in blood.

He was staring at the fast-flowing screen on the wall and listening to her. Movement in the corridor. Wheels on linoleum, boots, doors opening, flapping shut. How Scottish do you feel, Oliver Pablo? More Scottish than my English blood. Your blood is English but your *time* has mostly been Scottish. News. Rolling, non-stop: accidents and emergencies. We read: 'Police Attempt to Crack Down on Protests in Hong Kong.' Images of civilians defending themselves with… Look, umbrellas! 'Scots independence battle reaches fever pitch on streets and screens.' She sang, *I don't want the news I can't use it.* He said, Is Saoirse OK? Who knows she said. Next to her a child draped over their dad's shoulder began to cry, a toddler, big but young-looking. She looked at her chocolate bar. A Wispa is just chocolate with a chocolate filling but the filling has air in it which makes the chocolate somehow more… toothsome. You want some? No. Bet you've never heard me say the word 'toothsome' before. I've never heard anyone say it. She noted his outfit, the clothes he had put on that morning, now dried after their soaking, saggy joggers, her *Life Without Buildings* t-shirt. His old clothes look more like *boutique* clothes than his own clothes. Look at you! You're not very… let's just say you're shit at looking after yourself… and yet you're into this survival stuff, so, *clearly* you're determined to… Those survival equipment catalogues, are they not produced by the people behind the Innovations catalogue? Somewhere in Goole there's a warehouse full of surplus Innovations products being repurposed for the survival equipment market. Nose-hair trimmers converted into stun guns. He looked away then turned to the toddler whose body was limp but whose eyes were wide open, which made them appear as if full of fear. Here, catch. She chucked *Voices from the Emergency* onto his lap saying, I got this for *you*. I thought it might help she said. History is not homogeneous empty time he said. Oh! She reached out to him across the gap between our chairs but he flinched. He didn't say anything and stretched his arms out in a curious way then rubbed the back of his neck. *I am a patient boy, I wait I wait I wait.* She finished off the last of the chocolate with something like a sigh. He looked away from her and back to the screen. *Not my news.* She said, Don't you see, the emergency isn't *coming*, it's already *here*. It has been here for some time, it came sooner for some of us than others, or some of us just realized sooner. Whiteness *invented* capitalism. She said it so loudly heads turned to look at her. He got up. Walked off. Past the reception desk, the screen, passing the rows of people, to the other end of the room & she thought, White men: the first to speak, the last to know, and picked up *Voices from the Emergency*, reading another poem which she liked very much especially the line,

> May you take pride
> In being your own exception

which was written by the poet Nagarjun & he, stopping at a table with magazines on it, thought: Something to look at, something about TV shows I have never seen, will never see & turning to see where he'd got to, she saw him, with a shock: those joggers he was always wearing these days were *Daniel's* & in the heap of old papers and magazines he found an actual block, more of a pamphlet really, it was called *The Fuzzbuzz*, an old reading scheme block, the cover illustration a bizarre creature, head and body in one, blue with an indistinct outline like a pom-pom, red antennae, buzzed-looking eyes, a creature he remembered from his childhood & no longer in the mood for more news or emergency poetry, she took up her screen and plugged her earphones in and scrolled to find something to listen to and relax, into Sun Ra *talkin about…Nuclear War… yeah it's a motherfucker… Don't you know… talking about Nuclear War…* and then the song ended and the next track began but it was background noise from a loud bar, then she realized it was in fact an untitled voice recording & *this is a black box* he read; *buzz buzz buzz goes the black box, buzz buzz buzz; stop the buzz, stop stop the buzz; look! an egg is under the box, buzz buzz goes the egg; crack goes the egg, crack crack crack;* & and on the recording *buzz crack buzz* the sounds of the bar and voices and then her *own* voice, was that what her Kreol sounded like, ouch! and now Diego, speaking Kreol too, he was telling her a story, hard to make out, a sad story cos she was saying *Ayo!…* how could she translate that word into English? Was it even a word? It was more an exclamation, a sound, a feeling & *buzz buzz buzz* he read, *up jumps a fuzzbuzz; this is the fuzzbuzz, buzz buzz goes the fuzzbuzz, buzz buzz buzz; the fuzzbuzz jumps, the fuzzbuzz jumps up, up and up and up jumps the fuzzbuzz; and the fuzzbuzz goes under the egg;* & she remembered the argument she'd had in class with the old professor who'd told her there was no thought without language and she'd tried to say *but feelings are thoughts in another language* & *this is a house; next to the house there is a garden, this is the garden; in the garden there is a tree, this is the tree; there is a mattress under the tree; there is a fuzzbuzz next to the mattress, this is the fuzzbuzz; the fuzzbuzz is in the garden, he lives there, he lives in the mattress under the tree* & now it was conversation, random connections: lipstick, psychiatry, sarcasm, Seggae, invective, being gay in Mauritius, private beaches in Mauritius, rain and sun, cyclones, speaking Kreol, not speaking

Chagossian Kreol, the paintings of Clement Siatous, Arsenal, Mauritian literature, Edinburgh, islands, the Scottish independence vote, Dhall Puri vs gato pima, sisters and brothers and cats and dogs & as he was reading *The Fuzzbuzz* a hailstorm broke, a clattering, lumps of ice on the skylight above his head and he listened to the hailstones for a second and then went back to *The Fuzzbuzz* thinking, The sky is falling on our heads, and he remembered Daniel's MA show, an installation about the sky disappearing, she had not gone to the opening since she and Daniel had not been speaking at the time, and he remembered the snotty comment she'd made on hearing about the show, that it had sounded overly indebted to the work of Walid Raad & and now Diego was telling her about his sister Rose who was named for their mum, and when she asked what their mum had died of Diego had said, sagren & when he'd finished *The Fuzzbuzz* he went right back to the beginning and read it again with even greater pleasure, then looked around to see that no one was looking and rolled the block up and stuck it deep into the pocket of his joggers then continued to look through the papers and magazines on the table, mostly torn with pages missing but some new and bright, looking to him like a future era of fantastic life & sagren, this heartbreak, a fatal sadness that had killed, was killing Chagossians in exile & *the sadness* came back to him instantly, mostly and especially because he remembered the stupid thing he'd said about history not being homogeneous & then she had the strong feeling she ought to be transcribing what Diego was saying, and she scrubbed the recording back, this time trying to transcribe what she was listening to and realizing she would also have to *translate* as well as transcribe if she wanted to share this with him, and she thought of Walter Benjamin's country road, and wondered who she might pass as she walked along this road & he thought about the block about the Indian Emergency and he cursed himself because to deny that the desire of all politics to rule by states of emergency mostly undeclared was an extremely stupid and impractical way to think & then she had the idea that she would abandon the transcription/translation and instead rewrite what Diego had said but as she imagined Diego's sister Rose might have told it—Rose spoke differently to Diego, Rose was calmer, sharper, she desired different things, and her transcription of Rose's imagined words would be themselves a translation & and then he laughed aloud thinking how it was she who had suggested the music, the outro the family had given Daniel and he thought it needn't go on like this, it must not, because continuing *like this* precisely *is* the catastrophe, that's what Daniel had understood: not what stands to come but rather where we're at now. He made his way back past the row of people waiting, and saw she was at her screen, fingers hovering over the keyboard, her face in blue light. He held out the copy of *The Fuzzbuzz* to her, This is how me and Daniel learnt to read.

* * *

The tradition of the oppressed teaches us that the state of emergency in which we live is not the exception but the rule. We must attain to a conception of history that is in keeping with this insight. Then we shall clearly realize that it is our task to bring about a real state of emergency, and this will improve our position in the struggle against capitalism. One reason why capitalism has a chance is that in the name of progress its opponents treat it as a historical norm. The current amazement that the things we are experiencing are still possible in the twenty-first century is not philosophical. This amazement is not the beginning of knowledge—unless it is the knowledge that the view of history which gives rise to it is untenable.

* * *

Two months before Daniel entered his own personal state of emergency, he had made a new work. A video that begins with the clip of a man quoting from James Baldwin: 'Any real change implies the breakup of the world as one has always known it, the loss of all that gave one an identity, the end of safety.' The man, we found out later, was the Baldwin scholar Rich Blint, and the clip was taken from the Arthur Jafa film, *Dreams Are Colder Than Death*.

> … it is only when a person is able, without bitterness or self-pity, to surrender a dream he has long cherished or a privilege he has long possessed that he is set free—he has set himself free—for higher dreams, for greater privileges.

Copies of the clip successively expand out onto the screen, overlap, then disappear, Blint's voice and Baldwin's words, multiplying in echoes. Then a figure appears on screen, digitally rendered, blurred, naked. It's Daniel. 'Daniel' starts to stretch, in slow motion, shaking his arms—stretching as action and effect, he *looks* stretched, misshapen, and there's the temporal stretch of his movements. He's dancing. He is dancing like the go-go dancer who performs on Felix Gonzales Torres' white platform sculpture: Daniel's dancing is looped. He's a gif.

Alongside him a clip appears from the film by Bas Jan Ader, *I'm Too Sad To Tell You*, a close-up of the artist, silently crying. Daniel, still dancing. Daniel's dancing mocks Jan Ader's crying. Daniel's dancing is ritualized shame. Daniel's dancing is not-*living*, it is *dying*. In a loop.

To put white male sadness in conversation with Baldwin being quoted by Blint. To put the Jan Ader work in conversation with Jafa's film. To place that conversation against the backdrop of an unnamed sea: a loop of open water, and the sounds of an unseen small boat in motion. That Jan Ader went on to die in a foolhardy sea-crossing in a small boat, a mock mock-heroic project intended as an artwork. That it was the *Atlantic* that Ader tried to cross. That he tried, and failed, to do it alone.

* * *

The city is functioning again, the rain has run off the road, Melville Drive is drivable again, and cars are racing through the wet. We don't talk for a long time, all the way along the path that runs south of the Meadows which is not named on the maps, through the cold of the Meadows, the grass bluish and the coppery bark of the cherry trees. The eerie light after a storm. Saoirse is being kept in for observation and we are going home.

IV. GHOST

Edinburgh, November 2014. On the verge of morning. Sky a tender pink. He, sitting on the kitchen windowsill, screen opened at the higher timeframe chart, checking to see how bitcoin was doing. Market structure was bullish, a new 4 hour higher high painted. Feeling great, his bias confirmed. Looking down at the garden of their building, a lawn, an empty washing line, and wondering why we didn't sit out there sometimes. Too much coffee already, too early for a tube, too excited to go back to bed. His bag packed with a few clothes, the block he was reading and some of the special ingredients she had asked him to bring—the jar of her dad's achard, the jar of her gom's chilli sauce, a bunch of fresh coriander. Along with that, the news he had for her, about our bitcoin.

Cove Park, International Artists' residency centre, November 2014. Drawing back the curtains. Sky white. Loch too, and the mountains just emerging from shreds of mist. She made coffee which was not as good as his coffee, and went to the window: one whole wall of her accommodation, a converted shipping container, all windows. Outside, a wooden deck, a large pond, the water kept still by some mechanical device it seemed, its surface pure reflection. On the grass by the pond, stooping to drink, disturbing its surface, one of the highland cows that wandered the grounds, prehistoric-looking and fabulous. The wide skies, the loch below, and across from the loch, the mountains. When the sun was bright and the mountains green-black, she thought of Mount Ory in Mauritius.

At Gourock he boarded the ferry to Kilcreggan, feeling like how the water *looked*, enjoying the motion of being on a boat even while still moored, wondering what it was about boats that he had always loved so much, and then the boat pulled away and he breathed in the smells of engine fume and the cold wet salt of the breeze, thinking there was something in the order of his helpless love for dogs and also bicycles in his love of boats. Perhaps the joy of being on boats was just a distillation of all the time he'd spent on them as a kid, pedalos and dinghies and little sailboats, the best of their time as a family. And he laughed remembering the shitty little boat he'd saved up for with that gap year job at Argos in Dundee, those months of working in a basement that had bought him time out on the water in *Tomas*, named by the guy he'd bought it off in a junkyard in Arbroath. How he used to make Daniel travel in the open boot of their mum's car holding on to the

An hour later she set out to meet him. It took one and a half hours to walk to the harbour at Kilcreggan. She headed south along the coastal road. The sky bright blue, the smacking of the clear water on the rocks of the shallow shore. The sun rising up above the mass of hills to her left, behind these Faslane, the naval base on the peninsula's eastern side. Faslane, where the UK's nuclear submarines were berthed. When she had first arrived at Cove, one of the artists had told her that sometimes in the loch you might see a submarine surface there. Like seeing a whale she supposed.

At the harbour at Kilcreggan she stood looking out towards the mainland, though this bit of land she stood on was also part of the mainland, hanging out into the water like a bit of island, a peninsula, a *halbinsel*, and gradually she saw a boat heading towards them, the little ferry boat which seemed to be travelling very slowly, seemed to be barely moving. And there he trailer as they towed it down to the jetty at Tayport. The sky here so fuckin blue, the air so pure. He looked down at the water and thought of its eventual circulation around the world, how Daniel was now *in* the water. The ferry was heading towards the jetty where a small knot of people stood, and there she was! Climbing off the boat now and as she ran up to him and hugged him he heard her screen ping and thought, The markets.

was! The dear, familiar particularity of his outline and she thought back to the film she'd watched for the 3rd time the night before, *Chagos ou la mémoire des îles* that told the story of an historic trip made by members of the Chagos community back to their archipelago, what it would have been to have seen your islands approaching, then being forced to leave them all over again.

* * *

[0:04:49] Port Louis Harbour, Mauritius. 30 March 2006. A coach pulls up beside a large white ship, the *Mauritius Trochetia*. A few policemen stand around. A steel band playing 'Auld Lang Syne' off-camera, a crowd is singing, whistling, cheering. Cut to the crowds in the late afternoon light, waving handkerchiefs and flags. The bus doors open and out step members of the Chagossian community who will be making this historic trip to the Chagos Archipelago. Everyone is wearing the same white Chagos Refugee Group T-shirts, and the women are also in white headscarves. We see Olivier Bancoult, leader of the Chagos Refugee Group whose continued protests for the right to return, we learn, has seen the British government pressured into arranging this trip. He stands before the crowd, waving and smiling. Boarding begins. Close-up of a woman in the queue with a powerful expression, the Chagossian activist Aurélie Talate. The band plays Ton Vié's 'Peros Vert', the crowd waving and swaying to the seggae beat. A shot from the dockside up at the figures in white already on the ship dancing and waving large white handkerchiefs, among them Rita Bancoult, mother of Olivier Bancoult, who is now boarding and shouts out to the crowd: 'Retourn a later promi!' Then the band plays a Mauritian sega, 'Liberation Chagos' by Jalsa des Iles and Olivier Bancoult sings out: '*Liberasyon!*' The camera pans across the crowd, stops at a smiling man and closes in on his face. It is Robin Mardemootoo, lawyer for the Chagossians. In voiceover Mardemootoo says in English:

> I really wish I could have been part of this journey, to accompany Olivier and his people of course, but not only for that. I would have liked to see the Chagos archipelago as something other than the pile of files on my desk. I would have liked to set it apart from the smell of ink on paper, from its icon on my computer screen. I would have liked to give it shape in order for us to talk about it better in the hushed arena of the courtroom. Peros Banhos, Salomon, Diego Garcia, how many times have I heard the islands' names since the day Olivier and his delegation first came to tell me their story. For me, as the Chagossians' lawyer, Peros Banhos and Salomon are just two deserted islands while Diego Garcia is quite simply the biggest American army base outside the USA. But for Olivier, Annessie, Rosmond, Rita, Adeline and so many others who were born there, the islands have probably remained as fixed in their memory as they were on the day of their deportation. How are they going to bear seeing them again after thirty-five years of forced exile? How are they going to accept leaving

them once more? I hope they think the way I do because, as a jurist, this is my belief: this journey is a dress rehearsal for the true return that will come one day.

* * *

Walking to Cove Park. Along the back road, up past cottages and gardens now opening out into fields and woodlands. The sky and sun bright but the air cold. It had been days since we'd seen each other and months since we'd not seen one another for days. Here we are she said. Yes we are he said. On in silence, both smiling, though our smiling meant different things. The slow work of walking uphill on a country road, passing through light and shade. The smell of asphalt, damp earth from woodland, the woodland misted with ferns, the woody smell of the ferns, and past the fields, the sheep and sheepshit. The light here. Was it bitcoin you were checking? Yes. I guessed. What about the writing he said, how's it going? Oh so *well* she said. *Beautifully*. Look around you. We stopped and gazed. The lush fields, the blue sky, sheep nibbling with their long lips, and in the background, a noble stand of trees, straight from a seventeenth-century English landscape painting. You know my grandad was a guard in the Tate she said. Stationed in the Constable room. He always said *The Hay Wain* reminded him of Poudre d'Or, where he grew up. What I am writing she said is a kind of ghost story. No—what I am doing is *ghost writing*. Or maybe more like spirit writing. How could writing not happen here? He said, We could move here! I could trade bitcoin and you could write! Passing a stretch of woodland now, a clearing with a fallen trunk. Shall we stop he said, I bought crisps. We sat astride the log facing one another and he opened up the crisp bag, laying it out between us, like at a pub table. The birds calling across to one another, high in the trees, and below, our thoughtful munching. How is bitcoin doing? Great! Will you sell it or hold onto it? Neither he said. That's called hodling, that's not how I trade. The log we sat on was covered in lichen the colour of verdigris, which, close up, had the filigreed look of coral. I've been learning a *lot* about trading he said. I've been reading a lot about plants she said. If you're not hodling what are you doing? It's not about the linearity of rising prices but the exponential growth of compound interest. Fractal like ferns she said. That was the only bit of maths I ever got. That, and probability. So you mean small trades and just building your gains? He nodded. Look at that plant over there she said, that one with the green flowers. Those are leaves. No, they are flowers. They *look* like leaves, you don't *get* green flowers. No! come here. She dragged him off the log and pointed, *Those* are the leaves. *Those* are the flowers—no, don't touch! They leak an irritant. Madwoman's milk, that's the name of the plant. I have been reading about plants on Diego Garcia. Plants and ghosts. The Chagos Islands must be haunted. I watched that amazing film again, *Chagos ou la mémoire des îles*. And I have been reading more about that historic 2006 'heritage visit' to Chagos. I also found out about a beautiful painting that was made to commemorate the trip. Are you listening? But he was remembering the clearing, one like this, where we had gathered for Daniel. Afterwards all of us traipsing towards the sea. The tide had been out, so far out it had felt like one of those dreams where something desired perpetually recedes out of reach. He reached down for a crisp. She said in a kind voice, What have you been learning about trading? Do you know what Einstein said? He said compound interest was the 8th Wonder of the World. Then she said, Do you have any more food? Only your gom's chili and your dad's achard and some coriander. Let's go she said, I'm hungry. When we reached the back gate at Cove and walked up through the long grass he grabbed her arm. *Look!* The highland cows, mother and baby peaceably chewing, shaggy forms merging with the surrounding grassland. I like them from a distance she said. They are not scenery he said. I find them physically intimidating. Tell me more about the ghosts he said. Oh, they were laid to rest after that visit. Since the Chagossians who went on the trip were able to tend to the graves of their ancestors. But not all of them. Some people were unable to locate the graves of those who had died in their families. After I watched the film again I found photos online of the abandoned graves in Chagos. Broken gravestones, plots unkempt. One small cracked-apart grave that said 'Stillborn'. Heartbreaking. There are trees growing in the chapels now. Tomorrow is All Soul's Day he said. And the day after that is Chagos Day, she said. What is the date actually commemorating, the date the expulsion began? No she said, it's the date the High Court ruled the Chagossians had the right to return, in 2000. The ruling that got overturned in secret by the Queen. Trudging up to the studio units. The roofs covered with a sweet green moss lit up in the sun, still, glassy ponds reflecting the bluest of skies. Oh! he said. Could we not find some land? Buy a shipping unit like one of these? I'd do a garden. We could be happy here. We couldn't get a mortgage she said. We are credit ghosts. I will trade our way to one! If you leave a forest it will grow exponentially she said, like people if no one ever died and we could see the ghosts we live among.

* * *

[0:08:27] Night time. Rosmond Saminaden, sitting outside the British Embassy in Port Louis, during a mass camp-out by protestors for the Chagossians' right to return, says in Mauritian Kreol:

I often wonder, when they deported people, why was it done at night? No one can give me the reason. Why? It's because in the dark you can't see. Of course it is. When the boat leaves, it separates you from the island. The island is no more than a black dot moving away—no more light on it, no nothing on it. It's become like a desert island.

And beside him, Mimose Furcy, who must have still been a child at the time of the deportation, says, also in Mauritian Kreol: 'Do you remember, even in the dark, we waved our handkerchiefs as a last good-bye?'

Later in the film, when Rosmond Saminaden and other elders from the Chagossian community in exile arrive in London to testify to the High Court, who will go on to reject their right to claim for compensation, Rosmond Saminaden will say, in Mauritian Kreol:

I'm going to explain to the judge that we were fine in Chagos, we lived well there, that we don't know why—for what rea-son—they came and took us away to a country we didn't know. But that this act of domination they subjected us to is because of our black skin.

* * *

We first learnt about bitcoin in 2008. We were living with Daniel in his squat in Limehouse while we tried to finish our blocks. We shared a room, a huge room with a beautiful, broken ceiling. We were learning to be kind to one another, and to Daniel, trying to understand one another's language better. Living—trying to live—without consent to being single beings, as Edouard Glissant and Fred Moten said *they* wanted to do. But the writing was not happening: he had sold his block on a partial manuscript but by the time of his deadline still had 25% yet to write, with much less than that left of his advance. While she had finished multiple drafts of her block but had yet to get close to a version anyone but us considered readable. Meanwhile, Lehman's Brothers had collapsed. Disaster capitalists were studying and planning. Daniel, desperate, would keep him up all night talking, we called this *giving us the treatment*. In the day, too exhausted to sleep or write, he would go online, hopping from one topic to another. He would read the forums on bitcointalk.org. Alongside the financial stuff he'd learnt of bitcoin's inventor, Satoshi Nakamoto—who had in fact posted on the board. He learnt too that no one knew anything about Satoshi Nakamoto, not even whether they were a single person or a group.

He'd followed the whole story of bitcoin on bitcointalk.org:

The root problem with conventional currency is all the trust that's required to make it work. The central bank must be trusted not to debase the currency, but the history of fiat currencies is full of breaches of that trust.

He'd read:

Governments are good at cutting off the heads of centrally controlled networks like Napster, but pure P2P networks like Gnutella and Tor seem to be holding their own.

He'd read:

A purely peer-to-peer version of electronic cash would allow online payments to be sent directly from one party to another without the burdens of going through a financial institution.

He had also read how, that year, Satoshi Nakamoto had published a whitepaper called 'Bitcoin: A Peer-to-Peer Electronic Cash System'. They'd written the code and then mined the first ever chain of bitcoins which they called the *genesis block*. Permanently embedded in its code, hidden amid the thousands of lines of C++, was included the text: *The Times 03/Jan/2009 Chancellor on brink of second bailout for banks*. In 2009 Satoshi Nakamoto managed to transfer bitcoin from one computer to another for the first time, and then, the following year came the first ever actual purchase: 10,000 bitcoins paid to a guy in Florida by a guy in London in exchange for 2 large pizzas ordered from a local takeaway, paid for by the Floridian with $25 on his plastic. Satoshi Nakamoto (who by then had already disappeared) and the other posters on bitcointalk.org deplored the banks, especially the Federal Reserve and Bank of England and Bank of Japan. They declared that during The Emergency a person should buy silver and bitcoin because the pound/dollar/euro/yen was going to 0. And so it was that with the last £500 of his advance he had bought bitcoin. He'd watched with disbelief as the price of bitcoin had risen from $0.0008 to nearly $0.017, his £500 becoming more than £10,000 in less than a few months. He did not sell because the view on bitcointalk.org was that fiat would hyperinflate and bitcoin would rise *hundreds of thousands* of percent. But then he had watched, baffled, almost hurt, as bitcoin fell and fell.

She first learnt about bitcoin about a month after it had crashed. He was giving her a backie on his bike, the green one he'd built himself instead of writing his block. 4 o'clock in the morning she'd called him, trapped in the stairwell of a light industrial block in Hackney Wick. He'd strapped two sofa cushions onto the pannier rack, cycled along the canal breathing in the delicious woodsmoke from the barges. He'd found her in the carpark, sitting cross-legged on a pile of flattened cardboard boxes. She was transfixed by an unblinking woman performing close-up magic with a Rubik's cube. Back and forth he had rocked on his crossbar, pleading for her to *just come home*, the rear red light slamming round the walls of the carpark. He was holding out a tub of hummus and she laughed.

We rode back through the park because she didn't want to see broken things at the bottom of the canal, her leaning into him, telling him to slow down, to take the corners wide, to watch out for the kerb, bumps, potholes, broken glass, rats, stray dogs, urban foxes, telling him to pedal *smoothly* because why was there no suspension on this machine, and what kind of a fuckin bikebuilder was he anyway. Then she began to weep. Heterosex is nothing but a rape scam she'd said. He told her about his bitcoin, the whole story, how the £500 had become over £10,000 and how it was now worth much less than £500, all in the space of a few months. He told her how in the end it didn't matter, it wasn't about the money, and anyway bitcoin would become a measure of value that genocidal bankers couldn't control. She thought it might be true yes. But she did not believe that bitcoin would replace the monopoly of fiat to function as the currency for all the things the merchants of the world offer up for sale. As we rode into the pink-yellow light of dawn she said, The measure of value must contain value. What? he said. The measure of value... What? he said, I can't hear you. It doesn't matter! she shouted. She shifted her weight suddenly and the bike swerved. *Dear bicycle, I shall not call you bike, you were green like so many of your generation, I do not know why.* We can't eat bitcoin she said. The electric fizz of the streetlamps, the cold on our faces. She reached forward and inched the tub of hummus from his coat pocket. It slipped and fell and the hummus went *splat* like fresh cement. She laughed, he got angry, sped up, she shoved him in the back, we fell, swearing at one another, crashing onto the grass. His trousers were ripped, her cheek was throbbing. London is killing us she said. The birds began to sing.

* * *

Cove Park. Sitting out on the decking. We heard the trickle of the stream that fed the pond, the songs of birds we'd not heard before, and in the distance, the crackle of gunfire from the nearby military shooting range. A duck came in to land, tearing up the water. For lunch she had made miso soup. Have you missed me she said. I miss our mornings and I miss our walks to the library. And me? Oh no she said writing is going so *beautifully* it's almost scary. Like I am not writing it myself, like someone is writing *through* me. I thought that what I was writing was a kind of *ghostwriting* but actually what is it to ghostwrite the story of someone who never asked you to tell their story in the first place. Is that *hauntwriting*?

He was watching two people walk towards us, and the joyful dog weaving around their legs. It was the artist in the next unit with their girlfriend, visiting for the weekend. We are going to Helensburgh, do you want a lift? Why not we said. In the Cove Park jeep we sat in the back with the dog whose name was Bucket, looking out at the scenery replenishing itself, forests of pine trees like oversharpened pencils, while the artist Morgan pointed out local landmarks to their girlfriend Heather, also an artist. Heather plugged her screen into the audio and the car was filled with music, an unearthly voice, a woman's voice yearning and mourning, a rich country style guitar in lazy counterpoint. What is this we asked we love it. Two Wings said Morgan who had a light touch on the steering wheel. Glasgow band. We remembered that we liked Glasgow though it overwhelmed us in ways that Edinburgh did not. Much of the land we passed carried signs saying 'Property of the MOD'. Some of this land was strangely formed, humps of grass, as though the land were a carpet under which something misshapen had been swept. Back there is Coulport said Morgan. The arms depot housing the nuclear missiles for the submarines at Faslane. We became aware of Faslane's creeping presence, the unruly rolls of barbed wire, the distinctive anonymity of military architecture, low-level buildings the colour of sand or cement. It is through buildings like this that paperwork circulates, designating living people as ghosts. Heather said, There's something so threatening about the *sprawl* of it all. From the back of the car she said, I grew up on military bases, they look like home to me. Morgan told them how in the case of an independent Scotland, the MOD had indicated they would push for the designation of Faslane as sovereign British territory. So that the base could remain. Like Diego Garcia and the Chagos Islands! we said. We don't know about Diego Garcia and the Chagos Islands Morgan and Heather said. So we told them. We told them about meeting Diego. We told them about the expulsion of the Chagossians, about their struggle to return, about their confrontations in international courts of law with the largest powers on the planet. We told them the story of the dogs of Diego Garcia. After the dogs were killed the Chagossians were forced to board the boat that took them away from the archipelago. On that boat, where the people travelled in worse conditions than the horses on board. Some people died of an emotional-existential shock the Chagossians called sagren. People's bodies thrown overboard by the sailors. Some people threw themselves overboard. How the UK government and the US government lied and said these people were not a people. Heather and Morgan, silent. And then we told them about Michel Daëron's film and she told them all about the paintings of Clément Siatous.

* * *

[0:16:29] A workshop at the back of a house in Mauritius, a sign saying: *Atelier Raphael Louis. Reparations radios, cassettes et haut-parleurs.* On the radio 'Peros Vert' plays. Raphael Louis sits at his workbench crowded with tools and spare parts. He is holding a circuit board, into which he inserts a wire. The music stops. He reinserts the wire, the music begins again and he checks the voltage meter. As he works, he talks in Mauritian Kreol:

> They killed the dogs in the kiln. All of them! They made the owners catch them and put them in. All of them! Maybe 2,000 dogs! Everybody had 2, 3, 4 dogs. The dogs would have bitten them. They couldn't catch them. The owners had to do it. If you didn't bring your dog, you had to pay a fine. I was forced to put my 3 dogs in there. They were afraid. It's sad. Animals are like human beings. It's as if they killed a human being... They could have done the same to us. It would have been better. They should have killed us. Then it would have been over. Instead, they're killing us with grief. Not with bullets. But with disease, with heart-break. They're killing us in another way.

* * *

In Helensburgh we walked down the hill past the grand villas to the seafront. We walked along the shabby promenade of shopfronts that trailed off into shingled buildings and then we walked back, stopping to buy a poke of chips. We scrambled down the seawall then sat on the sand, leaning back against the wall. The wind whipping up and her hair stinging her face and the salt stinging our skin, the sky white. We ate the hot salty vinegared chips listening to the rush and shush of the waves. He said, I was thinking how Daniel is in this water. He's not she said. Well I know that he said, he is nowhere. No I mean he is not in this sea, this is part of the Atlantic and he is in the North Sea. All seas connect he said. Give me your screen he said suddenly, I want to check on the bitcoin. Can you trade on a weekend? You can trade cryptocurrency at any time of day or night. Can I tell you about my trading. OK she said. Purple shadows under his eyes. Do you know what I'm after? Yes she said, my permanent company. What I am after with my trading is—the wind suddenly whipping up. What? She said *Li*—he shouted, gesticulated—was he pointing to the sea?—*lick*—some of the crispier chips flung out of the paper poke that he still had a hold of. WHAT? She said LIQUIDITY!! I'M FOLLOWING LIQUIDITY!!! The wind dropped. She took the poke off him and peered into it. Only a couple of fat squidgy ones still stuck to the inside. She peeled one off. I'm learning to spot the patterns left by institutional investors he said, and I am following in their wake. Like the seagulls following the fishing boat she said. Are the actions of these big institutions so visible? Are they not more like submarines? You know that the Royal Navy calls them 'The Silent Service'? Sometimes they have this thing called *rig for silent running*: stealth mode to avoid sonar detection. Enforced rest for the crew. Playing dead—everyone in absolute silence to avoid sonar detection. During the Second World War a German submarine captain shot himself after cracking up during a depth charge attack—do you know about those?—but he didn't die instantly, he just lay there making groaning noises, so one of the crew stuck a pillow over his head till he went quiet. He looked at her. Sorry she said. Don't be he said, you didn't invent this shit. She said, I sure as shit didn't. Suddenly he leapt, holding his hand out as if stung. *What?* she said, What is it? She scrambled to her feet. *Bucket.* Tail wagging. Further down the beach Heather and Morgan, deep in conversation with a tall strong-looking woman in a silver shawl, a lurcher leaning against her legs. He didn't bite you? No he said he licked my hand. Oh she said, I'm not surprised. The chips! Bucket was now sniffing at the bits of chips on the ground. Doesn't mind the sand she said. Would you like more chips? Don't give him any more the greedy bastard, it's pointless feeding dogs they always want more. The woman with the lurcher walked away and Morgan and Heather approached, smiling and waving. Did Bucket steal your chips? No we said. We were just talking to that woman. She's been investigating Overtoun Bridge. You don't know the stories? Apparently it is the scene of a number of what some called dog suicides. Many dogs had leapt to their death there over the years. Some say it is the wild mink nesting below the bridge and the dogs leap over in pursuit of the scent, unaware of the sheer drop. Some say it is sonic disturbance caused by Faslane. Others that the dogs are picking up suicidal impulses from their human companions, who are drawn to this bridge. And still others—and the woman they had been talking to was one of them—believed that Overtoun Bridge was a *thin* place. What is that, we asked? A place where the veil between worlds is thin. It was starting to spit but filaments of sun lit up the clouds, and our faces were alive with the light.

* * *

[0:14:18] Robin Mardemootoo, lawyer for the Chagossians, speaks in voiceover, as black and white photographs appear on screen, archival images from the deportation, images of people who look in shock on board the *Nordvaer*, the ship which in 1973 took the last remaining Chagossians away from their islands:

> To examine the Chagossians' case, we had to return to the very origins of the deportation. And I came to realize that there were no official documents on that specific point. For example, there were no records allowing us to fix the number of accidental deaths or cases of suicide resulting from deportation. Our sole source was the testimony of the survivors.

* * *

[0:12:17] Lucette Azemia sits on the edge of a rope hammock that hangs by a wall of moss-covered rocks. Sounds of insects and a cockerel's cries. Lucette Azemia blinks rapidly as she speaks in Seychellois Kreol, her voice full of emotion:

> On Diego, the Americans arrived. They asked us to prepare our bags. They said we were going to Mahé. We didn't want to go but another group came with sticks and guns to force us to leave our house. They threatened us so we went to the wharf. With me I had my 5-year-old girl and my three boys. We didn't know where we were going. We couldn't even look back. The Americans were pushing us and forcing us to go forward.
>
> My daughter was behind me and my three boys in front of me. A truck ran into my daughter. And she was killed. I

turned to pick her up but they stopped me and forced me to board the boat.

Every day I suffer thinking about her buried so far from me. I can't look after her grave. If she were buried here in Mahé, I could grow flowers on her grave.

* * *

[0:14:52] Seafront café. Marcel Moulinier sits at a table. On it, two ashtrays, unused, and a cup. He speaks in English, with a South African accent. He repeatedly looks down at the table. In the middle of his story he raises the cup and drinks from it in two gulps, before continuing.

In 1965, I started working for my uncle who was the chairman of Chagos-Agalega.... He tells me that these islands have been selected by the American and the British to form an American base and therefore the Americans do insist that the whole of the islands, the Chagos, would be evacuated. And I was sent on and off to start the preparations to do the evacuations.

There was one very important item.... And that was the amount of dogs that we would be leaving behind.... we decided that the best way would be gassing the dogs. So I took one of the big caloriferes, kilns that we used to dry the copra. We made the whole calorifere, the bottom of it, first store, completely airtight, using the black plastic sheets. Then, on that, we put sea sand to keep everything down and every hole was blocked.... And then the two big holes on top in the wall so that we could put the exhaust pipes of the big trucks, the biggest trucks we had. It would be army trucks.

On the way back, Heather driving. The peace camp said Morgan and nodded to the side of the road. Caravans and lean-tos and handpainted signs behind a colourful picket fence. Morgan was making a film about it—about former military people who had joined the protestors. They told us how the protestors had a history of blocking deliveries of missiles with their bodies. From the back of the car she said, My dad used to drive the bloodhound missiles up to RAF West Raynham. She held her two hands out and splayed her fingers. This is what the missiles looked like—they were pointing out to Russia. Morgan turned from the front to look. Then they held out their own two hands and splayed their fingers like missiles too and Heather glanced at Morgan's splayed fingers her own hands on the wheel. Later, we saw the loch but we did not see any submarines. Morgan turned in their seat to look at us looking at the loch. Faslane will be flooded in time they said. In time for what? Heather said.

* * *

[0:25:15] Passengers in life vests leave the ship to board landing craft. Cut to a broken jetty on Salomon Island. Birdsong. Two soldiers stand in front of the palm trees, looking out to the approaching boat. We see the water, and the jetty. Its state is close to rubble. More soldiers emerge from the trees. Orange light. It is sunrise. The boat is moored and soldiers aid the older passengers in their orange life vests to disembark, speaking in English. On land, the passengers remove their life vests. Some can be seen kneeling and kissing the ground, others bowing to the island in salutation. Throughout can be heard the high-pitched weeping, perhaps even wailing, of a woman off-camera. A man can be heard saying, in English, 'sagren—sad—' in explanation to the soldiers. Cut to the interior of the island and the ruins of an abandoned settlement. Half-collapsed stone buildings among the vegetation, rusting metal equipment—what looks like a large wheel. At the cemetery, the Chagossians are busy with rakes, tidying up the graves. The mood is purposeful, chatty. A man bends to clear away large armfuls of dead vegetation that a woman has gathered with her rake. They are watched by two soldiers, one of whom is filming with a video-camera set on a tripod, while the other has a large SLR camera slung around his neck. Cut to two women. One is silent, and weeps, a large silver whistle around her neck. The other, in green baseball cap and white t-shirt, both bearing the CRG logo, talks about which of her family members is buried here: her grandfather, she knows, because her mother told her, and here her cousin Adeline and Adeline's older sister. Mo ena enn ser ki apel Matine kinn mor ar sagren, me mo pa kone mem ki direksyon, mo mere inn fini mor li osi, alor mo pa kone kot linn antere. A sister who died of sagren but I don't know where, my mum had died by then too so I don't know where she's buried.

Cut to the beach. In the distance, people in the sea, laughter, a surprised quality to it. Close up we see the people floating in the water, still in their clothes, while on the beach, a woman, stoops to pack sand into a bottle. A shrill whistle. A woman sitting with her back to the trees is staring out at nothing in particular and does not react to the whistle even when it is blown a second time. Cut to the jetty, soldiers stand in two inflatable boats, waiting to receive the pilgrims who line up to put on life vests, and climb aboard. As the boats leave they are watched from the jetty by three soldiers, and a man in an orange jumpsuit, some kind of maintenance uniform. One of the soldiers is an older man who wears a peaked cap and appears to be of more senior rank. He takes a snapshot on a pocket camera.

* * *

But why haunting? Haunting is the cost of subjugation. It is the price paid for violence, for genocide. Horror films in the United States have done viewers a disservice in teaching them that heroes are innocent, and that the ghouls are the trespassers. In the context of the settler colonial nation-state, the settler hero has inherited the debts of his forefathers. This is difficult, even annoying to those who just wish to go about their day. Radio ads and quips from public speakers reveal the resentment some settlers hold for tribal communities that assert claims to land and tribal sovereignty. The resentment seems to say, 'Aren't you dead already? Didn't you die out long ago? You can't really be an Indian because all of the Indians are dead. Hell, I'm probably more Indian than you are.' Sherman Alexie warns, 'In the Great American Indian novel, when it is finally written, all the white people will be Indians and all of the Indians will be ghosts.'

Erasure and defacement concoct ghosts; I don't want to haunt you, but I will.

* * *

Back in her unit he cooked us all dinner, ratatouille, and we ate with Heather and Morgan and Bucket. After we ate we watched *Chagos ou la mémoire des îles*. We felt confounded by its power, which seemed to expand with every viewing. The film's central focus was the Chagossian people's continuing resistance to the powers that had tried to erase them. We were struck by the Chagossian people's own power of refusal. Some people had refused to go on the 2006 'heritage visit' which had, after all been organized by the British government: Lorenza Piron, for example, who had been separated from her brothers and sisters in the deportation, taken to Seychelles while her family were taken to Mauritius. In the film, she says that the Seychelles, where she had lived for over thirty years, were not home, that Diego Garcia was home. When asked about whether she would go on the trip she says:

Pran mo plas pu al Diego? Mwa mo pe al vizit zil zame mwa. Ameriken? Pran pu li. Angle? Pran pu li—mo pa le.

Mo pa le. *I refuse.*

GARDE AND OTHER JOURNALWORKS
AN INTERVIEW WITH ROSE ANTOINE

Edited by Damaris Caleemootoo

Any translations from Kreol by Damaris Caleemootoo

Artwork by Rose Antoine

[i]

This is the very first one. It was for Diego. Very fine black pen, with coloured pencil.

I keep two sets, one with soft leads. The other, harder, sharpened to a point.

It's not a drawing of a police car, it's a drawing of a *toy* police car. I did it when we first went to live in Beau Bassin-Rose Hill. He loved that police car, like it was a teddy.

Diego always called me The Artist. It always felt like a complicated word when he said that.

Sad to love something so cold and hard and small. A *police* car.

One day Diego noticed that the lights on it were not symmetrical. He threw it away.

It was soon after our grandparents came for us. I drew the car for Diego because he was inconsolable. Because the toy car was wrong, because he'd had to throw it in the trash.

Diego was always throwing things away. Too sensitive. I find broken things interesting.

Admiring, affectionate, bitter, jealous. When he called me The Artist he was really saying: *Who am I? What am I?* I took to calling him The Poet. I was being nasty but I think it gave him ideas.

If I'm an artist then my day job is a kind of training. We are not called 'guards'—our official title is: 'warders'. But we guard.

Diego wasn't the name he was born with. It's the name he chose for himself.

I don't know if you could call what was in that notebook of his poetry. But it's not for me to say.

You could say it was his poet's name.

Mam was always suspicious of people in uniform. Diego too.

Me, I like order. Typical older sister. Typical *Capricorn*. But then again, I can remember the disorder.

Maybe I showed him the wrong poet. For a long, long time I stopped reading poetry.

The first time Diego came to see me at work I was on duty in Room 43. He could not stop looking at the Rousseau. That tiger with the very strange, very human face. Do animals have faces? I guess they have expressions.

I drew that car not as it was, but as it should have been. But the drawing made him sadder, somehow. He wouldn't take it. I didn't know what to do with it so I stuck it in a notebook.

If you read it in a certain way, it reads as poetry. Like looking at something with one hand over your eye.

All my work is in these journals. It doesn't exist outside of these pages. This is its form.

The title of the painting is strange: *Surprised!* It's not clear who's being surprised.

I sometimes give my work titles. They are like frames. But that first drawing, no. It wasn't meant as a work, but as a gesture. If I tried to give it a title now, after so long, it would be the wrong title.

I went to an exhibition once where the artist Quinsy Gario showed his works alongside that of artist-members of his family. His mum. His uncle. His cousins. His aunt. His brother. His great-uncle. His great-uncle's paintings were painted on board, using car paint. The paintings were of a series of buildings. Many of the paintings reminded me of Mauritius.

Rose Hill, where our grandparents lived, where they took us to live with them. Our dad's parents. But we didn't know them. We didn't know our *dad*.

One painting by Quinsy Gario's great-uncle Mauricio Onofra was of small huts on a beach that looked like fishing huts in Hastings, where I went for the day once with Louise. That painting had a title: *Bonaire Slave Huts*.

But a few of the paintings were labelled as 'no title'. Not 'untitled', which I have come to realize is a title in itself.

Our grandparents were Adventists. They took me and Diego to church. He used to love it! The singing. Me, I really liked the Bible stories.

If you look up pictures of those slave huts, you will learn that they were not big enough for an adult to stand up in.

And the library. My favourite books were the Ladybird books. This series called Great Artists. I loved the illustrations. *Van Gogh, Gauguin and Cézanne*.

The hush here is one of the things I love best. Even when it's busy.

When I arrived in London, this is one of the first places I came to visit. I spent the whole day in Rooms 41, 42 and 43, looking at the works of these artists. In the shop here I found a reprint of that Ladybird book.

I still can't believe this place. Like a *palace*. When they list the materials for works in museums and galleries, why, for some works, where this is relevant, do they not list 'time'?

London: how hard it was for me to really *see* London when I first got here.

Diego said, It's compound interest on the profits of enslavement. I said, I want to be with the paintings.

I had forgotten about that book until I saw it again! I was surprised to see how vividly I recalled some of the illustrations.

Gauguin, the white child on his tricycle, surrounded by admiring brown people. Cezanne and Zola, boyhood friends, bathing naked.

Looking at, and being with—two different things.

The paintings change all the time, because you are changing all the time, or are not the same every day. The paintings you notice, also. Before Diego mentioned it, I never really noticed that van Gogh painting, *Long Grass with Butterflies*.

Van Gogh in his room in the asylum, head being bandaged with great care. In the background, his bed bolted to the floor, the wall. Along the side of his bed, a row of metal rings.

And the illustrations in the book of the famous paintings are in *both* styles: Ladybird *and* Great Artist Master.

I often think about how 'guard' in English means to look after, to protect. The same in Kreol. Though in Kreol garde also means cop.

We have to wear name badges. We are labelled, like the paintings.

As a kid I never noticed the bolts or the rings in that picture.

Have you noticed, Diego said, you are all black and brown. Not all of us I said. I bet none of the curators are he said.

We guard these treasures with our bodies.

I'm the only Rose in the gallery. The only person called Rose. Of course there are hundreds of roses in the paintings.

On the website for the gallery you can search all their papers.

'National Gallery Technical Bulletin Volume 10, 1986. Brown and Black Organic Glazes, Pigments and Paints by Raymond White.'

The famous expression is English Rose. But I'm British Rose. Thanks to my mum I'm British, and I am Rose after her. She did it to give herself a second chance. In the hope she might come to feel more at home on an island she never wanted to come to, where she was not wanted.

Can you have two lives? Two homes?

Diego would spend a long time looking at this painting. He could not decide if it was terrible, or great. Funny, or very very sad.

There can't have been any roses on Diego. 500 miles south of the equator. Do roses grow that far south?

I love the names of roses. The names for the different varieties. Like the names for colours of paint.

Born on Diego Garcia but died in Mauritius. When I was 18 I was given her ashes. Me and Diego put them in the sea.

When our mum died we lost the language.

Some of my titles are in Kreol, some in French, some in English. Some have no titles.

It's the tiger who is surprised, but actually, it looks more terrified. What has 'surprised' it? Someone outside the frame of the painting. A man with a gun? The viewer?

Or the artist, in this very French-looking 'jungle', sitting at his easel, holding his palette and brush.
In fact he found his jungles in the Jardin des Plantes.

The only 'jungle' in France is the place they called the refugee camp in Calais.

After Diego died I read a lot of poetry. But not the notebook I found.

At Diego's inquest I copied down words which sounded interesting, or rather words being used in interesting ways. The way one of the nurses giving evidence did not refer to time but to *material* time. Like the *fabric* of time.

Light. That's what comes through. Like needles.

That is not what I imagine to happen when paintings are slashed, the way they can be by ill or angry people.

Which is something I must guard against. I am alert if I see someone act edgy round the works.

I'm less anxious about the works under glass, or the ones painted on cigar boxes rather than canvas.

I imagine darkness then.

Perhaps it was the artist himself who was surprised, by what he had painted. Sometimes I paint things that surprise me. This self-portrait I did here for example.

In painting that expression the artist painted himself into the painting. Diego said: I look at it and feel I *am* that tiger. Anyone with human feeling would.

The same for him being vegetarian from the age of 4, once Diego found out where meat came from. Soon after we came to Rose Hill. He just refused it.

The man who painted that tiger spent his whole life as a customs officer.

This is a self-portrait of me in my uniform. I painted it when Diego died.

Diego said, You know, I think it's that the tiger is surprised to be brought to life by paint.

The way words can bring things to life—can make it so: *You* have a British passport. *You* don't.

I like how there is no background. How I am floating. You can't see what it is I'm guarding.

[ii]

I've been in London since 2002, the year a judge ruled me British.

Not Diego though, born a year too late. Only those born between 1969-1982 to a Chagossian mother could get the passports. After that it's another generation.

They are always drawing lines around us.

If drawing could be a legally recognized language. Many Chagossian kids who were sent into exile never learnt to read or write: some stopped going to school because of the abuse, or because they had to work, to feed their families.

At the time I was back living in Rose Hill with my grandparents. It was after the divorce. I was saving up for a place of my own. I used the money to come to London instead.

Diego called me The Artist but I'm as much a *writer*.

You can make whole nations disappear, or invent them with words.

The night before I left Mauritius my grandmother made biryani. Diego didn't show up. There was an Arsenal game on.

He was crazy about football. *Arsenal till I die*. That's what he said.

I was working for a British company. British and American Tobacco. I worked in corporate governance. I attended to the legal requirements pertaining to the governance of corporations, institutions, etc.

I am good at filling out forms.

Diego said: Britain and America, a long history of working together in the business of death. He was a smoker himself. I pointed that out to him. He laughed and said that contradiction was the point, the *problem*.

It was when he started smoking that we discovered he had no sense of smell. My grandparents were always busting him for it and he couldn't work out how they knew.

In London I went to live with a friend of my grandmother's, Madame Lai. She came here in 1964 and bought a place with her husband. It's between Camden Town and St Pancras.

The house is tall and narrow and dark with small rooms, sloping floors, and a scrubby garden, more of a yard. It's worth a million pounds. I live at the top. There's no double glazing, the windows are old and rotting in their frames. It feels like a house from a black and white film. It creaks up there, under the roof.

I don't go to church with Madame Lai. I don't believe what she believes. But we don't talk about that. Madame Lai likes me to sit with her while she watches telly. I do that sometimes. Not that I'm interested in the programmes she likes. Soaps. Reality TV.

I sat him down in front of the fridge to test his claim, taking out piment crasé, achard mangue, a lemon, ketchup, mustard, poisson salé, some leftover Kari glenryck—nothing! He told me that instead of a sense of smell mwena mo sans.

Sometimes I help her out with her forms. Pension tax credits and things.

I find it restful to sit there, with her clock ticking, kind of sombre. Eating Marie biscuits and drinking vanilla tea.

This is London to me, the narrow pavements, the narrow houses. The greyness, the soot. The huge trees, so dusty they seem like objects cast from concrete, not living, green things.

Diego used to say, London is killing me.

Recently I have been using this dust as a material. I'd place an object on a new page of my book. It must be an object with a distinctive outline. I have done this with coins, with my mother's broken comb, with a pair of nail scissors, I like the curved blades. Then I paint the page around the object with white paint. 'Ivory white'.

The only thing I have of our mum's is that comb, and a photograph of her.

I put the book out on the windowsill during a dry spell. I leave it there for a few days. Eventually the paint dries, but all the soot in the air, from the road, gets mixed into it. I lift the objects off. They reveal their shapes on the page. I call this 'impressionism'.

The comb is blue. It has broken teeth. In French you would say 'she has broken teeth'. Not in Kreol, which is not gendered.

I remember little about our mum. She was funny about her things. Careless with them and jealous of them.

Two of its teeth are broken, snapped off. The blue of the comb is the blue of lapis lazuli, the stone used in pigments for many of the paintings at the Gallery. So expensive it was only used for the blue of the Virgin Mary's robes. Mined in Afghanistan. Now Afghanistan is mined.

That was one of Diego's. He did like to play with words.

In the Afghan war US warplanes took off from the base at Diego.

This blue is also the blue of the water just beyond the reef of Diego, or so I imagine.

Although I do like programmes with priests in. And historical dramas in costume in the English countryside with houses that look like the ones in the painting I guard. If the weather is nice I like to walk to work. On the way, I pass a Blue Plaque for Rimbaud and Verlaine. I go via the canal, and then by the churchyard of St Pancras.

I first heard of Rimbaud from reading Ananda Devi's *Ève de ses décombres*. How the boy Sad(iq) came to consciousness through reading Rimbaud's poetry.

Lorsqu'elle a fini elle a dit, ce poète s'appelle Rimbaud. Je suis votre frère.

When things first started to get difficult for Diego, when he was around 17 or so himself, I thought Rimbaud might help him too.

Je me suis armé contre la justice. Diego saw that and threw the book aside.

I tried to read him the note: *C'est-à-dire contre la pseudo-justice de la société telle qu'elle est.*

But he was against Rimbaud, he said, and what he stood for. Was it because he was homosexual? Is that what bothered him? Diego said I don't give a fuck who he fucked. But he became a fucking arms dealer in colonial Africa.

I should have given him the Devi instead.

Diego never enjoyed school, though he enjoyed words. He played with them but at school the words played him.

Me I like explanations and definitions. I always wanted to be a lawyer growing up, but I could never focus on my studies. I had difficulty concentrating. No confidence.

Where did that ambition come from? I had so few desires. Lawyers have a complex relationship with power. But then again I don't recall feeling powerless.

Not even when mum died, and we got removed to another life.

She hit me once for using that comb. Perhaps it was me that broke it. I don't remember.

A teacher at school told me about ICSA, the Institute of Chartered Secretaries and Administrators. I got a job at British American Tobacco. That was where I met my ex-husband. It is not an interesting story.

This qualification is recognized in Britain. Also: *Crown Dependencies and associated territories, which include the Caribbean, sub-Saharan Africa, the Middle East, Mauritius and Sri Lanka.* ICSA work seems very boring. But it is where all the details of power reside: in the paperwork.

Those experiments with the soot, trying to paint with soot, those are new. It was about the air. My mood.

I learnt the other day: Junior colonial administrators for the East India Company were called 'Writers'.

British Indian Ocean Territory: when the Foreign and Common-wealth Office created this, they presented the Chagossian people and their rights to their homeland as a fiction.

Here is a little watercolour of that comb. Underneath I have written in English: *whereby objects that are broken become things that I keep.*

This is a painting of my mum. It's in liquid watercolour. The colours are intense. A lot of red and blue.

I've only been back to Mauritius twice since leaving for London. For my grandfather's funeral, then my grandmother's.

I based the painting on this photograph of my mum. I don't know who took it. She's wearing a hibiscus in her hair. In the photo, she looks angry. In this photo she is not wearing her cross.

In my painting I haven't got the expression right, she looks a bit crazy.

I remember a little gold cross on a chain she always wore. Then one day it disappeared.

We were never encouraged to talk about her. Gradually we stopped.

You can see that the wall behind her is a very beautiful blue-green colour.

When I went back the first time, for my grandmère's funeral, Diego had just lost his job as a cashier in a minimarket. He was spending a lot of time down in Tamarin. One time he met a group of young people there from Pointe aux Sables. On a picnic for someone's birthday. They invited him to sit with them. He started hanging out with them. He told me stories they'd told him. Stories their parents and grandparents had told them about Chagos. He heard a story about our mother's mother, who we never knew. It wasn't a happy one.

Diego told me about losing his job. Turns out he was undercharging the old people who would come in for, say, a tin of pilchards or corned beef. Then he would make up his till by overcharging the people coming through with big trolleys full of frozen pizzas, fancy toilet paper. His till always balanced. But one of the shoppers with the big trolleys was a friend of the owner and she started to notice she was getting overcharged.

Only one of the walls in our flat was that colour. You can't see in the photograph but the rest were a dirty white. I remember the day Mum painted it. She said she didn't have enough paint for the whole room. What she meant was she didn't have enough money for the paint. She said the colour reminded her of the sea in Diego.

The day the soldiers came for them, rifles at their backs, rounding them up to get them on the boat. Washing still on the line. Waking up on the boat, seeing nothing around but sea, not even sure you were really awake. Some people jumped into the sea. They preferred to die in the sea.

When Grandpère died I came back to Mauritius. Diego hadn't had work in a while. He was depressed, thinking about our mum. Realizing how disconnected she must have been. How disconnected *he* was. He no longer hung out with the group.

He was now reading up about Diego Garcia though. The base there. He played me a sega by Menwar, 'Baz militer'.

This is what was left behind. A place where you never heard cars, just birds and the sea. Now the B1 and B2 planes screaming over-head. Concrete everywhere.

Also Ton Vié from Peros Banhos. 'Peros Vert'.

In an interview Ton Vié talks about how he never learnt to read and write—there had been schools on Diego, on Salomon, but not on the smaller islands.

The forms of knowledge that develop in the absence of literacy. The ways of remembering.

Kids arriving from Chagos who stopped going to school because they faced hostility. People mocking their Chagossian Kreol. And kids had to work. Doing hard adult jobs at 10 or 11.

An anthem for Chagos. The yearning of it. Diego sang it over and over as we packed up our grandpère's stuff in the home.

Chagossian women went out on demonstrations to fight for the right to return. Chagossian women faced police brutality, were arrested, imprisoned.

We are not part of the Chagossian community Diego said, for *the exact* reasons that there *is* a Chagossian community in Mauritius in the first place. The denial of the existence of the Chagossians as a people, with a homeland.

Chagossians were supposed to just disappear.

The Mauritian government should have settled the Chagossians on the coast he said, Not in the city.

Later, I remembered this. He didn't say 'us': the Mauritian government should have settled *us*. I remember this now because in London that changed.

What did our mum being from Diego mean to us, in the end? Only the loss of her. A name for her pain. And a measure of it. Nothing but a hole.

Before leaving Mauritius for London, I went to the CRG in Cassis, to see what I could learn.

I didn't tell Diego. I didn't think he could handle it.

The Chagos Refugee Group. It is a big villa in the Chagos colours—the walls orange and blue, the railings painted black. I asked to meet with Olivier Bancoult, head of the CRG. A lady took me to a meeting room where I had to wait. The walls inside were orange too. And covered with paintings. Many by the same artist, it seemed. As I waited for Olivier Bancoult I looked at these paintings, and took photos of them.

This one is of a large ship, a group of people on the dock as if posing for a photograph (as opposed to a painting). I think this must have been painted from a photograph. They are about to board. They look excited. All but one are dressed in white, some with green baseball caps, others with white headgear, all waving and smiling, the figure in the middle a man wearing what looks like business casual.

There's a panel of writing on the painting:

Ce tableau a été peint par Clément Siatous qui y a Reproduit la scène de l'escale à Diego garcia du Mauritius Trochetia le jeudi 6 Avril 2006 Artiste-Peintre CSiatous MSK

I was in London when this happened. Diego told me about it. He didn't go to the docks, ashamed of seeing his friends from Pointe aux Sables.

The ship is very carefully painted. The crowd is painted in a looser brushstroke, and gives a sense of energy, excitement, the joy of the whole group.

My mum should have been in that picture. Maybe she is, maybe among these figures there are also ghosts.

The first time Chagossians went home, after being forced to leave by the military, was a visit under military supervision.

Maybe the energy I see in the way they are painted is their spirits.

Above the ship is a fantasy painting of a tropical island at sunset and two small, motorized fishing boats—or perhaps speedboats?

When Olivier Bancoult entered I recognized him instantly. I had seen his photograph in the papers. And there were some cuttings on the walls.

He is handsome and looked very weary. Alone. In the way that statesmen are depicted in times of crisis.

In the foreground, a coconut tree in silhouette against the vivid orange of the sky and sea and, also, something that makes me think the painting is not of Chagos, even an imaginary Chagos, but Mauritius.

A thatched sunshade, the kind they put on the beach for tourists.

But maybe such things are found on the beach at Diego. Put there for the soldiers when they are relaxing.

I told Olivier Bancoult that our mum was from Diego but that we had grown up with Mauritian grandparents. That I was visiting from London.

I didn't know if these paintings were 'untitled' or 'title not known'. If they were all by the same artist.

I told him: I want to know my mother's story. Her death certificate said accidental overdose, age 25, but that's not her story. Just the end of it. Olivier Bancoult gave me the name of a person in Crawley I could speak to when I got back. Sabrina Jean, leader of the CRG in the UK.

We talked a bit about the paintings, he told me most of them were by a man called Clément Siatous, from Peros Banhos.

And this portrait of a woman whose name I wanted to know. She looks careworn in a way that speaks of the city, not the sea, as though she had been superimposed on this beach.

And this painting of an encounter. A casual encounter, a friendly one, two neighbours, a man and a woman, passing one another in the road. I love the way it is painted. It looks like an illustration from a Ladybird book. I would call it 'bon swar'. The bullock looks so patient. The woman's pink parasol and her pink sari. A country road. If these people had been painted by Gauguin, they would have looked different. The encounter would have looked different.

Gauguin's 'natural' was 'violent'.

Why are you so angry?

Good afternoon

I like how *casual* this looks. I have never seen brown people, black people, looking this *casual* in paintings in The National Gallery.

Siatous' paintings are amazing. Like photographs of memories.

I can't remember her laugh or her smile. But I remember that day. I remember that smell of fresh paint.

He lives in Crawley, now, Siatous. I often think about writing to him. Asking if I can meet him.

I love the names of paint colours, but I am mistrustful of them. They try to create a specific feeling. To sell you that feeling.

On my first ever visit to the gallery I saw colours I had no names for. Not in the paintings—on the actual *walls*. The walls were not white, as I would have expected. At least, I had no expectation of what colour the walls would be. But it was only when I saw them that I realized white is what I would have assumed.

In Room 43 I could not tell you what colour the walls are: grey-pink, purple-beige. I have tried to replicate it here but have not succeeded.

If I had to give this colour a name I would call it *chagrin*. But as it is used in English, not French: *Acute vexation, annoyance, or mortification, arising from disappointment, thwarting, or failure*. In French, the Larousse dictionary says 'sagren' means *État de déplaisir, de peine, d'affliction*. In Chagossian Kreol, the word *sagren* is the name given to the Chagossian psychic-somatic experience of exile. Actual heartbreak.

One of Diego's friends had a cousin who was one of the first Chagossian people to come to Crawley. They told him the story. How a man called Alan Vincatassin had had a vision that he should bring his people to Britain, since they were British.

Alan Vincatassin persuaded some people to go with him. They arrived at Gatwick. With reluctance and some bafflement they were let into the country. Who were these black people with British passports who spoke no English? They had nowhere to go, no money.

For days and nights they lived in the airport. Vincatassin was trying to get someone to help them but no one wanted to know. And then he told them he would go to the press. Immediately Crawley Social Services got in touch.

Now there is an established Chagossian community in Crawley. Also In Manchester and Derby.

In Kreol, *sagren* means *sorry*.

I read that in 1915 a Haitian poet called Edmond Laforest committed suicide by jumping to his death with a Larousse dictionary tied around his neck.

I know no words in Haitian Kreyòl. I remember no words of Chagossian Kreol. In this painting of my mum I have painted the whole room—that is, all the walls visible in the painting—in that colour that she chose. The colour of the sea in Diego Garcia.

Vincatassin and his supporters believe Chagos should remain under British control. The CRG wants self-determination, like Rodrigues has. And maybe other groups want Mauritian sovereignty to be restored. But what about the base?

Diego said: The base must go.

I am not sure if such structures can be torn down. Perhaps one must build around them.

Diego laughed when he first came to my work. What kind of colour do you call that he said. He meant the walls. Satini brinzel.

Satini brinzel would be wrong as a name for this colour, in this place. Too full of flavour.

Mum telling me this thing: that the queen of England thinks the world smells like fresh paint.

The paint swatch cards, with every shade between blue and green. Her getting me to read out the names to her.

Roses have nice names too. Odd names. Some for people, like 'Lady Di'. 'Sabrina Jean': that would be a nice name for a rose.

But now I am wondering: what stopped me from painting my mother beside the sea itself? That would have felt like a lie.

Since there is Clément Siatous painting what he remembers, how can I paint what isn't true.

[iv]

This is a sketch of Diego and Madame Lai. They are sitting together on the sofa, looking shocked, clutching each other. They are not looking at the viewer, or me. They are staring at something to my left.

When Diego came to visit me in London he didn't want to leave me. He couldn't stay legally. He didn't have the right to work here. To *be* here.

He got given a bike by a charity project and found cash in hand work as a cycle courier.

In winter he used to hang on to the back of buses to keep warm. He got ill from the fumes.

He started renting Madame Lai's spare bedroom. It turns out he loved watching television with her. He enjoyed all her programmes, especially *EastEnders*, *Coronation Street* and *Holby City*. *EastEnders* was their favourite.

In this drawing they are watching Phil Mitchell set the Queen Vic on fire while going cold turkey from his crack addiction, having accused his mum, Peggy Mitchell, of loving the pub more than she loves him.

When Diego couldn't stand the courier work any more he got a job as a cleaner. He used to go all over, a bingo hall, offices. He complained about not being paid the London Living Wage and they sacked him. But he made a friend there who got him into squatting. The people he lived with taught him electrics, plumbing.

I once saw them turn on the electricity for a whole tower block that a community—his friends and their friends—were trying to squat. It was winter, really cold. I watched Diego and his friend outside in the dark taking out some tool, a welding torch or some such. Then they opened up a lamppost.

They wired the torch's power lead to the panel in the lamppost. Then they used the torch to flip up a metal grid in the ground and then they hit a switch. The whole block lit up. The cheering!

After Diego left, I think Madame Lai got a bit lonely. She'd invite me to go on the church coach trips with her. They are really good value. It's a cheap way to visit museums in other cities.

We went to Hastings. There was a trip to Edinburgh. On the coach to Edinburgh I sat next to a woman called Louise. She told me a story about the founder of Adventism, Ellen G. White.

There is a long-running dispute among some Adventists on the matter of White's heritage: when it was claimed in a book that she had African-American heritage the White estate hired a genealogist to look into her ancestry.

Louise had grown up a Catholic but had a nervous breakdown. Then in hospital she met a kind Adventist so thought, why not.

When he started squatting, Diego was happier. He had friends. He had energy, schemes. He tried to get me to do portraits of people done to look like passport photos. To raise funds for his friends who needed the money for citizenship applications. Diego tried to sell these for me on eBay, but no one bought any.

Diego was a great believer in the online marketplace. He used to trawl charity shops for stuff he could resell for more money. He would make me presents of some of his finds. Clothes: he always thought I should dress more colourfully. He would always say he had bought these things for me from Gucci.

I told Louise when she admired my scarf, silk, marbled. Said that Diego had got it for me from 'Gucci'. On that trip we shared a room in Edinburgh, up by the foot of Calton Hill. Like an eighteenth-century painting!

And yet the light reminded me of Mauritius somehow—the light by the sea.

Diego and me used to go sometimes at the weekend, on our own. Down to Tamarin.

He started getting me art books too. He wanted to build me a library. One day he brought me a book on van Gogh from the Great Artists Collection library ('Five centuries of great art in full colour'). He wanted to know why van Gogh was Volume 1 in the series. I said Read it and see. He loved the paintings. Zot buze he said. And van Gogh's story.

Louise liked walking and I like going to galleries so we took the advice of the lady at the guesthouse and did a walk together. It's called the Waters of Leith. You follow this route along a low-lying river—a wide stream really. Walking at the edges and under bridges.

I loved the red and grey of the buildings, or the brick of a church we passed, mottled like a tortoiseshell cat's.

Although in the end it was confirmed by the hired genealogists that White's ancestry was 'Anglo-Saxon'.

The water shining, the pebbles shining. Both of us babbling. Louise has pale blue eyes that make her look eternally surprised. Louise talked about her breakdown and her lapsed Catholicism. She said: Everyone thought I broke down out of shame or guilt. But it was relief!

The different kinds of quiet. The different kinds of listening.

Realizing that if you followed these waters eventually you reach the sea. Louise telling me that part of the city is by the sea.

Two galleries, housed in mansions, facing one another, that's where the walk ends. I chose the gallery where I could see van Gogh's *Olive Trees*, painted in Saint-Rémy. I stood for almost an hour looking at it, Louise coming and going. That was nice—to be left alone, but returned to.

That night in Edinburgh we stayed up talking, both of us in our beds, addressing the ceiling. I told her about having been married, how he was a bully.

The house in Arles where van Gogh had hoped to set up as an artists' commune. The House of Friends.

Enn lacaz ec mo zami, Diego said. Mwena sa asterla. He meant the squat. He was so happy there.

I see now that he was the happiest I'd known him.

Louise came to see me at work once. She stood for a long time looking at the Lautrec painting *Two Friends*.

We went for lunch. Talking about the painting she said, I like how they don't give a fuck.

She was no Adventist. She said so herself. People were kind when I was ill she said. But I see now if they knew my heart. The one in the foreground is wrapped in something, not a shawl, it is too plain. A blanket? The hardness of her face.

Louise said, She looks like she's relating something to the other woman, who is sitting more erect, alert, listening. She's right in the middle of her story. Something difficult that has happened that she must relate to the other woman.

Louise said I have heard about this Adventist movement SDA Kinship. They have a group called KinWomen. Would you come with me to a meeting?

I don't know I said.

Diego was so happy in those days he even had a girlfriend. She was beautiful. Julia Contreras. Got him into reading. Gave him a story he went mad for, by an Argentinian writer. About these creatures called axolotls. I didn't know what one was then he showed me. They don't look real!

Diego's new squatting friends were involved in politics, in protests. He got back into reading about Diego Garcia. One friend, a student, told Diego that there was going to be a sit-in at my work. They were protesting the cuts to universities, to libraries, museums.

And our union was hearing rumours of outsourcing—our contracts transferred from the gallery to companies who guard bank vaults, buildings, borders, empty space.

I asked Diego to find out more.

They were going to hold a 'teach-in' in Room 43. Try to be there he begged me. They had chosen that room specially, because of two paintings there. The apples (and a pomegranate) by Courbet—painted in prison, when he was arrested for his part in the Paris Commune. Manet's *The Execution of Maximilian.*

Manet's paintings intrigue me. There is something *not quite right* about them.

I spend a lot of my wages in the gallery bookshop—I get a discount there. I bought a beautiful little book on Manet. Foucault says, Manet complicates our positions as viewers: makes us witnesses, rather.

We're not allowed to read while we work, not like in contemporary art galleries. You see them sitting hunched in the corner with their big tomes, ignoring you.

I found out when the protest would happen. Got myself put on that shift.

I like to look at what they're reading but they look resentful when you do. As though you've interrupted their privacy. If you want to be invisible wear a uniform!

I went to a contemporary art gallery once where one of the guards had a kid he was looking after.

This magical kid, running around the gallery like it was a playground, drawing her uncle into a kind of Musical Statues game.

That's the thing I notice most about this particular Manet, apart from the missing panels: the firing squad is central to the picture but what I notice are the *uniforms*. We are not allowed to read while we work but we can *think*. Which is like writing in invisible ink.

I'm always doing that. Most of the time what I'm thinking is nothing to do with what I'm looking at. I look at the art. I look at the people looking at the art. I look at all the ways they have of looking.

Looking but not seeing. Seeing but not looking. Staring. Looking via camera-phone. Contemplating. Looking in a way that suggests they feel they are being looked at. Want to be seen looking.

And then the people who come in to draw. Draw and look, look then draw.

Every time he spun round the kid froze, but her eyes were dancing. He kept pretending she was one of the artworks—and she was, and him too.

I stayed longer than I meant to, just to watch them play.

There are many episodes in history of people attacking artworks. We are told this on our training. You go on alert if you sense someone looking agitated around the works.

I felt a bit like this when the mass of students came in, near closing time, and sat on the floor.

I recognized Diego's friend. I announced that the gallery would be closing soon and that everyone should leave. But apparently, they were going to just sit there.

Diego had warned me beforehand. They wanted to write something together. A manifesto, to formulate their protest, to express their desire for change. I was scared for the art.

There was some discussion among the gathering: what were they doing there? Was it a teach-in or an occupation?

A fellow warder came in from Room 42. He was annoyed and stressed. He wanted to get home. There were protests outside in Trafalgar Square.

A protestor stood up and said, The reason why this brother wants to evacuate us from this room is because essentially there is billions of dollars of Capitalist assets in here.

I have always wanted to see Manet's *Olympia*. There was a coach trip to Paris with Madame Lai's church but I didn't go in the end.

The last time I saw Louise, we met up for a walk in Regent's Park. She surprised me: took me to the Rose Garden. The colours! You could almost taste them. I said, Diego would not be able to smell these. And the names!

They made me think of the paint names my mum had read out to me that time. I read them out as we passed.

Louise said, *The roses are named after queens and people of note.* That was when she took my hand and squeezed it, and told me how she felt.

I should have not pulled away. I should have said, Why not.

[v]

This is a drawing of common wireweed or *Sida acuta*. It only grows in tropical regions.

Though people of Chagossian heritage are unable to travel to the archipelago except under policed trips, organized by the government at their convenience, there have been many *many* research trips undertaken by scientists: to catalogue, document, etc. the flora and fauna of Chagos.

I learnt this from Diego.

In AN ANNOTATED CHECK LIST OF THE FLORA OF DIEGO GARCIA, BRITISH OCEAN TERRITORY BY J. M. W. TOPP, common wireweed is noted as growing in one specific place on the island: 'frequent in ruins of Point Marianne village'.

Diego was becoming more Chagossian than Mauritian. He became more confident, I noticed. He wondered why I didn't feel the same. I began to wonder this too.

I felt about as much Chagossian as I did Adventist. Which is to say, not much at all, though both must have shaped me. Before Diego died, this part of myself was hidden. Now I am trying to work it out.

When in 2010 the British government made the Chagos a Marine Protected Area, Diego went to meetings, rallies. The MPA was a cynical manoeuvre to keep the Chagossians out. How were Chagossians, a people who had always fished, meant to resume their way of life? Wikileaks confirmed that. As a 'no take' zone, no fishing could happen there, for example.

What were the rules around a 'no take' zone that had itself been taken?

I remember Diego going on his fishing trips to Pointe aux Sable.

And what is the point of a marine protection area with a huge nuclear submarine base in the centre of it?

Point Marianne village is where the copra plantation was. Where the Chagossian people on Diego Garcia who worked on that plantation had lived.

What the researcher's report doesn't note is that there are many uses of this wireweed flower in folk medicine. I read online about ritual plant use in West Africa. *Bathing in a decoction of this plant will help protect people seeking to escape from justice.*

I don't remember much about our mum but I remember she believed in magic. Witchcraft.

Diego went to a fundraiser in Crawley. Heard Sabrina Jean speak. She had got a football team together to play in a World Cup for stateless people. You should try out I told him. But he was too anxious.

One day I realized just how differently we felt, Diego and I.

Diego was sad. Julia Contreras had left the UK. Her student visa had expired. I said, Let's go to the Rose Garden in Regent's Park. I told him about all the roses. That they are named for people. A good place to go when you miss someone.

On the way we passed the zoo. The London Zoo we had heard about from our Grandpère who once came to London in 1977 with Grandmère on a visit to Madame Lai, and Pastor Lai, who was still alive then. The Lais had brought them here, where they had seen Guy the Gorilla and ate mint-choc-chip ice-cream. They had never forgotten the experience.

They had told us often how one day they would bring us to London and we would do this. Let's go for them, we said.

We walked around, depressed, for the animals, for how much it had cost us to be there, for Grandmère and Grandpère for whom this had been a lifetime highlight, for ourselves because we could not enjoy ourselves as they had.

Though we had a good laugh at the signpost, which I have drawn here: *Birds of Prey, Lions, Ladies.*

When we saw the sign for the aquarium, we went in. We might even see an axolotl. It was OK at first, walking through those subterranean passages in the dreamy silver light, though now I struggle to disentangle them from my last memories of Diego. His being ill. The sense of him submerged somehow. We passed the strange ugly nocturnal-looking fish that looked like nightmares.

And then we came upon it. The Chagos Reef Aquarium. An aquarium got up to look like a section of the Chagos coral reef. It looked like a Christmas display for Selfridges. We said nothing for a few minutes. Then Diego said, Anu ale and so we left.

He walked me back to Madame Lai's. We ate our dinner—kari pwason ek so satini koko—watching *Strictly*. We didn't say much about the zoo to Madame Lai, who told us her version of the story about Guy the Gorilla, though for her it had been Key Lime sorbet.

Whilst Diego and I had both found this experience of the Chagos aquarium unspeakable, the difference between us was that I also found it *interesting*. Colette said that writers should look closely at what pleases them, and closer still at what gives them pain.

Two years after they made Chagos a Marine Protection Area, the UK government changed the squatting laws. They criminalized the squatting of residential buildings: buildings designed and fit for human habitation. It became more dangerous for Diego, in the UK illegally, to squat houses. He feared the police, and arrest.

Some of Diego's fellow squatters who had been doing this for years were now finding their names come up on housing association lists after many years of waiting. His community broke up. Some moved into their own flats or left London for good. Then Diego started squatting commercial buildings. These weren't like the homes he had made with his friends. These people were harder. Desperate. Had big problems with drink or drugs, mental health.

He would come and stay with me in between evictions. He would tell me bitter stories of the police.

Madame Lai's son was starting to hassle her about Diego, asking when he was going to start paying proper rent. When I mentioned this to Diego we had a big row, back to how it had been in those first hard months, like he was blaming me for his life. He left.

To see him with all those bags. I can't say it was like leaving Chagos, because I was never there.

The Chagossians were only allowed one bag. He could barely carry all of his. God knows what was in them all. He looked shocked and hopeless.

He said he was going to Edinburgh. He was talking about the Rivers of Babylon, but I realized that he meant the Waters of Leith. He had heard me talking about them.

His friend from the gallery protest, the student, was working up in Edinburgh now. He could go and see her he said.

What I draw and what I paint are things around me. Or memories or things I want to remember. Writing too. More and more. Just bits of things I see or hear or overhear or read. There's no actual story.

He was not in Edinburgh long. Then he came back without all the bags. He came to my work.

I sensed him before I saw him. That feeling of being on alert, scared for the paintings. Then there he was, his back to me. Standing by the van Goghs. By *Long Grass with Butterflies*. A painting I had never really noticed before. So tense. He looked thinner, sadder.

In Pizza Express he eats like he has forgotten he was starving.

He rambled on about the painting. About never having really *seen* it before. How he'd always felt it was a non-painting, not about anything. The brushstrokes make you feel agitated he said, all over the place, like the guy couldn't keep his mind still.

He hated London but he didn't know where else to go.

I thought Norfolk, Wales. Somewhere near the sea. The country. Somewhere to calm his mind. Though it was colder now, February. Such places would be bleak. And he needed to be near me.

Sometimes I would catch him staring—just staring at the ground, frowning. That was it I realized. The subject of that painting.

In the end he finally agreed to go to the doctor's, when I told him we were going to a Safe Surgery. They will not turn you in for being here without the right papers.

This is a painting of me and Diego in a park. We're eating ice cream. We're eating ice cream on a beautiful day in the park. I tried to paint it like a picture from a Ladybird book.

Strange that I painted this, since I couldn't bring myself to paint my mum by the sea on Diego Garcia.

On the last day I ever spent with Diego he told me the story of that police car—of having to chuck it. He had forgotten about the drawing I did for him. I didn't mention it.

On that day we got off the bus in front of Lewisham Park, across the road from the hospital. For a moment I thought about suggesting that we go to the park to get an ice cream. He has always loved ice cream. Diego was always as greedy as a dog.

Though he loved dogs, would always share what he had to eat with a dog, would always have a kind word for a dog. If it was the kind that liked a grapple he would do that too.

I think of Diego's love of dogs and I think of the story. The one about the dogs on Diego Garcia: how they were gassed to frighten everyone. *Terrorize* them. Yes, that was an act of terrorism.

I was worried that if we stopped to sit and eat ice cream on a beautiful sunny day in the park, Diego would change his mind and the police would come. So I did not suggest it.

As we crossed Lewisham High Street and walked into the hospital grounds, following the signage for the mental health unit, I made sure to let him lead the way.

When we get to the unit, I let him open the door first, let him go through first. I let him call for the lift. At the door to the ward, I let him press the buzzer. I let him step through, into the ward, first.

the ward was like a submarine

the doors to the rooms like the doors to vaults, sealed chambers

the doctors were all white the nurses and cleaners were all black

only one of the patients was white

'Ivory black' is a name that has always twisted my brain.

'Bone black'. The pigment was originally made by grinding up burnt ivory in oil. *Historically, bone char was used in sugar refining as a decolorizing agent.*

I read online that the process of producing bone char yields a by-product, bone oil, a foul, filthy substance that was used in wartime as a 'chemical warfare harassing agent': during the desert campaign of World War II, it was used to render the water in wells undrinkable. Who came up with the idea of killing those dogs? Who formulated the plan?

The last time I saw Diego's face was as I was leaving the ward. As the door closed behind me I caught his eye through the glass. He mouthed, *Don't leave me.*

At home I read van Gogh's letters. The world knows about his brother but he had sisters too.

What can I tell you that's new, not much. I have two landscapes on the go (no. 30 canvases) of views taken in the hills. One is the countryside that I glimpse from the window of my bedroom. In the foreground a field of wheat, ravaged and knocked to the ground after a storm.

He texted me. *I won't be here for long.*

Where is 'here'. Where is 'there'. He told the doctor, *This isn't the place for me.*

The police who came to the door, who came with the news. If I had to name their expression I would say: *sagren.*

At the inquest I heard that Diego told the doctors that the ward was not the place for him. He especially couldn't bear it when the sirens went off, the emergencies.

I often wonder if what broke him down in the end was formlessness, or if his breaking down was because of his having no form, no name of his own, no sense of what he might call himself.

he never became what he could have been

husband or father or

poet

what other hopes he might have had then

lost over the years like things slipping

from a hole in your pocket that get lost

without you noticing

in the end I guess for him it was not enough

to be what he was

a friend a squatter

What a pity that one can't move the building here. It would be magnificent to hold an exhibition there, all the empty rooms, the big corridors

a bike courier a grandson, barely a son

but always

my brother.

[vi]

Since Diego died I've been dreaming a lot. Reading a lot. Drawing a lot.

At the inquest, I couldn't stop drawing. This is Sarah M, a nursing assistant on the ward. The last known person to speak to Diego.

The doctors had approved his going out, by himself. It was Sarah M who signed him out.

Asked to describe his demeanour she said 'cheerful, happy'.

Sarah M's voice trembled as she gave her evidence.

When the coroner thanked her and invited her to step down, her relief. She was crying: 'Oh thank you sweet Jesus.' As though she herself had been on trial, had been reprieved.

I never got in touch with Sabrina Jean. I didn't know how to. What to say. Now I realize it didn't have to be about telling or saying. It could have been about asking, or offering.

I have been thinking about Diego's passport photo paintings. If I could start doing these, try to sell some. To raise money for Chagossian people in the UK trying to stay. Though people might not buy them.

This is a pen and ink drawing. I did it in the notebook I found in his bag of things from the hospital. I haven't read any of the poems. They were not meant for me.

It's Diego, as an axolotl.

V. OUTSIDE

Edinburgh, November 2014. The cold on our faces. For a few days now on waking we could see our breath. *The sadness as always.* We wake up in the morning and we don't know what we're going to get. Scratching at his bedroom door. Smell of coffee. No reply but she shuffled in, still in her sleeping bag, we no longer put the heating on, we had taken to moving around the flat in our sleeping bags. He turned onto his side, pillow over his head. Do you think shell creatures *feel* naked in their shells? He didn't answer. *Crustaceans* she said, A word can't help how it sounds. She put his mug down on the floor beside his bed. Scattered there, a letter in red from the letting agency, a print-out of the story she had written at Cove Park: *'Garde' and other journalworks: an interview with Rose Antoine, edited by Damaris Caleemootoo (Any translations from Kreol by Damaris Caleemootoo. Artwork by Rose Antoine).* She said, I made you coffee. We did not like her coffee which was either too strong or too weak. She sat on the bed. So, did you read it? He didn't answer, he just lay there with his face under the pillow. Outside, a bus lumbering up the road, seagulls. She tried to yank the pillow off his head but he clung on. She bent to gather up the loose sheets of her story, placed them next to the shit coffee. From under the pillow he said, Bitcoin is tanking. She punched the duvet. You *know* the rule! He was not to talk about money before coffee, before we had smoked the first tube of the day. He was not to talk about money if we were hungover or underslept or if we were on a night out. Nor was he to talk of money just before bed, or if we were feeling happy or sad or while we were doing something pleasant such as eating a cardamom bun. He removed the pillow. His eyes were closed. *When*, then? When we're evicted? She stood up. Definitely not when *writing* is happening. She shuffled towards the door, swiping from his desk the latest issue of the *beautiful* magazine, which he had stolen for her because it was more expensive than a block. Let's get up and out she said. I want to go to the library!

The Meadows. Arthur's Seat lost in mist, a ghost volcano cut 'n' pasted. Strong wind, fine rain like mesh. His hood up, her scarf on. Feeling brisk, walking past people and not seeing them. His leg was better, or it wasn't as fucked, or it was just as fucked but he'd got used to it. Anyway he was no longer struggling to keep up. We need to talk he said. About my story? The *rent*: bitcoin is tanking. Fuck bitcoin, what about my *story*? I was going to read it this morning but you dragged me up and out. I need to get *on* she said. Anyway, don't worry about the rent, I just got an email from the *beautiful* magazine. I sent them 'Garde' a while back and… and they're going to take it! *Really*?? He threw his face up into the rain. You star! That's amazing! Yes she said. They want me to expand it. I love the title he said. I can't wait to read it. The rain, falling between us, drips from her hair, in her eyes. We were approaching Jawbone Walk. She was telling him that once her story was published in the *beautiful* magazine she would apply for money to develop it into an novel, she might even go to Mauritius for research, why not! She thought: Why not. The editors might still reply. How could they not? Mist like smoke still churning around Arthur's Seat, a witches' scene. At the junction of Jawbone and Middle Meadow Walk, a busker. Young, missing some teeth, no instrument. But their voice! He said,

(151)

Let's give them a fiver. Blue eyes shining in the rain. That's to pay for our breakfast she said. We can put breakfast on the plastic! The plastic is stressed she hissed, come on, let's just get a pie. Oh but we'll get, like, £200 for your story he said, the magazine pays *beautifully*. He dug in his pocket, brought out the fiver. Come *on*, they're singing about us! In those days every busker we passed in the city was singing about us. She wasn't listening. She was thinking about the pie from Greggs, buttery pastry, hot creamy filling. She looked at him. When had he last smiled? She took the fiver from his hand and put it in the busker's case. We stood arm in arm. Jacques Brel sung as Nina Simone had sung it: 'The Desperate Ones'. When the song ended we clapped and the busker smiled and bowed and we walked away. Passing rows of posters—posters for the YES campaign and posters for the NO campaign, wet, ripped, tagged—a defeat of imagination. Reaching Forrest Road. Flags flapping like kite tails. The newsagent with its neon numbers fluctuating. Everything the same. Everything the same but different.

* * *

The previous year she had entered a writing competition in the *beautiful* magazine. First prize had been a decent amount of cash and publication in the print issue. Runners-up won a subscription and publication online. She had come nowhere. The winning story had been a work of experimental fiction by a young white man whose story was a near copy of a work of experimental fiction by an old white man. The judges were three literary figures of power with no conception that the lenses of their reading glasses were so cracked as to be totally fuckin frosted. Reading between the lines of their judges' statement and looking at the stories they had selected, she'd had to surmise that they had read *experimental writing* by white men as experimental writing, and experimental writing by white women as *experimental women's writing*. And while experimental writing by black or brown men had seemed to read to them as *experimental writing by people of colour*, it was clear that to these judges experimental writing by black or brown women had read as *bad writing*. Whilst *revolutionary* writing by black or brown women and non-binary people—writing which threatened to tear down white forms of necropolitical sovereignty that circle the self in ever tightening spirals like water down a fuckin plughole—the judges had read as *mad writing*. In sending her story to the editors, then, mindful of her experience with the competition, she had composed her email carefully, she had taken time to *explicate* her work, to fuckin *educate* them:

Dear Editors, I am sending you this story attached is my piece please find attached my text my story 'Grief' my story 'Ghost' 'Garde'. 'Garde' is an attempt 'Garde' is a playful 'Garde' is an experimental an undoing 'Garde' explores the 'outsider' art practice of a Mauritian-Chagossian woman with British citizenship called Rose who works as a guard at the National Gallery in London. This story is based on a real-life This story is based on the transcript of an actual encounter in an Edinburgh bar with a man called Diego. Told by Diego in Morisyen, his first language Originally told in Kreol, it was recorded and then transcribed and translated by the woman he was speaking to, the author, me, myself, Damaris Caleemootoo, a British woman of Mauritian origin a British-Mauritian woman a London-born writer of Mauritian origin whose own Kreol is not fluent is imperfect is broken was broken by an ignorant broken by a neglectful by an act of colonial violence or let us say ignorance, that is to say indifference, though Diego's own first language his mother tongue, Chagossian Kreol, was denied to him was stolen by a political act whose violence traumatised into muteness robbed his mother of her speech language voice. Rose and Diego's story is mapped onto elements from the author's own biography own heritage her family her history family memories and stories told to her of her maternal grandfather, a guard for 20 years at the then Tate Gallery now Tate Britain stationed in the Constable Room, his favourite painting The Hay Wain, *which always reminded him of his childhood in Poudre D'Or, Mauritius. Also haunting also present also shadowing the story are elements from the memory from the biography from the life of the writer's best friend's brother, who last year died in tragic who last year committed last year committed to who last year took his own who last year ended his life—himself a gallery attendant, and, like Rose, an artist who also felt, in the end, outside.*

* * *

In Gregg's we chose a pie to share. He took out the plastic, she grabbed the pie and had a furtive go, biting into the pastry, tasting the creamy grey filling, her face falling. Furious disappointment of a tepid centre. He touched the plastic to the machine and held his breath. Declined. *Credit is truth.* She, pretending not to notice, had another go at the pie, a rough bite, somehow punishing the pie for not being hotter, the plastic for getting rejected. He patted his jacket pockets saying, We must have used the wrong card! He pulled his hood off, ran his hand over his head, stared at her, eyes shifting to the door, but she was too into the pie to care. He took our bag off his back and unzipped the front pocket, saying, Our *other* card must be in here. Dreamily, she rolled the pie around in her mouth—no actual chewing was required—the *joy*. She thought about 'Garde', which the *beautiful* magazine might yet take, why not? Sure they hadn't replied to her email yet but there was a lot in it to think about. As she had explained to the editors, what this story definitely was *not* was the story of a life. What interested her were the structures within which that life existed, which made that life possible, perhaps *im*possible for the person living it, though only that person could say. Could you stand to the side while you rummage please the cashier said, I've got *actual* customers to serve. Still holding the useless plastic uselessly he put our bag on the floor and unzipped its main compartment, thinking, Why did we give our last fiver to the busker? She's not going to get paid for her story straight away, you always have to chase the bastards. He started taking everything out of our bag, pretending to look for our other card, the existence of which he had almost convinced himself of. Then when the bag was empty he sat on the floor, trying not to catch the eye of the queue. He was starting to feel shit. He thought: *Debt is mutual, it runs in every direction, but credit runs only one way.* He bit down on his tongue until it started to hurt. She took another bite, thinking, I could make this story a *novel!* No, not a novel, a book, a *work* that expands on Diego's story in all directions, like a web connecting the personal elements of his life as he related it to me and I have reimagined it, to the people, places, ideologies, forms, epistemologies, and structures—social, political, historical, ontological, ecological, technological, cybernetical, astronomical, geological, ontological— that touch upon his story. He thought: What's she doing up there, not eating the whole pie I hope. Then he thought: I wonder what bitcoin is doing? If I can sell some? Make a transfer? He reached into her jacket pocket for her screen, brought up the chart. The cascade of red candles was levelling out, several green ones had appeared among the red, and one or two had started to lengthen, pushing up. The meagre value of our bitcoin! Around £150. Just about one week's rent. The low value was crushing but what was important to remember was the fact that soon bitcoin would no longer remain the preserve of a few crazed libertarians and anarchist traders, that it would go mainstream and surely become a measure of value that genocidal bankers/nationalists could not control. His head instantly felt light, the pressure dissipated and his mind began to clear. He thought: maybe it is a good sign she agreed to give the fiver to the busker, a sign of her confidence, a sign she's writing beautifully. Not only that but a sign that her writing is recognized, after all the *beautiful* magazine has taken one of her stories at last, after so many rejections. He began to marvel at how much she had written since Daniel died, while he had written precisely *nothing*. What *is* this ambition to write, which I used to feel so compelled to act out? Isn't the best kind of writing, for me, *no*-writing, *not*-writing, writing *nothing*? Shouldn't I be spending all my *not*-writing time supporting *her* writing? So that even if her writing doesn't sell, he thought, the bitcoin will sustain us when it recovers. She took another bite of pie, thinking: This story is not about Rose the sister and Diego the brother but Diego Garcia the island and the base that led to the forced exile of the Chagossian people from their homeland. By the time I have finished the story—no, *book*—I will have taken in Diego Garcia's geological history and its links to the mythological continent of Lemuria, its colonial history that saw enslaved people—ancestors of the Chagossian people—brought to the archipelago, its pre-military economy and copra industry, its status in World War II history and its *stellar* position in the history of astronomy, cartography and geodetic surveying, to its particular status in contemporary geopolitics: the military base, fighter jets, stealth fighters, nuclear subs, soldiers, administrators, engineers, ghost detainees, military police, torturers/medics and the support staff and reproductive labourers from the Philippines and Mauritius—though not from Chagos?—cleaners, cooks, gardeners, maintenance people, sex workers and entertainers—also the rendition sites operated by the CIA on the south side of the island, even the golf course built on the old dump site, and the bomb dump where Marines stagger at night scrawling messages of hate on the shells: ISIS EAT ME! DON'T FUCK WITH THE USA! YOU FUCKED WITH THE WRONG MARINE!! And above all the Chagossians, the indigenous people of the Chagos Archipelago and their descendants, born in exile in Port Louis, Victoria, Manchester, Crawley, and generations of the vengeful dead rising from their graves like mist. In this book I will connect the social death of the Chagossian people ghosted by the British government to the structures of intercontinental superexploitation too complex to represent through fiction alone, integrating instead elements of fact, transcriptions from all the documents generated by the ongoing legal narrative of the Chagossians' struggle e.g. the most recent case relating to the sale of the country code domain .io for BIOT. Oh yes she thought, licking her fingers. The blow my book will deal to the military-industrial complex! Still on the daily bitcoin chart, he saw a long downside wick: liquidity had been taken. We looked at one another. The pie had gone.

* * *

Soldiers have been banned from Greggs the baker in a bid to raise standards, it has been revealed.

Troops from the Balaclava Company, 5th Battalion based in Redford Barracks have been warned they risk making the regiment 'look unprofessional' and that 'under no circumstances' should they 'stand outside Greggs eating a pasty'.

A document about dress and discipline circulated around the unit in Edinburgh said soldiers should also refrain from smoking cigarettes in uniform or texting on mobile phones whilst walking down the street.

Non-commissioned officers, the backbone of discipline and standards in the Army, have been urged to enforce the edict. In the note seen by *The Mail on Sunday*, the middle-ranking troops have been told they 'need to have the fibre and moral courage to police this and be all over those who make soldiers from the Balaclava Company look unprofessional'.

However, some soldiers have vowed to carry on enjoying the banned snacks.

'If I have to go for my pasty in disguise, so be it,' said one. 'It is ridiculous for commanders to suggest that somehow we bring the regiment into disrepute because we stand outside Greggs eating pasties.

'We're not all fatties either and it's not like the food dished up at the Army canteen is any healthier than what we get at Greggs—and Greggs is cheaper.'

'The Greggs ban and some of the other new rules top brass have introduced are crazy.'

An MoD spokesman said: 'Healthy living and fitness in the Armed Forces is of vital importance.'

* * *

The Diego Garcia
dispute hits cyberspace

The dispute over the ownership of Diego Garcia and the rest of the Chagos Archipelago involves a complex array of legal, human rights, security and geopolitical issues. The United Kingdom wants to retain the islands it calls the British Indian Ocean Territory (BIOT). Mauritius wants to see the islands ceded to it. The United States wants to keep its military base. And many of the Chagossian diaspora who were forcibly removed decades ago want to return.

This multi-sided dispute has now been further complicated by arguments over ownership of the territory's internet domain—".io". It seems that digital players may be increasingly caught up in geopolitics.

BIOT received the domain designation .io, and the UK government left it entirely to the private sector to manage and profit from. As a result, the domain is "owned" by Internet Computer Bureau Ltd (ICB), a private company formed specifically to take advantage of niche domains. ICB in turn is now owned by US registry services giant Afilias.

The .io domain has turned out to be a big money spinner. As an abbreviation of Input/Output (an established programming maxim), .io is seen as a popular alternative for tech start-ups and cryptocurrency websites.

If Mauritius gains sovereignty over the Archipelago, BIOT will cease to exist as a dependent territory, meaning that the domain may be scrapped. As domains are based on the International Organisation for Standardisation's ISO 3166-1 alpha-2 codes, the removal of the BIOT from the standard would likely precipitate the end of the .io domain.

The retirement of .io would have severe financial implications for its administrators as well as for the many companies that use the domain. The loss of traffic caused by a domain change could be substantial in the case of many of .io's most visited websites.

On the other hand, many Chagossians and their supporters are wondering where all the money generated by domain sales is going – and how they might get their fair share. Domains can be big business for small countries. Control of the .io domain was reportedly sold in 2017 for US$70 million, and its value will have only grown in the years since.

Already, the "The Dark Side of .IO" website—established by two .io users—successfully encourages .io start-ups to donate the equivalent domain renewal fee to the UK Chagos Support Association.

The same association added the .io domain to their proposed list of income-generation mechanisms, should they be allowed to return to the Chagos. But as the British government does not administer the .io domain, this could create yet another impasse in the overall dispute.

There are also potential liabilities at stake. The .io domain is implicated in its fair share of criminal activity, including high-profile scams such as OneCoin and USI Tech, and many .io websites are implicated in child exploitation. Some European courts are considering whether to hold registrars culpable for illegal activity perpetrated on their domains. Any party that takes control over .io could be signing up for more than they bargained for.

* * *

The day Daniel went into hospital, bitcoin rallied to a blow-off top and we sold at twelve times our buy price. That was the last day he had ever *laid eyes* on Daniel. To lay eyes: to gaze like a caress, a blessing, which in the end was all that Daniel had wanted of him. They had looked at one another through the window of a locked ward door, Daniel on the inside and he on the outside. When there was nothing more to do except stop looking, he left, exiting first one secure door and then another. He walked down a corridor past trolleys piled with neatly stacked sheets, coming to a lift. He pressed the button. On the ground floor were two further doors *two horrific doors leading to the outside* the first he could pass through, the second was managed by a code. A security guard appeared on the other side and tapped into a keypad. Outside, he stood in the hospital car park. Eyes stinging, head empty. The sky was like a swimming pool. Then he set off alone, back the way he and Daniel had come, through the park, towards the railway tracks. He passed the ice cream van where, on the way, Daniel had asked to stop for an ice cream. He had said no, too afraid Daniel would change his mind about finally admitting himself into hospital. And Daniel, in his final state of incompressible meekness which could set him off crying non-stop or make him drop to the pavement as if electrocuted, had accepted this. Now he stopped by the van, but did not buy an ice cream. Instead he took out his screen and typed her a message: Where are you? Though he knew where she was, in Brussels on a writing gig. He checked our bitcoin. That was when he saw the huge green candles on the chart, and without thinking, sold it all in an instant. He took the bus back to the squat and stuffed some things—boxers, toothbrush, etc. into a bag, as he had done with Daniel earlier. Then he grabbed his passport and took the overground to St Pancras, where he bought a ticket for the next train to Brussels. He took the escalator up to the champagne bar and ordered a flute of their cheapest brand, then sent her a message: See you at Midi 14:15. When he came through the security doors he looked raw and underslept. She said, You smell of cheap champagne. He told her about our bitcoin. I'm on my way to the exhibition she said. Do you want to come? We left the station and walked its length along a dirty road, congested with traffic, past the sleeping places that people had set up within the building's recesses. As we walked he told her about Daniel.

It was an exhibition of work by Sophie Podolski. We'd heard about Podolski from the writings of Roberto Bolaño, a fan of her poetry: A Belgian girl who wrote like a star and died at 21. But she'd been an artist too. Inside the gallery, walking through rooms-within-rooms set out like the enfilade of a Brussels bourgeois apartment, we caught our breath. Walls covered with drawings on paper—in ink, gouache, felt tip, pastels, collage, coloured pencil, crayon, biro—pulsing with detail, colours so vivid we could taste them. Also, echoes of a young woman's voice, audible throughout: Podolski declaiming, intoning, riffing. We passed through the first room displaying Podolski's bedroom art, her high-school engravings, and into the next, the work articulated in a new language, somewhere between drawing and writing: a sequence of four calligraphic works, ink stains that struggled to come into focus, a blurring of something not fully formed, refusing form. In the final room, vitrines presenting pages from the handwritten and illustrated manuscript of Podolski's only book, *Le pays où tout est permis*. We stood together and read the wall text. Until 20, Podolski had been without nationality. She had been Belgian for one year when she had died by suicide. He said, Podolski's drawing-slash-writing is like Daniel's dancing. He moved off to look at the manuscript pages and she read on. Then ran to catch him up, saying, If you have no country is it necessary to invent one? She said, After she died her works were stored in forty cardboard boxes by her friend Joelle. It was the artist Joelle de la Casinière who made the film that was playing in the final room, which we now entered. Dans la Maison (du Montfaucon Research Center) was set in the artists' commune where de la Casinière had lived between 1969 and 1973, and where Sophie Podolski had found her people. A sequence of stills, a cast of gender-fluid kids, naked or in fancy dress. Oh she said, oh. A young woman seated, also naked, smoking. She was not looking at the camera. She was writing. Her name was Mariétou. Mariétou's writing, like Podolski's writing-drawing was still, and forever happening. The film had no sound, only that recording of Podolski's voice, echoing.

Her voice followed us as we made our way down from the gallery and out onto the street. We walked through the neighbourhood not speaking, looking up at the unfamiliar architecture, run-down buildings with surprising details, gilt mosaics or stained glass, the fruit and veg shops, the hardware stores, bakeries. Stopping to buy a Moroccan savoury stuffed with cheese and spinach, eating as we walked. We passed a square lined with lime trees in blossom, the sweet surprising smell of them, and he became agitated. She led him to a bench on the square, which was a circle, an amphitheatre, kids running in all directions. Have you heard from Daniel? He showed her his screen: *I won't be here long.* That's good? she said. Then, This kind of place is called a place. Yes he said, when you are here you are *here.* Two kids in rollerboots holding hands, in co-ordinated outfits. I bet they call themselves sisters she said. He said, I can't stop thinking about Sophie Podolski, her sing-song voice. It put me in mind of Chantal Akerman, *Saute Ma Ville*—that *lalala* voiceover that puts you right in her head. She dug him in the ribs. You know she financed that film by trading? He said, The smell of those trees is making me want to boak. We walked on, down a narrow street. At the far end a neoclassical building with a huge gold dome. The Palais de Justice. We walked along the narrow pavement squeezing past shoppers and greengrocers' stands. We passed a little gallery. Alma Sarif. In the window, portraits in soft grey pencil: Nelson Mandela, Mike Tyson, his face erased from below the nose. The artist, Mamadou Ba.

We walked on towards the Palais de Justice, which appeared to be at the end of every street. But in fact it sat on the old gallows hill, looking down on the city. We finally reached it via the Marolles, the oldest part of Brussels, a mesh of narrow streets and alleyways in the working-class neighbourhood that had been partially demolished to make for it. We took a lift up to the top of the hill. Police standing around, waiting for something to happen or waiting to make something happen. We walked up to, and then around the Palais de Justice, the marble blocks bristling with scaffolding. The original scaffolding had been up so long it needed its own support. At the rear of the building it felt like being backstage. We wandered up the external staircases connecting levels, amazed at how much interior space—niches and corners—were formed by its exterior. Some of these areas were curtained off by blankets into rooms. People living there, sleeping on marble. We sat on the balustrade, looking across the Marolles. The daylight was fading, the sky empty, lavender-coloured. We talked about the Podolski show, about the film, about her life. Who was Mariétou? we wondered. What was she writing? Where was she now? We lit two tubes. You know Akerman left Brussels soon after making *Saute Ma Ville* she said, but came back when she was making *Je Tu Il Elle*. I have been thinking: that would have been about the time the commune had to break up. I bet there was one big fuck off party. What if Akerman had been there that night! Imagine her hanging out with Podolski, with Mariétou! The three of them together! He said, You've got to write that story. She said, A year after that, Sophie Podolski died. Losing her community must have broken her heart he said. We didn't speak for several minutes. Then he said, Do you remember when we helped Daniel move and I chucked out what I thought was rubbish but it turned out to be works, those sheets of Perspex he had scratched into, how he kept saying *My Perspex my Perspex.*

* * *

Tout ce que je veux aujourd'hui à la fin de ma vie, dans la dernière ligne droite, c'est que mon œuvre ne finisse pas à la poubelle.

* * *

When we left Greggs it began raining hard and we ran for the Museum. In the Grand Gallery we stood, dripping. Drumming on the glass roof. The middle of the space, away from the exhibits. He was drying his glasses on the hem of his T-shirt. Her hair was drenched, spiking into her eyes. She took off her raincoat. He was looking up at the ceiling, head bent back to stare at the huge ornamental cage, the iron, the glass. Your *grandpère* was a drummer, wasn't he? Yes, she said, in the police band. He said, Who made the dead drummers in charge of the rain? Tinny voices echoing, unseen Gothic-sounding clock. She said, Are you going to read my story? Yes he said, give me space. He walked off towards a bench, and sat down. He pulled out the pages. She watched as he began to read, hunched over them, totally absorbed. He was sitting beside the atom smasher. Elements of its surface swarmed with reflected movement. It came to her then: *Bikini Atoll*. A sister atoll to Diego Garcia. Wasn't this the same story, in the end? The Marshallese forced into leaving Bikini Atoll so that the US could test atomic bombs. Relocated to an uninhabitable island where they struggled to survive. She wanted to rush over and tell him. But he was sitting *so still*. She turned and began to wander among the exhibits, stopping at a thin plait of coconut fibre from *Polynesia, Tonga, in the 18th century*. The plait itself came with a label, on which was written in a copperplate hand: 'A cord consisting of 5 folds: each of which is composed of 3 entire vegetable fibres; of which the islanders form many of their works.' It was signed 'M.E.' and underneath this, 'Friendly Islands'. She looked back and saw that he was still sitting there by the atom smasher, reading. Expressions passing so fast over his face she couldn't register them. Then he wasn't reading any more, he wasn't looking at the exhibits or the people but just staring at the page. Something in the way his back suddenly looked a bit more collapsed. Then he turned the print-out over to the blank side, eyes not moving from the paper. He took a pen from his bag and, bent, his hand started moving over the paper. He was... *drawing*. When he sensed her approaching he looked up. He thought: She's too much. He put the pen away, folded up the paper. He stood up and moved off down the gallery. Held up by a group of tourists in red raincoats, he tried to push through but they shuffled forward and he was swept along. He found himself in the glass lift, rising. When it came to a stop, the doors slid open and the tourists shuffled out. He saw her, on the landing, facing him, breathing hard and smiling. He didn't look at her but past her, to where a mother goddess sat, carved from bone, eyes turned upward. He decided he knew nothing. People were entering the lift, but she remained still, looking anxious. The doors closed, the lift rose once

(166)

again. When the doors opened, he saw her again, breathing harder still, looking right at him. This time he held her gaze, but he didn't move his mouth or change his expression. When the doors slid shut, he looked down through the lift's glass floor. She was running to the staircase, then up, taking the steps two at a time. Fourth floor. The doors opened and people got out, and this time she stepped in. Now we were alone in the lift. We watched each other without moving. She didn't know where he was going, he didn't know where she was going. We knew that right now she would go wherever he was going. At the fifth floor we stepped out. Up here near the roof the rain was loud. Every nation has its form of money, its form of drumming. He moved off down the corridor. She followed. He turned into a side chamber of the gallery and she did too. She caught her breath. Animal World. Soft light with no apparent source. Everything slow, like being underwater. Animals suspended from invisible wires in the central atrium. A giant squid. A hippo swimming in mid-air, stubby legs peddling absurdly. A stuffed great white shark. Sunfish. Is this a world? An installation from the future, showing us animals from the past? He walked right around to the other side of the gallery. He took out the folded-up pages of the story, laid them on the railing, then watched as she followed, feeding the railing through her open hand, not taking her eyes off his face. Now we were standing side by side, a whale's ribcage hanging before us. She picked up the folded pages of her story, opened them. He didn't move as she examined his drawing. Blue biro, cartoon scribbles. She recognized the bulbous shape of the atom smasher. Beside it he had drawn a figure, almost as big as the machine itself, a man in a lab coat, round spectacles, Einstein hair, mad grin on his face. Underneath it he had written the words: Atom smashing man. She said the words aloud, shifting their emphasis each time. She looked at him. His face so still, so gaunt, the bony nose looking like it might break through the skin. His head was in his hands now, shaking. She put her hand gently on his shoulder. Let's go.

* * *

We do not look at or speak to one another all the way to Arthur's Seat. The rain has stopped, the smirr has cleared and the sky is almost squeaking with sunlight. Arthur's Seat oppressive how it fills the eyes. The wind comes up. We climb, we move from the path to the wet grass and mud. Together at first, holding onto one another, then finding it's easier to make our way alone. At the top we step off the lip of the crater into its centre. Always that surprising domestic feel, intimate, the filled in-crater of the extinct volcano always smaller than we remember, now covered in long tufted grass, the gentle depression giving shelter after the exposure of the ascent.

She looks at him and says, Tell me about my story. He is looking up at the sky, tilting his head back as though looking at the ceiling. The sky looks like a painting he thinks, *one that gives an impression of peace and balance at first, but then strikes him as deeply disturbing.* He rights his head. It's OK, she says, you don't have to tell me. We begin to walk slowly inside the crater, around its circumference, arm in arm. Round and round we walk, light draining from the sky. Still he says nothing.

We climb back up the lip. On the edge, looking down onto the city. Light grey sky, an orange tint. We can just about see as far as the Meadows. So often we'd be over there, looking across at the figures swarming up here, the vertical strokes for people, the dogs as dashes. I'm hungry she says, are you hungry? Wish we could go to Kebab Mahal for a tinda curry. Just saying that makes my mouth water! Juicy chunks of marrow and that tangy sauce! I'm not hungry he says. I'm going to go now she says, to work more on the story. I had an idea in the museum she says, I thought of a connection. Bikini Atoll she says, and the US government's nuclear testing there. They made all the islanders move to another island where in the end they were left to starve.

You can't just graft one story onto another he says. No she says, but you can connect the abstractions. He stops. Pulls his arm from hers. Why map Diego's story onto Daniel's? Out of solidarity. Isn't what caused Diego's suffering in the end connected to what caused Daniel's? He looks at her and says, You got it wrong. Diego was undocumented, right? They would not have let him into the hospital without checking he could pay. And even if they *did* let him in, they would not have let Diego out. They let Daniel out because he was white, middle class. Because he could speak their language. He managed to convince them he had 'capacity'. True she says. He says, You could have given Diego's story a different ending. You could have imagined a future for him. It's just a story she says. Yes but not *yours*. Diego could be anywhere. He is alive, I know it. And he pulls away from her and scrambles up to the lip of the crater, cupping his hands to his mouth shouting Diego! She climbs up to where he's standing, takes his arm. The sky is turning silver. She thinks: What about the future?

The wind comes fast, suddenly wild. She's struggling to make herself heard. What? He tries to shout back. She grabs him, pressing her mouth to his ear... she was singing: *It's hard to live in the city... It's hard to live in the city...* Now she is walking off, he watches as she picks her way down the face of the dead volcano, her eyes fixed on her feet. Then she reaches the bottom, walks away across the grass, disappearing into the city.

He sits on a rock and unfolds 'Garde', examines the reverse of the pages. He looks again at his drawing, reads his words: Atom Smashing Man. He takes out the biro. He draws an atom—a circle transected by the orbit of its electrons. He gives the atom a face, like a character from a '60s government public service film about nuclear power. Its face is also its body, arms coming out of its sides, oven gloves for hands. He adds legs, bent jauntily at the knees. He stands the atom on a wall, sketching in one or two bricks and a bit of moss. He gives the atom a mallet. A big stupid grin on its face. The mallet hangs just above the head of the man in the lab coat with the Einstein hair, poised to slam down on his head. When he's finished the drawing he has a bad feeling.

The sky goes dark.

DAMARIS & OLIVER PABLO

To: Oliver Pablo Herzberg
Date: 19 September 2020
Subject: Wandering lines
Attachment: Notes for Garde-HWBAW

O, dearest O.

The globe is now transected by lines of love, everyone writing to their everyone's asking—are you OK?

Are you OK, O?

These cracks appearing at our feet—the earth crazing, is crazed

Tell me you haven't fallen in

Tell me what your life is like, how you've been.

We can talk about *before* or *after* but in the end that's just oppressive, I mean for those who don't get to 'say when' there never *was* anything else but this, this *here*

After we got off the train at King's Cross and went off in different directions—

Before we left Edinburgh, *before* we lost the flat—

(How I remember you: crouched on/like? a rock on Arthur's Seat. And then I made my way down and I didn't look *behind* me)

Prepositions, I have been thinking about prepositions.

+++++

I sent you a present though today is not your birthday. I don't know if you got it. Are you still there?

Here I am in Brussels since August 2015, living in the place we stayed that time when we went to the Podolski exhibition at WIELS.

After King's Cross I headed up the Cally Road to Gom's. She hasn't changed. Still fighting me at the kitchen sink to do the washing up aged 93. In the end I'd say, *I'm not going to fight you old woman!*

I didn't like to stay too long because she was anxious about her benefits, what with that spiteful bedroom tax.

Every day I'd walk to the British Library and write. I wondered if I'd see you though knew I wouldn't. I'd go and sit in Business and Intellectual Property where you always liked to hide though I always preferred Rare Books.

Then I heard about this sublet in Brussels and I took it on.

Not long after that, the bombings. The city was full of soldiers and tanks.

One day, Dina, the little girl who lives in the flat below asked me, *C'est quoi, 'soldats'?*

My first experience of a lockdown. That uneasy quiet. If you want to know what it was like then watch this amazing film by the artist Sara Sejin Chang, *Brussels, 2016.*

Sometimes when I'm walking around this city which reminds me of Edinburgh and Paris and Amsterdam, a badly maintained fever dream* of these cold cold Northern European cities with their grey stone faces I think and I think, How am I here? I like it here as well as anywhere. It feels a bit familiar, there are correlations with other cities I've lived in—beyond the fact of the urban—but it does seem arbitrary, that I have ended up in *this* country as opposed to *that* one—

but then I think about my family and our history and I think, Well it's always been this way. The Hakka the Indian the Creole. Though me with my freedom of movement.

My landlady reminds me of Gom. She lives on the ground floor. An apartment with those rooms within rooms, *enfilade.*

Do you remember the name of this road: Rue d'Angleterre. Did you notice that all the streets round here are named for countries? Living near Midi, it's dirty and run-down, that long filthy road, crawling with traffic. But until March this year I could walk 5 minutes down the road and get a train to Paris, Marseille, Cologne, Amsterdam, Luxembourg... and London. Which feels furthest away of all, these days.

A dark house that smells of the basement and everyone's different cooking. Like home.

The other tenants are Macilia on the second floor, then Souad and Dina on the third floor.

It gets very hot up here in the summer but I just climb out of the skylight and sit on that bit of flat roof where we had our tubes. Only occasionally now. It's heavily built-up round here and there are few gardens, mostly tiny yards, so we're all up against one another, and in summer, when the windows are open, sound ricochets across the concrete and we are all in one another's lives.

There's an old formica kitchen table just next to the window I found in the basement and use as my desk.

On my desk are books and one of them is new: a dictionary of untranslatables: a philosophical lexicon of '400 philosophical, literary and political terms and concepts that defy easy translation from one language to the other'.

I looked up the word 'sagren' but it is not there.
I looked up the word 'hogra' but it is not there.
'Hogra' is a word I learnt at New Year.

+++++

Are you still trading? I've been reading about trading's environmental impact. And the military's.

Are you still not writing? I feel now that you refusing to write felt like you refusing whiteness

Daniel's refusing to live feels now like Daniel refusing whiteness

Q: What does it say about extreme depression that it engenders a kind of 'feminized' behaviour—passiveness, quietness, etc and what does that say about patriarchy.
A: nothing we didn't know

Daniel's books are here now. My sister and her family moved to Mauritius. They shipped the boxes to me when they were packing up the house. They tried to get in touch with you. I can't believe Tats has done this: reversing the journey our parents made. Thanks to her I am now applying for my Mauritian citizenship. Why not. I could never feel good about flying to Mauritius. But to live there for a while. To hang out with family.

What if you could put your whiteness into the service of refusing whiteness. Is that possible?

Is writing for you a process of interiorizing, of individualizing—of burying yourself alive in your white man's body? (What Daniel did, trying to escape.)

If so, what if there was a way to write *outside* yourself?

I have a teaching job in the Netherlands, working with art students on their writing: I *love* it.

The search for new forms of expression/knowledge sharing—in these times this feels like the most urgent and necessary form of *uselessness*: the only thing worth doing if you cannot be a truly *essential* worker. The search for new forms *for our times*, if not a *fuckin cure*.

I have been asking myself, Why write? But also, Why do I write?

I write, if I'm honest, to be reread.

Fiction as a political tool for putting possibilities into language.

I didn't understand theory till I realized it must be read as poetry.

+++++

As I write I am listening to the album by Big Joanie called *Sistahs*. That's the present I sent you. I don't know if you got it, if you still have your record player.

(I remember the story of how you bought it, with the money you earnt working at Argos in Dundee one holiday—the summer you spent in a basement, when the manager took you aside and told you about the future you had there.)

It's a New Year and I'm still here...

Do you know Big Joanie? The first time I saw them, two years ago, they were supporting Parquet Courts so the room was full of middle-aged white men (and one middle-aged brown woman). I bought two copies of *Sistahs* from the merch stand. One for you. At that gig they played 'Crooked Room'—singer/guitarist Stephanie Phillips explaining to these old white guys (and the odd brown woman) about the song's title—from Melissa Harris-Perry's description of Black women's struggles to orient themselves amongst an assault of violent preconceptions as being like trying to stand up in a crooked room. The generosity of this explanation.

And I wondered how it must have been for them at this gig, three young Black women, looking out from the stage at all those old white guys who have always claimed this music as *theirs*. Reminded me of feeling so conscious of being the only non-white kid in the audience at gigs, trying not to be seen.

I hear Big Joanie and realize what futures have been denied; what the future must look like.

The second time I saw them was just before lockdown. They were headlining. All three band members play together in a line, front of stage. A *her*-archy.

Track 3: *Remember when we used to be friends? I'd like to be / friends with you / but I only / feel hatred.*

Since lockdown ended I go out walking a lot more than before. In anticipation of the next lockdown which will surely happen before winter.

I often walk up to the Palais de Justice. Do you remember it? I've been up there a couple of times with Macilia who is obsessed with photographing it.

What happened at New Year was this: I was supposed to go with Macilia for a walk but I had bad period pain . So she went out alone. When she came back she told me this story.

She went up to the Palais de Justice with her camera and took a few shots. Then she headed down into the Marolles, down an alley towards one of those little streets full of sleek retro furniture shops and shops selling wildly expensive houseplants. There were people at the bottom watching something happening. When she got there she saw that they were watching a group of police dragging this guy into the back of a police van. He looked dazed, the people watching looked dazed. There was blood on the man's head. No one was doing anything. No one was filming. Macilia's camera was around her neck. She'd shot her roll of film. She did not know if she would have been brave enough to take photos had she had film. She did not consider at the time the idea of pretending she still had film in the camera—pretending to take photos. A policewoman trying to disperse the crowd was violently asserting that there was *nothing to see*. Yes said Malicia, she was representative of an institution that could mediate our reality to the extent that what we were seeing was not in fact happening. 'Police' is an uncountable noun but Malicia counted 8 of them. They shoved the man into the back of a van with no windows. What would happen out of sight? She said that all she could think was she hoped the guy had not seen her standing there with a great fuck-off camera around her neck, not taking any photos.

Nothing to see here—in a *tourist* district.

Then Macilia told me the Arabic word *hogra* which as I understood it from the French means a kind of official form of contempt and humiliation, or abuse of power by authorities towards individuals from oppressed groups.

I thought of that Duras text in *Outside*, her article about the flower seller and the gendarmes.

In the summer I went back with Macilia to the Palais de Justice, to the Black Lives Matter protest. 10,000 people gathered for George Floyd and those others murdered by the police. I thought of Kaya too, and also those who have died at the hands of the state: Sarah Reed, Paulette Wilson and others from the Windrush generation. All the Chagossians who died of *sagren*. Deaths of despair.

Big Joanie's best track isn't on this album. 'Dream Number 9'.

Kicks in with a proper moody post-punk bassline then shifts into shimmering girlgroup harmonies (the Shangri-Las; The Pixies):

Despite myself / Only Dreaming / Despite myself / Half here, half full/ Despite myself I'm whole again.

(And that 'only' in Only Dreaming sounding so *English* or do I mean *London*? Do I mean *British*?)

They played this when I saw them last. That was in February at Beursschouwburg. The last gig I went to before lockdown.

That middle 8 breakdown, the fucked up VU freakout of it just undoes me.

+++++

I met Macilia at my French lessons at the commune. I used to go before covid. Our group of students came from Colombia, Portugal, Rwanda, Romania, Macedonia, Tibet, Poland, Turkey, Morocco, Haiti and the UK. We all had to give our reasons for wanting to learn French. The woman from Macedonia said, So I don't have to be a cleaner all my life. The woman from Tibet said, So I can get a cleaning job. We were all women and our teacher was a man. We each had to write something about our respective countries and their characteristic qualities, to share with the group. One of the things on the list he wrote on the board about Belgium (which did not include 'colonialism') was 'l'auto-dérision': the ability to make fun of oneself.

Macilia was looking for a place and Mariette had a studio to rent so voilà.

During lockdown I kept thinking of the New Universal Embassy, everyone in our building looked out for one another, and our lives became more intertwined.

It was an intense time. Souad lost a lot of work. So did Malicia. But they spent their time making masks on Mariette's old sewing machine—she had worked as a seamstress in her younger years. I helped to homeschool Souad's daughter Dina who I call the *Why Why Girl* after the Mahasweta Devi story.

(For a long time all this time I have been thinking about how I live, how I should live, if there is any other way to live—what is it to refuse the heteronormative family unit, though perhaps it was never refusal, perhaps it was choosing something else which had always felt until now conditional, provisional, near-future focused?

But then like everyone we got slammed into the ever-present tense and all we can think of is how to live right now, at this moment, with what we've got.)

Do you know about the Universal Embassy?

I discovered it through an artwork by Hito Steyerl, a short video in a group show at WIELS.

At the outbreak of the Somalian civil war, the Somalian embassy here in Brussels was abandoned, and a group of sans-papiers activists claimed the space.

Brussels is a labyrinth. Online too. Lots of dead websites. Or just... nothing. Streets have names in two languages. I appreciate its multivalency.

The last reference for the Universal Embassy I can find online is this, from 2003:

The Universal Embassy is a star.

Clandestinity is an absurd journey, at the end of which there is the loss of identity. A resident from Somalia, that vanished country, wanders around in the city wearing a Zorro mask. In the centre fermé he would have held incoherent speeches... A migrant grandmother rings the doorbell of the neighbouring building, convinced that her daughter lives there: the Embassy of Saudi Arabia. She has spent seven years on a journey, during which reality dissolves... She is 77 years old. Clandestinity becomes a state of suspension in a parallel world, an evaporation of one's own substance.

The Universal Embassy is a concentrate of weakness. When someone comes here to find shelter, then it is because the precariousness of their situation has become unbearable.

Fear is the clandestine's shadow. Fear of everything and everyone: of taking the bus, of working, of moving. One must take care not to be conspicuous, not to loiter in the shopping centres. Those who have nothing to buy, have no reason to loiter there... Every action holds its own measure of risk.

It is the justice system that holds one together. The hope is minute, and everyone settles into waiting. Always, always waiting, everything concentrated on this waiting. Wearing out in wearing through the procedure, for months, for years. One seeks encouragement in thinking that it is still better than risking certain deportation. Obscene labyrinth.

20, 30 years old, with no future, no possible life plan. Clandestine migration extends the bitter experience of a lost youth. In order to flee from a leaden society or unemployment, migration becomes a life project in itself, the hope of a possibility. This dream retreats back to itself. The project becomes unreal. There is no more desire that could be articulated. The hypothetical day of regularization becomes devoid of meaning, none can be invested in it. The only constant is that there is no solution.

The loss of self is at work here. Becoming a driven, exploited animal, a criminal and a victim. No more reading, no more writing, earning three euros in an hour, even less as a woman.

Souad works in a local bakery. One of its biggest sources of revenue is catering for weddings and celebrations, all of which got cancelled during lockdown. Souad earns 6 Euro an hour.

Today Souad brought fekkas back. These are my favourite. They were slightly burnt. She has a lot on her mind she says. There are burn marks on her forearms too.

It is amazing how little French Souad and I need to enjoy one another's company. A lot is communicated through food, through laughing (often at things Dina says and does). But it is interesting to see which words Souad knows in French. When she was describing her job to me, she was very clear that where she worked was in the *back* of the bakery. How she was *cachée*. In a limited vocabulary the words one knows beyond the everyday basics are telling.

(That crappy school recorder on *Eyes*! Queer punk!)

+++++

Brussels reminds me of my all-time favourite literary form—the fragment.

I like the cold I like the rain and I wonder if this is me being British or a writer. I am still writing. I have been trying and failing to make something of 'Garde'.

Prepositions again: students of mine have written about Trinh T. Minh-ha wanting to speak *nearby*. Not wanting to speak 'over', or 'for'. Not even 'with'.

I am getting to know some artists here—and some we knew before in London (Mel, Chris, Will). It's a nice community. I don't know what I can contribute except writing so am working out how to do that.

Writing is a practical skill, writing is the most practical thing I can do.

But what to do with it?

How to use it?

What I call writing is me trying to grab the questions that come at me. And when I can't do anything with them I can't do anything.

I am reading about writing, Audre Lorde alongside Bhanu Kapil:

Right now, I could name at least ten ideas I would have once found intolerable or incomprehensible and frightening, except as they came after dreams and poems.

And:

I want a literature that's not made of literature.

One of the questions I think about is why is poetry so poorly paid and who is making money out of poetry. Poetry is essential, we all agree. Poets are Essential Workers.
I think of form and I think of what I want to say and the form for that is poetry but I am not a poet.

The very last time I was in a room full of strangers, before the cancellation of all social life here, was on a weekend of art events in Saint Gilles.

First I saw Will at his launch for the latest *F.R.David*. It was at Alma Sarif—do you remember the gallery where we saw the drawings in the window? (I have since got to know the artists who run it, Monica Gallab and Joseph Kusendila who you would love.) Chris and Mel were there too.

Then I went to see Kate give a reading. It was at a gallery called Damien and the Love Guru where the artist duo Slow Reading Club had invited Kate to present her novel-in-progress at their finissage. We all sat on the floor of the packed gallery, trying to avoid touching one another—at that time, for reasons of social awkwardness—listening with great care. The scene Kate read was intimate and solitary, it featured a woman alone in a flat with her baby. I remember it now and think of that woman as self-isolating. Maybe that's what life with a newborn is like. Afterwards, we all crammed into a tiny bar, all of us who had just arrived from Düsseldorf, from Hamburg, from LA, from Rotterdam, from London. The following night Mel and Chris had an event at their studio. Mel and Anna and Dana did readings and Chris and Will performed and Jessica and Katja DJ'd and Aglaia and Willem and Mai and Benjamin and Perri and Kevin and Graham and George and Marnie and Clare and Castillo and Robin and Bojana and Monica and Joseph and Sara and Reem and Mohanad and Keira and Paul and Timmy and Emma were all there. People you don't know but I am beginning to. Looking back now it was magic; at one moment I had a shock, a body-memory, or perhaps it was an actual feeling, of *standing* next to Daniel. I was so often with him in such spaces.

After that night, things seemed to change rapidly. Or my awareness of them did.

Early in the lockdown I was listening to John Maus on repeat. *On the walls of silence / It's written on the walls of silence hey! / Hey* with the window open marvelling at the silence in the streets. I was wondering if it might be possible to meet a friend in the park for a walk. If I could measure out 2 metres of ribbon, and if we could each take one end of ribbon and walk with it taut. What it might look like if everyone in the park were to do the same. The new choreographies of walking. All the angry men who hold their lines and don't make way. Those who don't realize or feel able to care that we should not be walking too close to one another right now. Who might never have realized or felt able to care before this happened. I think about Daniel. I wonder how people already isolated are feeling now.

In those early days I had a dream about Daniel. It was the end of the world.

In the dream I was on my way home, wherever that was, but decided to stay and spend some time with him, because I knew there wasn't much time left.

The day after, I took Daniel's books out of their boxes and put them out on my shelves, where they could breathe. I have been reading his copy of Fernand Deligny's *The Arachnean and*

Other Texts. (Deligny's concept of the 'wander lines': the way we move now.) Now when I come across highlighted pages they no longer undo me: I don't hear his voice in my head anymore. I just see the words.

'What a shame that humans didn't place heaven at the centre of the earth when they elaborated their mythologies.'

At the *F.R.David* launch, I was talking with Monica and Joseph who asked if I might do something at the gallery. They had seen me read at Kantine, this great space run by two artists, Perri MacKenzie and Kevin Gallagher. I had written something about our time in Edinburgh. That time we sang with the busker when we were mad with grief: well, in the reading I had to sing that bit on my own.

I told Monica and Joseph about Daniel's books. The ones he used to read when he first started reading seriously—books by clever white men with fascist death drives. And the ones he came to right at the end, the books that were full of love and joy and pain and the huge labour of reckoning—e.g. all the Moten works. (Perhaps the process of assimilating the loss of Daniel is complete for you now: perhaps you have completely regenerated. Or perhaps you recognize that you will always be broken. But in seeing your own brokenness, and seeing it in others, Moten gives you a way to survive it.) Ferreira da Silva. Verity Spott. The second wave of Daniel's reading. I told Monica and Joseph how, inspired by Daniel's books, maybe even presenting Daniel's books, I would like to set up a temporary library of political joy and love. How we might connect that up with the neighbourhood, the school. Monica and Joseph liked the idea. But that project could only happen with you.

On the Alma Sarif website M&J have posted a view down the length of the street. At the end of it looms the Palais de Justice. It's the same street that Dina's school is on. When the kids come out of the door, that's the first thing they see.

+++

There's a new documentary I watched online recently, *Another Paradise*, an account of the Chagossian people's continuing resistance through a portrait of Sabrina Jean. Do you remember I wrote about her in my story, 'Garde'? The Chair of the Chagos Refugee Group in the UK? *Another Paradise* was made by a Belgian filmmaker, Olivier Magis, who lives in my neighbourhood. It's a wonderful film.

One minute Sabrina Jean is mopping school corridors in her day job, the next she's flying to Washington to address graduate students on the political injustice perpetrated against her people by the governments of Britain and the United States and Mauritius. These are David Vine's students, the author of *Island of Shame*. Sabrina Jean is a radical. When she tells David Vine of her plan to launch a clandestine trip to Chagos by boat he listens carefully then takes her to see a lawyer friend. She looks crushed and it *is* crushing when the lawyer urges her to give it up for her own safety: The US military will *hunt you down*.

You remember Chagos has a national team and it's led by Sabrina Jean? The documentary shows her with them at the 2016 CONIFA World Cup. CONIFA is a federation of football associations excluded from FIFA. They hold a world cup of 'nations, de-facto nations, regions, minority peoples' and 'sports isolated territories'. The team loses. Total wipe out. But not for want of Sabrina Jean's drive. They should have put her out as striker.

The film's final scene is devastating. Sabrina Jean's father, Serge Aristide who lives with her, was born on Peros Banhos. In this scene he is sitting on his sofa in Crawley, visualizing his homeland. He is looking straight to camera. Then he closes his eyes and says

Mo pa le mor dan later kolon
Mo le mor dan mo later natal

I don't want to die in the land of the colonizers.
I want to die in the land of my birth

and he intones the names of the animals of the land and the sea and the air, the names of the trees of that island that he remembers from his life on Peros Banhos:

Anture ek sa bann zanimo sa bann zwazo bann pwason
Anter mwa dan mo landrwa, Peros Banhos
Sa mo dezir
Mo nam pu repoz byen anpe
E pa dan langleter, later kolon
Se sa mo panse

He opens his eyes. Looks into the camera.

There was meant to be a screening of the full film here at the Millennium Festival, but it's been postponed for Covid reasons. When it happens it is hoped that Sabrina Jean will come for a live Q&A with the director, if UK residents are allowed to travel then.

After watching the film I got in touch with Olivier Magis. We went for coffee. I asked about the film and how he came to tell the story of the Chagossian community in Crawley. He told me that he'd originally planned to make a film about the Chagos Islands football team, following their progress in the CONIFA cup, but after an initial meeting with the team's management he'd been so struck by the force and brilliance of Sabrina Jean's personality that he decided to tell the story of the exile and the Chagossian community in Crawley through Sabrina Jean's activism.

When we met up I told him about us meeting Diego, and how since then we had been reading about the story of Diego Garcia, the military base and the exile of the Chagossian people. I told him how, as a writer, if there is something you can't stop reading about, it's something you need to write about. But how to share a story that needs to be told, if it is not your story?

We talked about how this move of telling others' stories has been made by documentary makers, by lawyers, anthropologists, activists outside of the Chagossian community, in support of Chagossian testimony and what it might be to do this through *literature*. What might be achieved specifically by that. He mentioned Shenaz Patel's *Le Silence de Chagos* and I had to confess how I still hadn't read it yet, how I'd been too anxious about my French. But there's an English translation now, by Jeffrey Zuckerman, who translated Ananda Devi's beautiful *Ève de ses décombres*.

I found an interview with Sabrina Jean online. She is talking about travelling, as one of a group of second-generation Chagossians-in-exile who went on a so-called 'heritage visit' in 2011. How, as the boat approached Peros Banhos, she went onto the top of the boat:

> I said 'I want to go on the top, I want to see the beautiful island of my dad!' It was so beautiful. To see the beautiful

island, to see the blue sky, the seaside... it was so beautiful. It was so beautiful...

I looked up government information about these so-called heritage visits:

The trip will be physically tiring with long hours spent on aeroplanes and boats and will require a certain level of mobility and resilience. A medical letter will be requested from all successful applicants indicating they are fit and well with no terminal prognosis. As such, you should consider your ability to cope with such a trip before applying.

In the interview Sabrina Jean says:

I was in the Youth Group that started in Mauritius in 1989 when I left school. I know a little bit about the culture, the history, the struggle of the community, so when you are here on the island, even if you are not a natif from the island, you can feel the sadness. The way the natifs talk to you about the island and then you see it with your own eyes, it was very painful. Very, very, very, very painful.

When I think about Diego Garcia, I think about disappearances. Ghost flights. Extraordinary renditions. At the island's centre, a hole. A legal hole. Remember that journal article we found: all the treaties on human rights, on the environment, ratified by the US and the UK governments, *with exemptions for Diego Garcia*. The island is claimed by the British state, the military base by the American state, but somehow it functions, legally, outside both.

Since we began to research the story of Diego Garcia, there've been developments: I wonder if you've been following them. If you have been in an OK enough state to do that. Did you see the ICJ proceedings relating to Mauritius' claims to sovereignty? You can watch it all online. (Presumably this is what those members of the Chagossian community, who'd travelled to the Hague to attend, had to do in the end, as they were not admitted, for fear they might 'disrupt the session'). It is quite a thing to see those 15 judges lined up all wearing black robes with white cravats, each lacy in an individual way. All the documents relating to proceedings are lodged online. And in the judges' legal opinion, which they published last February, they included this amazing summary of the history of sovereignty over Chagos through legal events:

Geographic location of Mauritius in the Indian Ocean— Chagos Archipelago, including the island of Diego Garcia, administered by the United Kingdom during colonization as a dependency of Mauritius—Adoption on 14 December 1960 of the Declaration on the Granting of Independence to Colonial Countries and Peoples (General Assembly resolution 1514 (XV))—Establishment of the Special Committee on Decolonization ('Committee of Twenty-Four') to monitor the implementation of resolution 1514 (XV)—Lancaster House agreement between the representatives of the colony of Mauritius and the United Kingdom Government regarding the detachment of the Chagos Archipelago from Mauritius— Creation of the British Indian Ocean Territory ('BIOT'), including the Chagos Archipelago—Agreement between the United States of America and the United Kingdom concerning the availability of the BIOT for defence purposes—Adoption by the General Assembly of resolutions on the territorial integrity of non-self-governing territories—Independence of Mauritius—Forcible removal of the population of the Chagos Archipelago—Request by Mauritius for the BIOT to be disbanded and the territory restored to it—Creation of a marine protected area around the Chagos Archipelago by the United Kingdom—Challenge to the creation of a marine protected area by Mauritius before an Arbitral Tribunal and decision of the Tribunal.

From Olivier Magis's film we learn that among the things Sabrina Jean does for her community is to act in the capacity of *écrivaine publique.* I don't think this expression/concept exists in the Anglophone world. I guess historically this was the person who would write letters for people who couldn't write at the market. Now it's the person who helps those who don't have written French or are not literate in the language needed to negotiate state administration. Especially in connection with immigration, and citizenship. It's what the children and grand-children of working-class immigrants do for their elders.

I love the term *public writer.*

I love teaching. I'm more interested in other people's writing than in my own. It doesn't make me any less a writer, more that I want to be a different sort of writer now.

How to be a *public* writer?

Do you remember Plum? Getting together all the writers and readers we loved in London for a night. How we started out holding it in that bar, the former toilet, Public Life. My high-lights: Kathryn Simmonds, Sara Heitlinger, Yair Wallach, Robert McGill (Bob!), Brian Chikwava, Rattawut Lapcharoensap—darling A. and June!—Sandeep Parmar, John Doran, Megan Bradbury, Megan Barker…

I could suggest to Monica and Joseph a project around this idea of the public writer. To host a public writer for the neighbourhood. Forms yes, but help with any kind of writing.

Lately I've been thinking about 'Garde'. About my making up a story about Rose, about Diego. That it needs to be *un*made.

Last night I had the first ever dream about Daniel in which he was actually dead. That is, he featured in the dream as dead. A group of us (I don't know who *we* were but we were an *us* for sure) were discussing his work.

The next day I went back to 'Garde'. I don't want to write like that now. And so I send you this instead, gathered from the notes I made while writing 'Garde'.

D.x

[NOTES FOR 'GARDE', OR HOW WE
BECAME A WRITER]

1.
You and I came to writing from different directions, at different speeds—me, directly, but cautiously. You, circuitously, but getting there faster.

The first time I took acid I invented a word but didn't know its meaning. The beginning of a new language.

The second time I took acid I remembered this word and realized its meaning was: 'here I am again'. It was in my recollection of it that this word acquired its meaning.

Have I told you that for a long time I have been writing fragments but fragments without a form to call a home, that don't add up to much

and when I think about these fragments I think of a word, a new word, that means something like: white/*blank*-black.

Specifically: the points at which this intersects my backstory, that is to say my mother's backstory; how she was mothered. And how she mothered me: my writing and my reading.

And then there is your reading, and your not-writing. I remember the day you stopped; the day I couldn't stop.

———

The *weather* and how we kept saying *the weather*. The wind and the rain, the rain in the wind, the sun in the rain. All at once.

You met me off the train. I'd been in Brussels. We were going to see Daniel in the hospital.

Later there was to be a meeting with the hospital and your family, to discuss whether Daniel ought to remain in hospital, against his will.

But first we were going to see the work of an artist we needed to see.

When we think of Diego Garcia and Chagos, and how this story is part of a history of political barbarism, we think of the work of Kader Attia, who speaks of the madness, the pain, the grief and the despair—the *injury* to *bodies*—inflicted by power.

But Attia speaks also of *repair*: human gestures and rituals of healing that quietly refute all the strategies of power, attending with care to those injuries.

Walking around those darkened rooms lit up by flashes from fragments of mirrors, reassembled to question the notion of 'whole', we did not speak.

We both felt, but did not mention, the presence of Daniel. We both felt but did not mention how the show would have spoken to him.

We both admitted, later, to hiding from him our plans to come here; how we knew this plan would hurt him.

We both felt but did not mention our feeling when walking around the show that by that time Daniel was already dead.

2.

Attia has a video work, *A Thread of Light*, in which we watch the artist's hand etching into black scratchboard fragments of his mother's memories, drawn from an ongoing filmed conversation about her life and experiences over 20 years, but which remains private.

Attia's Berber mother was raised in Paris by an uncle who refused to let her learn how to read and write. He even painted over a window in his home that overlooked a school. Attia's mother would scratch into that paint to glimpse these other children.

In the video the only audible sound is the scratching of Attia's stylus as he forms his mother's words.

When I ask how you learnt to read, you do not remember, as though it happened naturally.

I was taught to read at age four by my mother, in English and French. My memories of that experience are fearful, imbued with what felt like my mother's anger, but which I now realize was my mother's fear.

Fear of what happens to brown girls who don't learn to read, who don't finish school despite their promise, who leave their A-level studies (art and English) to get married whilst still a teenager to escape an unhappy, overcrowded immigrant home in an unwelcoming country, a watchful father, a pathologically disengaged—clinically depressed—mother.

My mother was taught to read aged three by Mamzel Gigitte, a young woman who lived with her mother in a *lakaz tol* at the end of their street in Cité Martial.

My mother remembers being told one day by her father that there would be no more school.

Ki ou pe di? she said, Mo pa pu al lekol enkor? When she tells this story she is remembering her child's rage: disappointment, incomprehension, powerlessness.

The place had burnt down.

Mother and daughter, both dead. The fire had been caused by a candle: Mamzel Gigitte had been in the habit of reading late into the night.

Who had taught Mamzel Gigitte to read? What did she read, and where did she get her books?

Did Mamzel Gigitte *write*?

What books might have been written had Mamzel Gigitte and her mother lived in a *concrete* house, with electricity.

My mother's mother was suspicious of language, could barely read. Could barely speak.

Was dark-skinned where her sister was light-skinned. Their mother Creole, their father—lost—white.

Her sister would be taken out, my grandmother left at home. Their mother worked in a *maison close*.

What happened to Mamzel Gigitte sounds like a fairy story: a tale of theatrical violence told for the pleasure of our disbelief, to present as fantasy a violence we refuse to acknowledge as reality.

3.

Your mum studied History then trained as a primary school teacher specializing in remedial literacy, working with dyslexic children.

You and Daniel were born 18 months apart. Your mum, exhausted, would take you both out to the park, letting you loose like dogs to run and run while she sat and read novels obsessively. She forgot about History. Until the day you decided to study it.

Aged 6 you remember the teacher who used to get you kids to stroke her bare legs as she read to you. You remember wanting to miss play-time because you had no friends. So you asked to continue working on your story, *Ragnar The Brave*, about a Viking boy and his pet eagle. You wrote right through break. How writing could stand for sociality.

You first got the idea that it was possible to *carry on writing* from the boy in your class who did not stop even after the teacher had asked you to put down your pencils. The teacher, impressed, had allowed him to continue.

But in the end he was punished when it was discovered that he had not been writing a story at all, just the same word over again.

How authority requires legibility of those who answer to it.

You can't remember which word.

Benjamin on Kafka tells the story of Potemkin taken to his bed with one of his periodic bouts of depression; his refusal to sign state papers, to the consternation of his officials. An insignificant clerk, Shuvalkin, persuades them to let him try. To their surprise he comes out with all the papers signed. Only, it is then discovered that Potemkin signed them all as *Shuvalkin*.

You tell me you did not learn how to *really* read until you reached university, and once there could not stop, reading everything with great hunger, scepticism, desire. *Life A User's Manual* on a bike trip round France, shedding pages as you read, the book getting lighter the further you travelled. But the first book you ever loved was *Sunset Song*.

In *Sunset Song* the protagonist was a woman although the author was a man.

The day your history professor kept you back from class and claimed you were a genius was the day you responded to his seminar brief to embody an historical perspective on migration to America by speaking in the voice of a character you had created—an enslaved woman from Guinea. You had just read Alex Haley's *Roots*.

Your mother has spoken about her brother, your uncle David, adopted from Ghanaian parents by your white Methodist grandparents. How he had been severely dyslexic. How the teachers attributed him not thriving at school to 'stupidity'.

When I started school I could already read and write. My teacher, Miss Brown who was white, chose me and Donna Augustine, the only two non-white kids in her class, to appear together in her animal alphabet pageant. Together we were 'm' for monkey.

By this age I had already lost my Kreol. A teacher at kindergarten had instructed my parents to stop speaking it to me or I would not learn English.

4.
One day you found on the floor of a girlfriend's room—a poet, who would write you tiny poems on Bible paper—an application for a prestigious writing programme you never heard of. Until then it had

never occurred to you to write. But now it seemed obvious—when considering the gaps in the historical records you studied, why not write in these gaps, in these margins?

Every year I sent off for that application form and every year I did not dare to apply. Until the year I was made redundant and thought, Why not.

The first time I met you was in a seminar room. I thought you looked like Kafka. One day our teacher, a famous German writer who was preoccupied with Kafka—too discrete a man to manifest obsessions—remarked on how much *you* looked like Kafka.

It was our German writing professor, as fascinated by Benjamin as he was Kafka, who told us Benjamin's story of Shuvalkin.

The first time you came to my flat you were eating a veggie hotdog bought from the greasy spoon across the road. You sat on my sofa, eating this hotdog, dripping ketchup on the floor and talking at speed with your mouth full about the book you were writing—and how you were going to sign up with the most famous agency in the world and publish with the best publisher in London, though neither at this point had heard of you.

5.
There was fear when learning to read, but also wonder: I can still remember illustrations from one book I learnt to read from though I have never seen it since. Lately I wonder if it was one particular book I remember, or if I have been imagining a palimpsest of all the books I read with my mother at that time.

When I learnt to read we were living in Hong Kong. Whenever people learnt that my dad was in the British Air Force they always expressed surprise. Him being Mauritian. But both my grandfathers had fought for Britain in the Second World War.

I grew up on air force bases. The militarized architecture, the high security—armed sentries (ammunition: live), decommissioned tanks and fighter planes as décor, the rows and rows of blank ugly houses with identical interiors and furnishing, down to the same scratchy white blankets, the miles and miles of barbed wire fencing—this environment was familiar to me, felt like *home*. I look at images of the base in Diego Garcia and it could have been the airfield at RAF Sek Kong in Hong Kong where my dad was based for 3 years.

In the early 70s my dad spent 9 months on RAF Gan in the Maldives, just 200 miles north of Diego Garcia, refuelling aircraft. The island of Gan is part of Addu Atoll. British military operations were wound down on the island in the mid-70s, with the establishing of the base at Diego, following the forced expulsion of the Chagossian people from their archipelago. RAF activities in the Indian Ocean were now to be supported by the airfield at Diego Garcia.

My parents still have the box of seashells he brought back. Broken bits of coral. Red coral.

Gan was in the Indian Ocean, which my dad had crossed five years earlier, by ship, from Mauritius, to Britain, which he then left 7 years later, to travel to Gan.

The first time we went to live in Hong Kong, our plane stopped to refuel in Gan. I remember the steamy heat we stepped into, when leaving the plane.

A strange position to be in: in Hong Kong on behalf of the colonizers, my parents themselves subjects of a former British colony, my dad with a Chinese mother.

When we returned to Hong Kong for another posting, I was old enough at 12 to feel our presence as something complex.

There is a photo of my mum taken on a trip to what we knew then as Stonecutters' Island, but I have since learnt is Ngong Shuen Chau and no longer *an actual island*, having been connected to the mainland by reclaimed land in the 90s.

Wikipedia continues: *During the 60s, 70s and 80s, the island became used as a 'Rest and Recuperation' resort, having several chalet style bungalows built around the Navy, Army and Air Force Institutes shop, restaurant and swimming pool complex on the South Shore. During the 70s and 80s, the island was also the forward operating base (FOB) of a Royal Navy Hovercraft unit deployed to assist the Hong Kong government with anti-illegal immigration operations.*

We were told about desperate people who would try to cross the South China sea in small boats, who would drown or be attacked by sharks. Whose side were *we* on?

In Hong Kong my dad did our cooking, our food shopping. Never at the NAAFI, where other RAF families shopped for imported British goods. We went to the market, where we saw baskets of pigs' ears, the piles of bitter cucumbers that looked like sea creatures.

My mother is wearing a hibiscus in her hair and she looks pissed off. I think of Gauguin: *Why Are You So Angry?*

My Mauritian-Chinese grandmother first learnt to read in French. When she was 7 her mum died and she was sent to live with a Chinese family who sent her to Chinese school. When she ran away to live with her aunt, her aunt sent her back to French school. Then her dad came for her and sent her back to Chinese school. When her dad got sick and she went back to her aunt's she was once again sent back to French school. But all schooling stopped for her at 13 when she was needed at home to look after all the small cousins, while the elder ones went out to work or continued with their studies. And all this time her country was in fact British. The only things she reads now are her Bible, in French. The letters from the council, or the organizations they contract out to, she asks us to read for her.

The British presence on Chinese land. The higher status of the British over the Chinese, and the Nepalese—the Gurkha unit in the British army, and their families. The Gurkha soldiers were paid less than the British soldiers. They fought for years for the right to settle in the UK and to receive equal conditions. My family, our Mauritian origin and brown skin, my parents' own history as colonial subjects—in this most British and white of institutions.

———

You told me that when you were at school you had a friend whose dad was in the RAF. He lived on the nearby base. This is now defunct but when operational, during the Cold War, it was home to fighter plans that patrolled UK airspace by the North Sea. You went to his home once. The walls were covered with artworks by his dad, whose subject was female cyborg women with weaponized breasts.

Years later the friend wrote to you telling you he'd changed.

We passed the base on the way to the forest where we gathered for Daniel's memorial, by the sea where you and your family scattered his ashes. You said that going to your friend's house had felt like going into a prison.

At New Year, the last year of Daniel's life, he rang you in crisis. He was outside a prison. He had gone there in solidarity with the prisoners. He had been writing to one of the prisoners regularly, part of a project he never realized. He had not known what else to do.

Four months later, packing up his things, you find notes for a project about the National Gallery and the prisons nearby:

GET BLUEPRINTS FOR:
—NG
—Prisons around London

Then underneath, references to numbered National Gallery post-cards and a map sketched out, with Goldsmiths, his art college, at the centre.

6.
Your brother once gave me a book: *The Book of Colour* by Julia Blackburn. He would trawl charity shops for stuff to sell on eBay. He bought it for me because the author had Mauritian heritage, and the novel was set there.

When she first arrived in London as a teenager my mum liked to go to this bric-a-brac shop on the Hornsey Road. She particularly liked to look at the old books. One she bought for 4p was called *Othmar* by Ouida and featured a character called Damaris. She named me for her.

The other books my mother bought from the bric-a-brac shop: books from Volume 1 of *Encyclopaedia Britannica*'s Great Artists Collection including van Gogh, Gauguin and Constable.

In London my grandfather got a job at the Tate Gallery across the water from MI5. He was stationed in the Constable room. His favourite painting was the *Hay Wain* which he claimed looked like the Mauritian countryside of his childhood in Poudre d'Or.

His mother was an Indian labourer in the sugarcane fields, illiterate, the willing mistress—or so my mother was told—of the French plantation manager, my grandfather's father. She was killed, my grandfather always claimed, by voudou.

Motherhood allows for a species of narrativization. Our mothers gave us a love of this.

Once, in London, the family were watching *University Challenge* and my grandad got a picture question on Constable correct.

When I was a child my mother took my sister and I to visit galleries. To the Tate to see my grandad. I remember hearing about *Equivalent IV* and being disappointed to see that it was an *arrangement* of bricks and not a pile.

Taking the suburban train from Bexleyheath to Charing Cross my mother would take us often to the National Gallery. Our favourite rooms were rooms 41, 42, 43 and 44.

Once, I had just drifted away from a painting when the guard on duty called out. Everyone turned and I saw my mother recoil, ashamed—she had reached out to touch it.

She remembers this as van Gogh's *Sunflowers*, while I remember it as van Gogh's *Wheatfield with Cypresses*. I have always wanted to reach out and touch its toothpaste clouds.

As a teenager I would get the suburban train into London by myself and visit the bookshops on Charing Cross Road. It is where I found books by James Baldwin and Kathy Acker and Paul Bowles. I would read these in Bunjie's Coffee Shop, alone and feeling lonely.

At the time I was studying German A-level. My German teacher gave his class of four girls set texts by four men: Frisch, Brecht, Remarque and Lenz.

The German language assistant lent me his tape of Nina Hagen. I felt sorry for this cool guy from Berlin stuck in Bexleyheath.

Bexleyheath was the same part of London where Stephen Lawrence was murdered.

In protest at Stephen Lawrence's murder and the police's contemptuous handling of this, we marched to shut down the headquarters of the BNP, near where I lived. This place, the organization claimed, was a 'bookshop'. I remember a countermarch by fascists. The police protecting the 'bookshop', the fascists.

I remember you telling me how you first had a sense of your Jewish heritage: you were going to see *Schindler's List*. Your dad told you why he would never go and see it.

Before your brother went to Goldsmiths he made works alone, in his squat, never showing them, like his series of 'scratchings' on Perspex: scenes of Jewish people fleeing from the shtetls.

Your father spoke German but did not pass this language on to his kids.

Not far from where the BNP 'bookshop' stood, my dad got his head kicked in on the way home from the pub one night.

At the hospital I watched as a policeman tried to take a statement from my dad who was still groggy. The policeman asked, *What did your assailant look like.* I saw my dad struggling. I tried to help:

Was he taller than you, shorter than you? Was he white?

Do you remember him shouting out anything as he was kicking you?

The police never found the attacker and closed the case. My dad didn't want to pursue it.

Years later my dad had a fit which was later ascribed by doctors to this beating. He passed out in a pub. When he woke up his mind was a blank.

7.
You were a vegetarian from the age of 4, having learnt where meat came from.

You recall that as a kid you suffered from a high degree of empathy, and claimed to have had a visceral understanding of the pain of others.

I ask myself if your brother was similar. And if he was, I wonder at his capacity to contain this. The doctor at the inquest claimed he could not detain Daniel under the mental health act because he had 'capacity'.

When you were kids you went to summer camp for the first time. While you were there your dad was in a hotel in Pitlochry undergoing rebirthing therapy—being guided through his past lives by a hypnotist helping him to locate the source of his depression which he believed was focused on his birth, his mother, her past, her traumas. In one life or one narrative of a life, he was in a pirate ship, up on a crow's nest.

When you were a very little kid on a seaside trip to Anglesey you saw a kid in a wheelchair.

His lips were sore, puffy. He was dribbling. You couldn't stop looking at this boy, trying to feel what he felt. For the rest of the day you chewed on your own bottom lip, so that by the end of the day it was red and raw like the boy's had been.

In our writing class many people would comment on how unfeeling your protagonist was.

The day after Daniel died I stayed away. You were with your family. The day after that, when you asked to meet we went to the park, walking round and round, jumpy around the big London dogs.

You talked and talked, barely stopping to breathe.

You were describing how Daniel had looked as you went with him to the hospital, the sore on his forehead from where he constantly rubbed it, trying to erase thought.

The obsessive plucking at his bottom lip, and as you were talking *you* were rubbing at your forehead and plucking at your bottom lip

Telling me you were scared that what happened to Daniel was happening to you or that you were becoming Daniel that Daniel was you and you looked me dead in the eyes asking

if I thought this was true, were you going mad did you look like you were going mad

and I said No

it was one of the few times in our friendship I was conscious of telling you a barefaced lie.

8.
The RAF paid for the children of servicepeople to go to boarding school, so my parents sent me to a convent school, where I made best friends with a girl whose family owned a bookshop.

I was not a Catholic so inspired dislike and suspicion in certain of the teachers and nuns.

The Maths teacher who delighted in having caught me reading under my desk. *Ho ho! What have we here!* She snatched the book but could not conceal her disappointment that it was *Jane Eyre*.

Another teacher who taught Latin and lived with her best friend the Geography teacher.

The Latin teacher spoke many languages, had studied at Cambridge, had been involved in espionage in the Second World War, where some of the girls she had known were murdered as spies. She wrote in my report that I would write a book of my own one day.

The male lecturer at my university who convened the Commonwealth Literature class. His eyes seeking mine as he apologized to the class in his introductory seminar for all the bad things white men like him had done.

The white guy I dated at college who turned out to be violent. The apology he sent years later, the confession that part of his violence had been jealousy of my writing.

In all my time of studying reading and writing, all my teachers have been white.

9.
The book that had been doing the rounds when I had been caught with *Jane Eyre*: Linda Goodman's *Sun Signs*.

Your brother was a Virgo. That Capricorns and Virgos had difficulty communicating was apparent in our relations.

The low point came when you were away on a cycle trip and without you to manage our tempers we fell out.

We did not speak again until your book launch 6 months later.

In the end it took you and me twelve years in total to write our respective first novels.

Not long after our first conversation at my place, with your mouth full of veggie hotdog, you sold your novel to the best publisher in London on the basis of six chapters and a plot synopsis.

It sold in a three-way transatlantic bidding war between major metropolitan publishing houses—a deal executed by the world famous agency you'd had your eye on.

While I finished my book after years of struggle, and had it turned down by every publisher in and outside London, except for one small press on the south coast who offered for World Rights 0.7142% of the total sum that you had received on the sale of your UK and US rights alone.

In the meantime, you were struggling to complete the remaining 75% of your novel. Your writer's block was made worse by the stress of having already spent that portion of the advance already paid out—on an electric piano you did not know how to play, a Canondale Bad Boy that got stolen, and the deposit on a peach-coloured studio flat in Norwich that looked like sheltered accommodation and lapsed almost instantly into negative equity. You were too depressed to live there.

You realized then that you had no interest in writing the book that the publishers believed you to be writing.

You had no interest in being the kind of writer you had thought you wanted to be. You stopped writing altogether.

Increasingly desperate, you looked into funded teacher-training programmes which might allow you to repay the paid-out portion of your advance and to find a meaningful career.

You overshot your deadline by two years. At a party thrown by your publisher that I persuaded you to attend, the man who acquired your book asked you for a light. I realized he had no idea who you were.

You developed anxiety, then fear, then stopped feeling anything.

Later you would ascribe this to the intensity of Daniel's own state of mental deterioration and his dependence on you and how scared you were of letting him down, how scared you were to go back to the squat every evening in case you found him dead.

In the end, I offered to help you write some of your book: two chapters in the form of diary entries by the protagonist's long-ago lover. I would do it as long as you did not interfere. OK you said. You cook I said, and buy me tubes and pints and drugs. OK you said.

After your world famous agency had read the full manuscript and you'd revealed my contribution they expressed unease. Your publisher reacted similarly: what if I wanted my name on the cover...? Would I want *paying*? What about the terms and conditions for literary prizes? What was the position on collaboration?

We'd already decided between us that since those two chapters constituted 10% of the book, you would pay me 10% of your advance. Which percentage was considerably more money than 100% of the advance on my own book.

And after the books and the reviews—with one interpreting your acknowledgement of my part-authorship in the endnotes as a tricksy literary manoeuvre, believing Damaris Caleemootoo to be another element of your fiction—after the no-sales and the no-interest had come, for you, the no-writing, and for me the non-stop writing and the not-finishing.

I wrote an article about writing those chapters of your novel. Daniel read it and wrote to me:

it's good to get an insight into what, from the outside, is a fascinating relationship

I could think of nothing to do for Daniel, once he was in the hospital. But I sent him a book. I didn't know if he could read. It was *The Odyssey*. Emily Wilson's translation. Something he could read *aloud* if he could not read at all.

When I wrote to him asking if I could visit him in hospital he said, Yes, but I won't be here for long.

I remember him reading an early draft of my novel. He said, Do you realize how many times you use the word suicide in this book?

When it was finally published he came to the launch and wrote a review of my book online. He titled it, 'A heartbreaking complex tale of sibling love'.

The last time I saw him was at an event where I had been reading.

I read my translation of an excerpt from a radio interview with Marguerite Duras: a story Duras had told about being terrified of the police, of being so terrified she could not shoplift from bookshops like her friends.

He told me that he too would be doing a reading soon.

But I was in Brussels at the time. Later, you showed me the text he had written.

It was a letter to Kafka. A response to Kafka's assertion that 'there is hope, but not for us'.

10.
We gathered in a forest: you and your family, Daniel's friends, family friends.

When you spoke about Daniel you told us a story he'd told you when you were accompanying him to the hospital.

About the toy police car that he'd loved, and then hated. That he'd had to throw away once he'd noticed that it was *wrong*.

In the hospital Daniel had said to the doctor: *This isn't the right place for me.*

You talked about how Daniel had been inspired by the work of Fred Moten, and read a quote you felt described Daniel's relationship to the world:

'The world was ever after, elsewhere… no way where we were was there.'

But since then I have learnt that the Moten quote is Moten *quoting*:

from Nathaniel Mackey, his ongoing decades-long poem 'Mu', one of what Moten calls two massive, braided streams of retrospective invention—

'that follow a mysterious, migrant "we" through the rhythms and currents of the world'.

At the gathering you described the video work Daniel had made, two months before he died. It opened with a quote from James Baldwin:

'Any real change implies the breakup of the world as one has always known it, the loss of all that gave one an identity, the end of safety.'

You described the video ending with Daniel dancing. You said: *Happiness occurs in spite of difficulty. Joy happens, I think,* because *of it. For Daniel, acknowledging the things that are wrong in this world was a necessary prerequisite to finding joy.*

Then you read the rest of the Baldwin quote:

'… it is only when a person is able, without bitterness or self-pity, to surrender a dream he has long cherished or a privilege he has long possessed that he is set free—he has set himself free—for higher dreams, for greater privileges.'

Then you said, Well, Daniel has set himself free.

After the forest everyone walked to the shore where you and your family waded into the water and released Daniel's ashes.

The tide low, the light too, the wet sand and the water shining.

In my mind, remembering this, it is Daniel I see, wading in.

11.
I took many photographs of you that day, in the gallery.

The works and your encounters with them felt charged. In one you are contemplating a large spherical work that looks like it is stitched together from broken mirrors. You peer at it closely, as if waiting for it to speak. There is an aura around you and the work, the spotlight and the darkness.

Leaving the gallery to take the train to the hospital: the *weather*. It is at the station that the police call you, to tell you that Daniel has gone missing.

We go to his place. We press the buzzer. We are both instantly relieved then confused when a voice answers that we both immediately take to be him.

But it is not him, it is the upstairs neighbour's teenage boy who is afraid to let us in. His mother has told him not to open the door to anyone.

You go round the back to break in. I wait at the front door. You take an age to open it. When you do, I try to read your face. He's not here you say. I walk in. We wait.

You are on the phone. With family, with the hospital, with the police.

The sense of a life interrupted. Discarded clothes, the unmade bed, the dishes in the sink, the pot plants that need watering. The smell of him. Outside in a pot the small plum tree he grew from a stone discarded in the street.

A thank-you card on the mantelpiece; the unutterable sadness of Daniel having put it there at all.

I look at his bookshelves. I always used to look at his bookshelves, to look for books of mine I was missing.

I go to the back door and look out into the garden, which is overgrown. Below the garden, train tracks, the constant sound of trains on their way to somewhere. Trailing over the fence, honeysuckle, a flower. Something in its complicated structure, its grace, that *yellow*—is him.

In his notes for a work called FAMILY SNAPS that reads like a Kafka text:

Flowers grew from his mouth: roses and sometimes lilies.

When there is a knock at the front door I open it. You come out to join me in the hallway.

The two police, a woman and a man, ask to come in. I wonder if the upstairs neighbour kid who would not let us in had heard the breaking glass and reported it.

Is that why you're here? I ask the police. But you say, I think I know why they are here.

I don't get it. Even when we are sitting down in the front room, at their insistence, even when they begin to tell you the news, I still don't get it. But immediately, you do.

The way the policeman is speaking—as if he were reading from a script. Reading aloud, not speaking. His repetition of the word *regret*.

The sense of Daniel being *narrated*. And later, at the inquest too.

Your crying sounds like something mechanical that has rusted up. And that is what you feel like when I hug you.

The gesture of opening a thank you card from a work colleague, then putting it with care on the mantelpiece. Not like him. Yet it was what he was brought up to do. At this point, he was automated. At this point he was very lonely.

What he was brought up to expect and what he didn't get and what it did to him not getting it.

When your family arrives, I leave. I can't remember how to get back to my sister's. Eventually, on the platform at Finsbury Park station, I sit on a bench. I take the notebook, the old nearly new notebook

I found the other day, a present from my sister who understands that the only present I ever need is notebooks—only a few pages used, I'd torn these out, then bound the edges with washi tape the same yellow of that honeysuckle—a book in which to make my notes for the Kader Attia exhibition.

All I had written in the gallery was *oil + sugar (a description of the process/image)* and *hygiene precarity (shitting outside)*

Because after that I had stopped writing and had only taken photos. Now I begin writing. I do not stop for four days.

Is the writing brain a lizard brain an alien brain that notes, that records, as the body experiences, a kind of psychic bodycam
    Birdsong and how it always goes on

In one of Daniel's notebooks I found this:

the weather was fine. The world was disintegrating.

Days after the gathering in the forest, I looked at the work you had referred to: the one where Daniel was dancing.

You wanted to leave everyone at the gathering with an image of Daniel experiencing joy.

Though that dancing was not joyful.
I found among Daniel's books his copy of Moten's *The Universal Machine*. The first chapter, called 'There Is No Racism Intended', is prefaced by an extract from an interview transcript: Emmanuel Levinas in conversation with an unnamed questioner. The extract begins with Levinas saying: 'I always say—but under my breath—that the Bible and the Greeks present the only serious issues in

human life; everything else is dancing. I think these texts are open to the whole world. There is no racism intended.'

everything else is dancing. Your brother highlighted that in blue, and circled it. In the margin he has written, *title?*

There is a lot of highlighting in blue right up to page 19, where the corner of the page is turned down.

The rest of the book is unmarked.

To: Oliver Pablo Herzberg
From: Damaris Caleemootoo
Subject: Judge Gaja's question
(Notes for an essay: On a literature of solidarity)
Date: 13 January 2021

Dearest Oliver,

Thank you for the birthday present/card (so clearly one of your books! That you have written in it as though it were a card! So YOU!). It just arrived.

I love it. And the promise of a letter to follow made my heart sing.

I'll wait. I have *so many fucking questions* but I'll wait.

I saw *Who Touched Me* in rile* the amazing bookshop here, but I bought *Ban in Banlieu* instead.

I don't know Wu Tsang's work but I want to explore it now— *Wildness* sounds amazing. And I loved this: 'she experiments with how to be accountable to the communities that she documents'.

I only know Moten's collaborations in terms of his conversations, but not this one. Thank you.

And I love the look of this text: how it is performing friendship and thinking together.

'Wu Tsang's works explore hidden histories, marginalized narratives, *and the act of performing itself*'. I am reading through— around? Within?—Daniel's Fred Moten books—so it's hard not to read Daniel's death in terms of performance: performance or non-performance though? I still don't know.

I ask myself sometimes, Where is Daniel's privilege now?

+++++

my *half century* wow. And still not a *grown-up*.

Are *you* grown up now? Is that why you don't write? Does it make you suffer?

Are you and Diego somewhere together? I am a bit obsessed with that—whether you found each other.

Remember that bit in *Chagos ou la mémoire des îles* where the Chagossian pilgrims on the *Mauritius Trochetia* arriving in DG are briefed by some English Navy prick who sets out the terms of the 'visit'—

Photography is not allowed, 'it's a *sensitive* island'.

He says: 'We're all *grown-ups*.'

What did he mean by 'grown-ups'??

Fully interpellated subjects?

A 'grown-up' knows the difference between fact and fiction.

There's something particular about the use of fiction and narrative as a strategy by the UK government in the story of the Chagossians' deracination that I still can't believe e.g. that FCO memo headed 'maintaining the fiction'—from the John Pilger documentary—cynically stating the intention to misrepresent the Chagossians as itinerant workers instead of a *people*.

You see I'm trying to write an essay, and I wanted to think it through with you...

It's enough to feel you're reading at least: your reader's voice in my head as I write.

This all began because I finally read *Le silence des Chagos* by Shenaz Patel.

Someone in the book reminded me of Diego, one of the three people featured, and to whom the book is dedicated:

A Charlesia, Raymonde et Desire, qui m'ont confié leur histoire. A tous les Chagossiens, déracinés et deportés de leur ile, au profit du <monde libre>...

I feel in *Le silence des Chagos* that Patel herself is playing with the UK and US government's instrumentalizing of fiction and narrative—highlighting it through her novelization of her interlocuters' lived experience.

Sorry, this is not a letter perhaps.

Do you remember John Douglas Miller's article about Guibert's photographs of Foucault in *Tinted Window*? That beautiful letter of Foucault's he republished? *That* was a letter! So not a letter but notes for an essay then I guess.

++

NOTES FOR AN ESSAY:

Magic

I have a photo of you on my wall. It's the one I made you pose for, the restaging of the Guibert photograph of Foucault in his robe. Dina asked who you were. I said I didn't know. She comes up here to read with me sometimes. It's made me think back to the books I loved as a kid. I don't care how much fuckin 'magic' is in a book, if it doesn't attempt to reimagine the structures of our world but with every word *enforces* them, it's about as magic as a breezeblock.

Empathy v solidarity

What I notice about the most amazing children's literature is there is not much of what gets called 'empathy' in it. 'Empathy' in literature—litfic I should say—is an impoverished thing: centring your understanding as a reader and a writer of 'the other'.

But then there's Elena Ferrante, making a performance of how little she understands her characters or they one another, or themselves.

Chris Kraus's luminous consideration of Simone Weil's radical empathy in *Aliens and Anorexia*.

Octavia Butler's worldmaking empathy: her 'sharers', her *ooloi* (I just finished *Dawn*).

What does a fiction of solidarity look like? I guess this is Patel's project in *Le silence des Chagos*. I am trying to think/feel through this for an essay—about three writers from outside the Chagossian community who have written about the Chagossian people's forced exile. Patel, Lindsey Collen and Saradha Soobrayen.

Maybe translation is one of the purest forms of writing as solidarity. Spivak and her translations of Mahasweta Devi.

Solidarity requires us to get over ourselves. *Outside* ourselves.

I can't talk to anyone the way I talk to you. It's unnerving you not talking back. Is that how it was all that time ago? Me talking at/over you?

Pronouns have been preoccupying me; prepositions too.

I need to go now, though, sorry. Souad and Dina are coming for dinner.

Version/Hag
They've gone. It was lovely. We danced. Dina was DJ, playing her gloriously terrible autotune faves.

Dina used to turn her nose up at my cooking until I started cooking Mauritian food for her. She loves it! Especially *ladob poul*, which I cooked tonight. I never cooked that for you, obvs.

Dina pointed out to me that my hair is falling out. She said it like she was being helpful. Thanks Dina!

I've been going through the menopause, perimenopause, symptoms are peaking now—hot flushes—covid false alarms—which I don't mind, like flashbacks to the 90s and coming up on an e.

I can't wait to be a Hag. Like Ariana Reines says about Duras (and 'Sucking' is the model for my structure here, I see now—so maybe what I'm thinking about here in the end is just *good* writing vs *bad* writing…).

I go to Tai Chi now like Gom and all my great-aunties. In lock-down I saw a group practising in the park and I remembered Hong Kong.

Listening / Voice
It's crazy now to think how many times I tried and failed to read *Le silence des Chagos*—the fear of my French failing me, the fear of mistranslating Patel, if only to myself. But now I live in a Francophone place. *Je me débrouille…*

The book draws on Patel's journalistic background. She tells the story of the Chagossian community exiled to Mauritius through the experiences of three people she came to know—Charlesia, Raymonde and Désiré—their stories shared with Patel in conversations spanning a number of years.

There is something powerful in the force of narrative fiction combined with testimony—it's fiction in the sense that Patel uses the techniques of a novelist to tell a true story, to *inhabit it* as a writer. Interesting to consider it alongside Svetlana Alexievich's project of testimony, her *novels in voices*.

Patel is drawing on the *feelings* of Charlesia, Raymonde and Désiré as well as their stories. A different strategy to Alexievich's. But both feel like radical acts of listening.

Charlesia Alexis's voice
Charlesia in the book is the activist and singer Charlesia Alexis who died in 2012: she was in Daëron's film and of course we have read about her in countless legal documents, research papers etc. She was one of the elders who took part in the original women's protests and hunger strikes and was a founder member of the Chagos Refugees Group in Mauritius.

I'm listening to her album on Spotify now: *La voix des Chagos.* Chagossian sega.

Charlesia Alexis's voice is incredible, raw, like a voice sounds when someone has cried so much they can't cry any longer—or like she *refuses* to. Patel writes *voix de cendre et de sel.* You can *feel* it. And the sound of the tambour, how the fingers play on it, a kind of knocking, or rapping, like on a door, no, perhaps more the tapping you would do on wood to replicate hard raindrops as sound effects for a story. But more rhythmic. A sort of shuffling of the fingers. It's mesmerizing. And on one track in particular, 'Wiyem alé'—elemental.

Patel writes about this song in her novel, written by Charlesia and her group for a fellow musician who has died, a tambourier, Wiyem. So this instrument is the song's heartbeat.

Testimony and fiction
Do you remember watching *Chagos ou la mémoire des îles* with Heather and Morgan at Cove Park? Charlesia Alexis is one of the members of the Chagos Refugee Group who come to London in 2003 to testify in the High Court. But I have since discovered that for complex funding reasons Michel Daëron made another film covering that same period, *Il était une île, Diego Garcia*, focusing on this court case.

After the judge rules against the Chagos Refugee Group members there's a scene in their b'n'b in London where they read out reports of the case from the papers. Some of these reports highlight derogatory remarks made by Judge Ouseley about Charlesia Alexis, who is then seen blaming herself for the outcome of the case. I went and found Judge Ouseley's 300-page summary online. He's highly critical of the credibility of the

Chagossian witnesses, but is particularly contemptuous of Charlesia Alexis, accusing her of lying.

In the film the Chagossians' lawyer Robin Mardemootoo says:

Amongst the archives in London we found many things we didn't know existed. Because around 1997-98, certain documents were declassified, came into the public domain and became available to anyone. Hence the wonderful exchange—today I can say 'wonderful'—between the British Minister of Foreign Affairs and the American Minister of Foreign Affairs where the American writes: 'Nowadays, with all the independence debates taking place in the United Nations, it must remain secret. We must create a fiction that lets it be known that these islands were always uninhabited.'

Three weeks later, the British replies: 'I would go further, not only must we create a fiction, but we must maintain that fiction. We must engage a political plan to this end.'

Point of view
In Patel's book, it's from the POV of Charlesia Alexis that the story of the forced displacement is introduced. Charlesia Alexis was one of the Chagossian people who went to Mauritius on routine business (medical care for her husband) and was suddenly prevented from returning—told *Zil inn fermé*. How can you close an island? Like a factory shut down.

Charlesia Alexis returns to the docks again and again to ask about her passage home and is always turned away. 6 years later in 1973 she is once again on the docks when she sees the *Nordvaer*. The passengers are being escorted off by soldiers, among them a woman she recognizes from home. That is when she realizes that she will never be able to return.

How Patel tells the story through the specific perspectives of the individuals she writes about but also, how she allows these individuals to *see* one another. In Charlesia seeing Raymonde come off the boat, in Désiré seeing Charlesia at the port, there is an affirmation of Charlesia, Raymond and Désiré's recognition of one another as people from the same community who understand one another's experiences as only *they* can, a move by Patel that at once acknowledges her power as the story's writer to *mediate* this story, but at the same time, *refuses this power*, giving it up to the people she's writing about. *With.*

Boat
An incredible section which could only happen in a novel.

It features Désiré, nicknamed Nordvaer since he is born on the ship that has taken the last of the Chagossians still living on the islands into their forced exile.

Because of his birth at sea and the way the registration is fucked up by careless administrators, he lacks valid ID papers.

Désiré ne savait plus où il en était. Mauricien ? Il avait toujours vécu ici, mais n'en avait pas la nationalité. Seychellois ? Il n'avait jamais vu ce pays. Britannique ? On voudrait encore moins de lui là-bas. Chagossien ? Il ne connaissait pas ces îles ou il aurait dû voir le jour. Son lieu de naissance était un bateau, qui avait disparu.

In trying to sort out his identity papers he ends up writing to the national library of Norway, where the ship was originally in service. He receives some newspaper cuttings about the ship.

What follows is a trippy sequence, a dream, where the boat's 'life', and its role in the deracination, is imagined in close third person, which could also be read as Désiré's perspective, given the ambiguity of the ship's masculine gender (afterwards we read that: *Toute la nuit, ce bateau a parlé dans sa tête*).

The story of the dogs' extermination is recounted as something the boat 'hears' one of the passengers confessing. The boat 'witnesses' the suffering of the Chagossians, and is haunted by it:

Ils resonnent en lui, les cris silencieux que ces hommes et ces femmes ont étouffés au fond de leur gorge, tellement fort qu'ils ont coulés de leurs yeux en longues trainées salées.
C'est ce jour-là qu'il a commencé à rouiller de l'intérieur.

They resounded in [it/him?], the silent screams those men and women had stifled deep in their throats, so powerful these had leaked from their eyes in long, salty streaks.
It was on that day that [he/it] had begun to rust from the inside.

The ship, an object, shows more feeling—more *empathy*—than the 'humans' who executed this deracination.

In a beautiful review of the book, the writer Ariel Saramandi tells us that Patel first wrote about Chagos as a journalist, 'but she always felt like it wasn't enough. "I wanted to give flesh and voice to their story, tell it from the inside."'

From the *inside*. So perhaps solidarity is to write from the *inside*. Back to prepositions again... Trinh T. Minh-ha, and '*speaking nearby*'. From an interview with Minh-ha: 'Nothing is given in the process of understanding the "social" of our daily lives. So every single work I come up with is yet another attempt to inscribe this constant flow from the inside out and outside in.'

NB 'nearby', not 'beside'. The difference between solidarity and empathy.

Concrete
Reading the book made me think of Diego, and of Daniel.

I thought of Diego when Désiré tries and fails to get a bank account so he can get paid for his 2 days' labour on a building site, the episode that leads to his trying to sort out his paperwork.

And I thought about Daniel when I read about Désiré's brutal experience on the construction site—

Tout ce gris refermait d'un coup sur lui. La tour, déjà haute, obstruait le ciel, le ferraille hérissait le béton froid, la poussière de ciment fardait indistinctement l'herbe rare et les chevaux des hommes. [...]

La poussière de ciment lui collait au corps, son acidité lui rongeait la peau. La grisaille asphyxiait ses muscles et sa volonté.

What Daniel wrote about the concrete dust of London:

Liquid concrete seeps through the synapses and it doesn't just make it hard to think—it hurts. Concrete is killing the planet, I read. Of course it is. What would be the smallest possible degree of concrete and would it fit in a brain cell. There's no doubt; my brains cells have toxins of all kinds in them, concrete dust too I'm sure. Can we at least form a community around this. Toxic Brain Anonymous, in which we can cry and look at pictures of each other as smiling children. Remind each other that there was a time when we were not really thinking all that clearly and it was ok.

In *Chagos ou la mémoire des îles* the pain of seeing the Chagossian elders setting foot on Diego Garcia for the first time since the expulsion, falling to their knees and kissing the ground—concrete.

In/visible
At the end of the book, after Charlesia has told Désiré the full story of the deracination, the struggle to return, and the story of life on Chagos before the British forced them to leave, Désiré asks Charlesia if it was really as wonderful in Chagos as everyone remembers. Charlesia tells him, *C'est comme ça dans notre souvenir. Et le souvenir, c'est tout ce qu'il nous reste.*

The book ends on a really beautiful formulation about remembrance.

You will be able to read it now, thanks to Jeffrey Zuckerman's translation. Or you could let me read it to you one day. I could translate it for you.

Patel's *book* is an act of remembrance.

I think that too of Clément Siatous' paintings.

Memory as resistance. Resisting erasure. I saw Clément Siatous in an interview online. He was being filmed painting. He said, in Mauritian Kreol, When I'm painting like this, I am *there*.

I go back to Daëron's film, to Rosmond Saminaden's question, why the deportation was *at night*. And the only possible answer he can find: so that the island would no longer be visible to the Chagossians. But this is what Clément Siatous does: *he makes the islands visible*.

But I haven't even reached Collen and Soobrayen yet. Tomorrow?

'Tomorrow'
In fact it's 2 days now, sorry.

I had to go to the commune to fetch my new residence/ID card, to allow me the right to stay.

To collect this you go to guichet 12 from 8–12pm. I went yesterday but forgot a particular piece of paper. So I had to go back again.

Souad and Dina have a parrot that matches their sofa, down to an exact match in colour/shape of the orange splodge on each cheek. Whenever they let it out of its cage, which they do every day, it likes to sit on the top of their fridge and nibble the edges of the important papers for appointments etc that Souad has attached there with magnets. The effect is quite artistic.

Learning to read Lindsey Collen
In the same way it took me a while to read *Le silence des Chagos*, it took me a while to learn how to read Lindsay Collen's writing. There was something I struggled to connect to it, an energy that disturbed me, but which I now find exhilarating. Writing as an intense kind of speaking. (Reading Mahasweta Devi helped.)

Mutiny
Collen's novel *Mutiny* features a Chagossian character, Mama Gracienne, although the story of the Chagossian exile is not centred in the novel, but connected to a wider narrative: the state's monopoly on violence.

It's set in 1998 in a jail cell of the women's maximum security prison on the main island of Mauritius, in the few days before a powerful cyclone is due to pass over the area. The narrator, Juna, is a computer expert imprisoned on the charge of 'allegation', a fiction. She shares a cell with the young Leila, banged up for causing an 'effusion of blood'—aka punching a policeman. They are joined by Mama Gracienne, a Chagossian elder, in for 'confession'—accused of murdering her daughter.

As they wait for the cyclone to hit, they swap stories of their 'crimes' and share recipes for the dishes they most crave— (including *bred sonz*, my mother's favourite) and Juna lets them in on a secret: her plans to circumvent the prison's computerized locking systems and release all the imprisoned women, a plan that the approaching cyclone will make possible.

The narrative is punctuated by Juna's transcriptions of pointed legal definitions copied out from books in the prison library e.g. the definition of the state of Mauritius (from the Constitution of Mauritius Act), encompassing among other territories the Chagos Archipelago, including Diego Garcia.

Struggle / pronouns
The book is being written by Juna; there is a focus on the labour of her writing, her struggle to obtain materials. The book honours storytelling and writing as acts of resistance.

But what I am intrigued by, in connection with Collen's representation of a member of the Chagossian community, is her use of pronouns.

Collen has organized the narrative in sections named for pronouns e.g. 'We, us' (the three of them), 'She, her' (the story of young Leila), 'You in the plural' (the story of a nascent political party told by Juna), 'I/me' (Juna's story) and 'They/them' (the guards, or 'Blue Ladies'). Throughout, Mama Gracienne is addressed directly, as 'you': her introduction into the story is presented in the section 'You in the singular'.

As though this whole structuring device was about this 'you'; created to support it.

This 'you' feels like an acknowledgement, an honouring.

Lindsey Collen and Charlesia Alexis
Collen, a white South African woman, is writing from the POV of a woman of colour, a character apparently based on her friend also named Juna, a trade union activist who was wrongfully arrested on this same specious charge of 'allegation'.

I find it interesting to consider Collen's position in relation to the essay by Claudia Rankine and Beth Loffreda, 'On Whiteness and The Racial Imaginary: Where writers go wrong in imagining the lives of others'. Have you read it?

Arguments refuting cultural appropriation in Anglophone litfic seem to centre around the writer's right to have unimpeded extractive rights to the world's narrative resources.

Bur Collen's project feels the opposite of extractive.

Her linguistic situation is interesting: the dominant language of literature in Mauritius is French; the language in which Shenaz Patel, Ananda Devi, Nathacha Appanah, Barlen Pyamootoo write.

Collen is one of Mauritius' few Anglophone writers of literature.

Collen is a lifelong activist, involved in the anti-apartheid struggle and has lived for most of her adult life in Mauritius, a founder member of the radical leftwing political party Lalit. In the acknowledgements for *Mutiny* she writes:

> 'For sharing an arrest and a trial in Port Louis in 1981 with me, thanks to my seven co-accused, all women from Diego Garcia, the Chagos Islands and Mauritius Main Island; and to our lawyer Kader Bhayat.'

I wanted to know more about the trial. I looked online and found that one of the women who was tried with Collen—for protesting about the deportation, and in support of Chagossian women on hunger strike—was Charlesia Alexis.

I read more about these protests in 'Charlesia Alexis: The Struggle of the Chagossian Women', an article by Laura Jeffery:

> "We were just women; there were no men at all in those days," Charlesia mentions. Why not? "When we did demonstrations, the police beat the men … so we decided to use a majority of women and a minority of men." The Chagossians' struggle was also supported by Mauritian members of the radical Women's Liberation Movement, who joined in the demonstrations. "The government doesn't care about us," the protesters chanted, "Send us back to Diego Garcia!".

That chant in Kreol is *Rann nu Diego* which also means: *Give us back Diego Garcia*. In other words, the Chagos Islands.

Here are some sentences I copied from *Mutiny*:

The same state that can bomb a market place can arrest a drunk beggar in another market place for disturbing the peace.

In sizing up furniture as potential weapons:

legs can be arms.

Also:

the beauty of the story is in the listener.

She looks unbelieving. Disbelieving. Can I blame her? I can hardly believe it myself. That's what the state does to us. Puts us in a state of disbelief.

What is it to read fiction but to willingly suspend disbelief?

That is what the UK and US governments wanted the world to do, with the fiction that they created.

There's an irrepressible spirit of political joy in the writing of Collen's that I have read so far.

She refutes Kafka's formulation, the one Daniel wrote back to so bleakly:

there is hope, but not for us.

Collen's writing makes me believe there *is* hope, for all those who despair.

I note that *Mutiny* is dedicated to the memory of her brother John (1952–1975).

Saradha Soobrayen

Finally, an amazing text by the British Mauritian poet, Saradha Soobrayen, 'Out of place, out of language, out of home: Fifteen pieces of poetic inquiry'. In these 15 verses Soobrayen gives an account of her experiences as poet in 'non' residence on the AHRC funded project CHAGOS: Cultural Heritage Across Generations.

I love how Saradha Soobrayen makes visible in the poem the institutional framework of this project, staging the difficulties she experiences in trying to think through her poetic enquiry (and testimony). And how she shares her personal reflections on the complexity of this experience for her, how her time with the Chagossian community touches upon her own experience of diaspora.

What I loved most: some lines I have copied out from Saradha Soobrayen's work:

Having lacked the sinew and muscle for an essay

She writes:

I have struggled to find a form that stays afloat, only to find my hands bloody with the guts of poetry and a Chagossian woman's lament, 'not another book'. (from *ii*)

And:

I learned about sagren, the Chagos Islanders dying of sadness from the film Stealing a Nation *(Pilger 2004). I rejected both of my governments. I was appalled and riddled with guilt, complacency and a wish for another poet to respond.* (from *vii*)

Also:

At the 2016 launch of 'Kayo Chingonyi: A Creative/Critical Residency on Migration', I read a short poem on the long poem as a space for marginalized voices: '[a] poem can buckle under that kind of expectation to represent or speak for another, there needs to be self-doubt, writing with a sense of failure' (Soobrayen 2015a). I find myself questioning the ambition of such a poem while no one with a marginalized voice was present at this event or writing poetry, and why would they be? The Chagossians were writing letters to the UK Home Office, requesting visas for the children and family left in Seychelles and Mauritius.
(the whole of *viii*)

But most of all, this:

As a child, I could trace around the shape of Mauritius from a keyring, the souvenirs, a small blue photo album with a few out-lines of the nine districts. As a British child I didn't completely understand the Kreol spoken aloud and I did not understand how much it would matter. (from *xiii*)

I want to read more of Saradha Soobrayen's work.

Judge Gaja's Question

Did you notice the subject heading of my email? Did you get the reference? Lord Gaja's question. That was the one question asked by any of the 13 international court of justice judges in relation to the advisory opinion requested by Mauritius, about its partial decolonization by Britain, which hived off the Chagos Islands before granting independence.

Judge Gaja's question has been tugging at me while I've been thinking about these texts:

'In the process of decolonization relating to the Chagos Archipelago, what is the relevance of the will of the population of Chagossian origin?'

I come back to Charlesia Alexis's album. To Clément Siatous' art. I guess I am wondering why you and I felt—I still feel—so compelled to engage with this story as writers.

How as a writer do you tell a story that needs to be shared, if it is not *your* story?

I meet people all the time, people from the UK or the US who are otherwise well informed and politically engaged who've never heard about Chagos or the Chagossians or what the UK and US governments did to them in the name of 'freedom'; what they continue to subject the Chagossian people to. How the Chagossian people are resisting. But are asking for support, solidarity.

I went to an online conferencce organised by Chagossian Voices, a platform for the global Chagossian diaspora. One of the organisers, Frankie Bontemps, spoke of the issues facing Chagossians in the UK today: the struggle and huge costs to secure British citizenship for younger members of Chagossian families excluded from the legal ruling on this. The struggle for Chagossian groups to secure any of the £40 million fund supposedly allocated to the Chagossian community in the UK.

At the webinar I saw blank squares with names I didn't recognise and wondered if one of them might be Diego.

Sometimes I think about the thing Diego wrote in his notebook. *Some poems are not for you.*

I thought perhaps you might like to write this essay with me?

writing with a sense of failure: I cherish these words of Saradha Soobrayen's.

Cake
I had Souad and Dina up here for tea and cake the other afternoon: I thought it might be nice for Souad to eat some cakes she hadn't made, for once. I found a recipe for napolitaines online: those little pink sugary cakes you get in Mauritius.

In Saradha Soobrayen's poem she writes about learning to make a Chagossian coconut cake called matouftwa, a sweet coconut cake: *I will choke you.*

D. x

To: Damaris Caleemootoo
From: Oliver Pablo Herzberg
Subject: Re: Judge Gaja's question
(Notes for an essay: On a literature of solidarity)
Attachment: Debt
Date: 13 January 2021

dearest Dam

I have loved your letters. Thank you for writing.

The ideas for your essay—yes!

And Public Writer. Beautiful.

As for everything else, all that's passed. It would be easier to tell
you these things in person. But since I'm in London and you're
in Brussels we must make do with what we have. Like we always
did. What we had wasn't much, although it was something, we
were good like that. I've been trying to write about it. I've
attached it. I don't know what else to tell you except maybe how
I came to write it at all—the first real writing I have done since
before we left London.

That day on Arthur's Seat, when I read your story about
Diego/Daniel—I watched you getting smaller and smaller as
you made your way down the hill, half-knowing you'd not come
back. I had the feeling I was made of glass. Finally it got too
cold to wait so I went home and you weren't there. Do you
remember the sketch I made that day? At the museum—
inspired by the atom smasher. I recently found it, tucked
between the pages of *Island of Shame* by David Vine. I had
picked it up to reread for reasons I will tell you. A bookmark for

a work that marked me in ways I'm only now starting to understand. You too, I know. Looking at my sketch and all its crazy elements I haven't the faintest idea what I was trying to communicate. You came back home that night but things were changing fast between us. Was it that same week we lost the flat?

After that, I moved to different places, looking for somewhere to live that *wasn't* London. In the end there was nowhere else to go. Right now I'm in Daniel's old place. Remember Nora? Her huge paws? Her velvet snout? She's still here. Ula had a kid so Nora started coming to me. She's here now, sleeping. We're inseparable.

We watched the ICJ hearing together, Nora and I. I had it streaming on my phone for the entire week. When the vote came in 116-6 requiring the UK complete the decolonization of Mauritius and get the fuck out of Chagos, me and Nora celebrated with a walk around East London, all night nearly. When the UK refused to comply, surprising no one, I felt something like rage. I let it boil inside me for a few days. Nora and I continued our night-time walks, sniffing at abandoned bikes along the canal, tiptoeing around the tents on the eastern side of Victoria Park—more and more of these. As we walked, the feeling of rage started to change. It was no longer totally wrapped in sadness, it became something that made me want to question or do I mean search for an answer.

I thought about our time in Edinburgh, about what fools we were but also what a beautiful, sad time it was. I thought about Diego and hoped he was OK. I looked at my notes on Diego Garcia, re-read *Island of Shame*. What Fred Moten says about his ambitions for *Who Touched Me?*:

The book that took place. The book that happened, and was gone, like a rocket stage, a kicked-away ladder.

Well when I read *Island of Shame* it was like that for me, and when I reread it too. I didn't just absorb the information, though I felt shaken all over again by the hard facts, the testimonies. This time I read it as a call to action, David Vine himself responding to the call, the call of the Chagossians. Rita Bancoult:

do not make the mistake of thinking that we are a harmless bunch. We may not have education and arms, but we have our faith in God and the will to fight injustice.

There is nothing else to do but join the fight, as David Vine says.

(Damn, Dam, I need more blue paper)

Several times I tried to write about our time in Edinburgh, about meeting Diego mostly. Whenever I opened my computer to do so I got that sensation of being made of glass again, a feeling of being completely invisible. I stopped writing. I read some more. Then I went on a protest to Yarl's Wood detention centre. That was two days ago. I still have the taste of smoke in my mouth. You know, D., *this* is what I wanted to write to you about, I see now.

The afternoon was dark, was misting over as we gathered in a car park near London Bridge. I had already boarded the bus that would take us past Bedford and on to Yarl's Wood when I saw, walking towards us through the mist, banners and luminous vests, megaphones, a sound system, torches. Organizers from Movement For Justice By Any Means Necessary. It looked like a science fiction film. They boarded the bus and spoke to us.

We were to arrive at Yarl's Wood, walk the perimeter of the barbed wire fence, playing loud music so the women inside could hear our approach, we'd come to a stop at the back of the building, gathering where the women could see us from their bedroom windows.

I had gone with friends from Akwaaba, a social centre for refugees I've become part of. I was involved in a bike project there, fixing them up etc., and then we started a storytelling group. Until lockdown we were meeting every Sunday in a dilapidated primary school in Dalston where we wrote and read together, sometimes we recorded conversations, interviews, and then we transcribed the recordings, editing them together afterwards, preparing for something whose form no one quite yet knows.

On the bus, which was moving at last, I felt kind of drugged. I hadn't really slept for the past couple of nights. I heard my name being called from the back. There was Amy, part of the Akwaaba storytelling group. She was wearing a hi-vis vest and carried a megaphone and she was beckoning me to sit beside her. In 2015 she had been detained in Yarl's Wood for a month and a half and it was there, she'd told us, she'd lost all her teeth. We had become friends and used to meet at least once a week in the Dalston Library, where we would write to her solicitor about her asylum case or try to collate her medical records or find photos of her kissing girlfriends to include in her file, all the time redrafting her asylum statement on my laptop.

The bus ride went smoothly. I felt cold at first, but as we left the city and drove past parched fields and empty truck stops, the temperature rose and I had to take off my coat and jumper and open the window. I watched the landscape until it became too monotonous then I started reading *Island of Shame* instead. When we pulled up at the roadside there was no sign of Yarl's Wood so we waited. More buses arrived. There were speeches. People painting banners. Amy opened a foil package and gave me a dumpling that was incredibly delicious. This is war she said, and we set off on the fifteen-minute walk to Yarl's Wood.

I will tell you in full sometime about the protest. How we stayed into the night banging pans with wooden spoons, kicking at the fence, fixing yellow flowers into the wires. How we talked to the women inside via mobiles hooked up to the PA. How they spoke of the abuse at the hands of the Serco staff and how badly detention was affecting their mental health, especially those who were locked away from their kids. How when we shouted, *We can hear you! What do you want to say?* they responded: *Freedom.* How later the drumming started up again, how there was dancing, singing, how we shouted, absurdly, obscenities at the Home Office, and messages of hope to the women inside. As we left the perimeter fence to head back to where the buses were parked we lit flares.

On the bus Amy and I sat in silence. The white lines of the motorway, bright in the headlights, rose up before us and my eyelids started dropping. From the window I saw or sensed fields, trees, powerlines appearing out of the darkness. I became cold again and wrapped myself in my jacket. I fell asleep for a while. When I woke up the bus was stopped at some traffic lights. I looked across at Amy, who seemed very tired, her eyes heavy, empty, staring far off into the lines of cars. Someone shouted for music and the driver turned on the radio and now dance music blended with the noises of people chatting. Amy picked up *Island of Shame* and opened it at the first page. Is it good, my dear? she asked. I started telling her about the book but I felt nauseous and trailed off. I feel strange I said. Like glass. I didn't say the bit about glass, I only thought it.

It took us exactly 40 minutes to walk from London Bridge to the squat. I didn't know this until Amy told me later, I don't know how she knew, since the whole way we were chatting, or rather Amy was talking. She said that when she was in Yarl's Wood she fought hard and made a lot of trouble for the guards, because that was the only way she would not be deported. She told the guards she'd rather die in Yarl's Wood than go back to her country. Look at me she'd said to the guards, I am half dead anyway, so let me finish dying, bury me here and you don't have to waste the plane ticket. Then she hit her head against the wall. I passed through a lot, my dear, she told me, My heart is very strong. They brought a guard in, he was Spanish, and she said something that made him run out. They brought in a Caribbean guard, a tall man and I told him that he was just an immigrant like me. You fought to do this rubbish job? Leave it for the English people. That one went back, she told me. I was so tough and very aggressive because it is war. She told them that they wouldn't get her on a plane. She told them that the only person she would respect is a dog. Bring a guide dog she said. If a guide dog tells me, 'Enter the plane now,' I will go. But not a human being. She told me that after that they started beating her like never before. Very big men holding her. That's why being fat sometimes is good she told me, because they couldn't lift me easily. Every time they tried to put her on a flight, they returned her to Yarl's Wood because the blood was too much.

We stopped at the squat and I went in and collected Nora and we carried on walking and talking. A lot of the girls were not like me, Amy told me. They were very quiet. I met one girl at the migrant centre. She couldn't speak English very well. She had a very sad story. She had come to the UK as a teenager with her mother and younger brothers and while her mother worked as a cleaner she looked after her brothers. She was fighting to stay with her family in the UK but after four years she was arrested and taken to Yarl's Wood and she was deported but not to where her family was from. She was from Chagos, my dear.

Yesterday Amy sent me a message. A photo of her Facebook page but I don't have Facebook. She had posted this quote:

> The coalition emerges out of your recognition that it's fucked up for you, in the same way that we've already recognized that it's fucked up for us. I don't need your help. I just need you to recognize that this shit is killing you, too, however much more softly, you stupid motherfucker, you know?
> —Fred Moten.

The following day I sat down and wrote the story I've enclosed with this letter. It came out in a wave. I haven't looked at it since (I want you to read it raw and unprocessed because our time in Edinburgh was just like that).

Xx O.

To: Oliver Pablo Herzberg
From: Damaris Caleemootoo
Subject: *Il était une île, Diego Garcia / AUKUS*
Date: 3 November 2021

Dearest O.

Thank you for the story.

I haven't read it yet because I didn't want to. Not straight away.

Not after the *letter* you wrote me. This letter is incredible to me!

Who you are in it.

That you're *in* it.

I see now it was never *Diego* who disappeared—he just left our sight, left his bags behind, reappeared somewhere else. It was never about *our* point of view, in the end.

It was you who disappeared—it began the moment Daniel died.

But in your letter, I see you reappearing. Your story, I will read tonight.

So much I want to ask. Could we call sometime…?

Meanwhile, all is well at Rue d'Angleterre, 11.

Souad and Dina have started a 'garden' in the tiny yard that gets no light. It's all in pots. I went with them the other day to the nice nursery co-op up the road. They persuaded me to get something. So I too have been trying to grow something, out on my bit of flat roof. Honeysuckle.

I still love my job in Rotterdam, my colleagues, the students.

Last time I was in the Netherlands an artist told me that the Zapatistas were in town. That she had been to a 5-hour meeting with representatives of the community who had sailed over to Europe in May, and were travelling, meeting with organizations to share their knowledge and get support. I did not know this. Did you? Chiapas and Chagos. It's Chagos Day today, did you know?

It's always a shock when the train pulls into Brussels Midi from the Netherlands. The crumbling cement, the dirt, the careless-ness, the disrepair. The people who are sleeping—living—within and around the building. It hits you.

Travelling the other way I'm struck by an orderliness I once found desirable and now find oppressive as I get used to Brussels. Walking around NL you are aware how it became world-leading in the establishment of mercantile capitalism. There is a reckoning now with the so-called 'Golden Age' and the primitive extraction and murder that funded this.

And wandering around Brussels you cannot forget that a former King set up a personal colony in Congo with a regime so unde-niably genocidal that his fellow colonizers were aghast (*everyone will notice*), and forced him to cede direct control over to the state—whose bourgeoisie sought to screen/embellish the horror with art nouveau.

In the park is an empty plinth where a bust of him has been removed. It is a haunting work.

In the road leading up to this park is a strip of land where there is a medicinal garden. It was set up and is maintained by volunteers. Souad takes Dina up there.

There's a flight of steps leading up to this park. At the top, turning back, you get a majestic view of Brussels, directly facing the Palais de Justice. Once I saw two police on horses taking a selfie here, trying to get the Palais de Justice in the background.

+++++

In your letter you mention your interviewing project with Akwaaba. I'm more and more intrigued by this form—of the interview, of the conversation.

Earlier this year I went to Utrecht to see the Kader Attia show, *Fragments of Repair*.

Some of the works I recognized from *The Museum of Emotion*, where we went the day Daniel died. But here the emphasis was on film works, not objects. And since most of the films were interviews, conversations with others, this exhibition felt less *authored* somehow. The central work—physically too, in terms of its location in the space—was *Reason's Oxymorons*, a video installation comprising 18 'chapters': a series of interviews with psychiatrists, healers, storytellers, poets, ethnologists etc., many with migrant backgrounds, people whose life's work is dedicated to the kinds of cultural concepts of 'repair' to which Attia himself is committed. I found myself searching the works for references to sagren.

And it was the interviews that struck me most in Michel Daëron's films. I watched *Il était une île, Diego Garcia* again the other day, after reading about the announcement of AUKUS. It doesn't fucking *end* does it??

Some of the scenes in *Il était une île* are amazing. E.g. some footage shot by Olivier Bancoult on a handheld digicam. It's from the 'heritage trip' on the visit to Diego Garcia. Olivier Bancoult is filming from a boat as the island comes into view. Then his camera zooms in to the base; the footage has the feel of being clandestinely filmed (everyone on the base just going about their business, unaware of being filmed). I *felt* it: the vastness of this military operation, the whole machinery behind it. When the passengers disembark, two Chagossian men in the pilgrims' white T-shirts kneel down alongside one another on the concrete of the harbour, while base personnel look on. The men kneeling are side-on to the camera. They bend to kiss the ground. The man furthest away breaks down, crying as he declares his return to the island of his birth, where his umbilical cord is buried. The other man is composed. His face in profile shows no emotion. Still kneeling, he turns his head to find the camera, glances into it. Then turns back to look straight ahead. He begins to speak: slowly and deliberately, the pause between each phrase incredible, as though he's leading a prayer, listening to a silent repetition of his words:

Later:
mo mama
mo granmere
mo granpere
mo bann aryer anset

Then he gets up off his knees, walks off, his back to the camera. In Kreol, *Later* means 'land'.

I have since learnt that the man who makes this declaration is Fernand Mandarin, leader of the Comité social chagossien in Mauritius, who died in October 2016. He wrote a book *Retour aux Chagos!* about the history and culture of Chagos, his recollections of life there, and his people's struggle to return. He wrote it with Emmanuel Richon, curator at the Blue Penny Museum in Mauritius, where the two had worked together on an exhibition. It was published a few months before Fernand Mandarin died. I'm trying to get hold of a copy.

The man kneeling beside Fernand Mandarin in the film, I am still trying to identify.

Then there's this scene with Charlesia Alexis right at the end. She's come back from Crawley to Mauritius. Her son has died. She sits on the steps of her family home, surrounded by her grandchildren. It's such a beautiful shot. She talks in Mauritian Kreol, the subtitles say:

I can't explain his loss of life to you. I wasn't here. I don't know why he did what he did. All I can say is that despair probably got the better of him. Last month, when I was in England, I heard that five Chagossians had died. Now, with my son it makes six. Nothing comes of it. My son is dead, my brother is dead. I keep thinking if we were on Diego they would not have lost their lives.

I thought of Daniel. And I think now about the document of the Committee Fraternelle, the organisation that Charlesia Alexis was a key member of, who *refused* the official individuation of deaths of despair caused by the forced exile; who ascribed *unequivocally* a unifying cause of each of these deaths: sagren. A *political* cause. Because who caused this sagren? The British government. The British Government caused these deaths same as they did Paulette Wilson's, and all those of the Windrush generation whose deaths were brought on by the stress and fear of trying to reclaim the identities stolen by what they believed to be their government.

I want to write about the work of Clément Siatous. His painting of the *Mauritius Trochetia* and the pilgrimage of 2006. He said in an interview that this painting is called *Pep derasine*. A deracinated people.

Now I'm going to read your story.

++++++++++

I just read it.

Then I reread it.

Though I almost couldn't bear to. It's beautiful.

Though so strange to find myself written *about* in this way. I feel I want to add to it. Add my voice.

I was hoping you might come to see me in Brussels.

That when you get here, we could figure out together what to write next.

D.x

Sources

Origins of long quotations used, in order of appearance.

Dambudzo Marechera, *The House of Hunger* (1978).

Theodor W. Adorno, *Minima Moralia*, translated by E. F. N. Jephcott (2005).

Marie Cuillerai and Maria Kakogianni, 'Greek money and the "new idea" of Europe', *Radical Philosophy* 186 (2014).

David Fairhall, 'Indian Ocean island of Gan returned to Maldives', *Guardian* (2015).

Fred Moten, *Black and Blur* (2017).

UK Chagos Support Association: https://www.chagossupport.org.uk/

Silvia Federici, *Caliban and the Witch* (2004).

David Vine, *Island of Shame* (2009).

Rita Bancoult, 'An Open Letter to the British High Commissioner in Mauritius' (2011).

Stewart Motha, *Archiving Sovereignty* (2018).

Voices of Emergency, edited by John Oliver Perry (1983).

Colin Harris, *The Fuzzbuzz* (1994).

Sun Ra and His Arkestra, 'Nuke', *Nuclear War* (1984).

Walter Benjamin, 'Theses on the Philosophy of History', *Illuminations*, translated by Harry Zohn (1968): slightly altered.

Arthur Jafa, *Dreams Are Colder Than Death* (2014).

Michel Daëron, *Chagos ou la mémoire des îles*, Vagabond Films, MBC, SBC, France Télévisions, Filao Films (2010).

Satoshi Nakamoto, bitcointalk.org (2009).

Eve Tuck and C. Ree, 'A Glossary of Haunting', *Handbook of Auto-ethnography* (2016).

'Troops warned eating at Greggs makes them "look unprofessional"', *The Telegraph* (2018): slightly altered.

James Mortensen and Samuel Bashfield, 'The Diego Garcia dispute hits cyberspace', *The Interpreter* (2021).

Big Joanie, *Sistahs* (2018).

Tristan Wibault, *The Universal Embassy* (2003).

Audre Lorde, 'Poetry Is Not a Luxury', *Sister Outsider* (2007).

Bhanu Kapil, *Ban en Banlieue* (2020).

Fernand Deligny, *The Arachnean and Other Texts*, translated by Drew S. Burk and Catherine Porter (2015).

Olivier Magis, *Another Paradise*, Clin d'œil films (2019).

Shenaz Patel, *Le silence des Chagos* (2005).

Laura Jeffery, 'Charlesia Alexis: The Struggle of the Chagossian Women', *Eviction from the Chagos Islands, Displacement and Struggle for Identity Against Two World Powers*, ed. Sandra J.T.M. Evers and Marry Kooy (2011).

Lindsey Collen, *Mutiny* (2002).

Saradha Soobrayen, 'Out of place, out of language, out of home', *Crossings Journal of Migration and Culture* 10 (2019).

Stefano Harney and Fred Moten, *The Undercommons* (2013).

Michel Daëron, *Il était une île, Diego Garcia*, Vagabond Films, MBC, SBC, France Télévisions, Filao Films (2010).

Acknowledgments

Our deep appreciation, respect and thanks to Chris Kraus and Jacques Testard for their early interest in the book, and for the encouragement and conversations as we wrote it. We acknowledge here also the great influence of Chris Kraus's own writing on ours.

Our thanks to Hedi El Kholti for his sensitive reading of our work, and for his tremendous patience.

Thanks also to Clare Bogen at Fitzcarraldo and Juliana Halpert at Semiotext(e).

Our collaboration on this novel began in 2011 and was completed in 2021. Throughout we have had many conversations with people who helped us to think through our project, which is ongoing.

We thank Sabrina Jean, chairperson of the Chagos Refugees Group UK, and the artist Clément Siatous for their time and conversations about the forms of their activism.

We also acknowledge other members of the Chagossian community in exile, Serge Aristide, Rita Bancoult, Lucette Azemia, Mimose Furcy, Annessie Jaffar, Raphaël Louis, Rosemond Saminaden as well as Charlesia Alexis and Fernand Mandarin who have since passed away, whose powerful testimonies (along with Robin Mardemootoo's in his capacity as legal advisor), we quote from in this book.

We thank Remmie Najjuma for sharing her story with us.

Thank you to Olivier Bancoult for making time to meet in 2015 in Mauritius, and to Frankie Bontemps of Chagossian Voices for the invitation to attend the online Chagossian Voices conference, which helped us to learn more about the issues facing the Chagossian community in the UK today.

We thank Michel Daëron and Olivier Magis for their great generosity in sharing their inspiring work with us, and for their kind support for this project.

We thank Stefan Donnelly of the UK Chagos Support Association for the ongoing conversation.

We thank David Vine and Laura Jeffreys for their kind interest and help with research sources at the very beginning.

We thank Lindsey Collen, Shenaz Patel and Saradha Soobrayen for the guiding example of their work, and for our conversations around this.

In writing this book we have been inspired by the decolonial practices of Mai Abu El-Dahab, Taylor Le Melle, Olivier Marboeuf and Sara Sejin Chang, and we thank them for conversations that have happened along the way.

Thank you to Eve Dickson and Benjamin Morgan for your friendship and your inspirational approaches to activism and collaboration.

For their support, friendship, conversation, and their inspiring example of feminist community building around writing and art, special thanks to Kate Briggs, Daniella Cascella, Melissa Gordon and John Douglas Millar.

For the precious conversations around family, shared heritage and our work, Sophie Soobramanien.

For the stimulating conversations around writing and practice we thank our colleagues Marloes de Valk and Steve Rushton, and our students on the Lens-Based Media and Experimental Publishing Masters Programmes at PZI in Rotterdam.

Thanks to the following for their kind interest in the project, and for the wonderful conversations so far:

Castillo, Paul Becker, Gerry Bibby, Megan Bradbury, Brian Chikwava, Andrew Cowan, Bojana Cvejić, Chris Evans, Monica Gallab, Kevin Gallagher, Oscar Gaynor, Joseph Kusendila, Will Holder, Estelle Hoy, Sara De Bondt, Nadia Hebson, Juliet Jacques, Graham Kelly, Ghislaine Leung, Perri MacKenzie, David Musgrave, Robert McGill, Richard Misek, Francesco Pedraglio, Ariel Saramandi, Max Schaeffer, Reem Shilleh, Luke Skrebowski, Robin Vanbesien, Phoebe von Held, Yair Wallach, Eleanor Ivory Weber, Caroline Woodley and Nariman Youssef.

We thank our partners Lucy and Rob, and our daughters Iona and Iris, for their love, patience, and understanding.

Special thanks to Rob and his amazing mother, Agnes Dijkstra, for the kids' camping trips that gave us time to write, and to Natasha's sister Natalie and her husband Stan for their interest in the book, and the childcare. We also thank Amelie, Laurie and Elijah for being such great fun, and helping to keep Iona and Iris company.

We thank Heleen Eijkman and Virginia Wright and Georgie and Marie-Claire and Isabelle Soobramanien for being keen to read, and Arlette Ta-Min for her much appreciated support and thoughtfulness. We thank Gom for being Gom.

We thank Natasha's parents Lina and Dédé for their kind support for the book, through their generosity with their stories and with the beautiful care and food that helped to sustain our writing.

We thank Luke's mum Hilery for her patience, kindness and unceasing support for the book. We thank Luke's sister Thea for the trips away with Iona giving us precious writing time. We thank Luke's dad Martin for his enthusiasm and, together with Wendy Dover, the wonderful writing time in Perthshire.

Finally, we would like to acknowledge Daniel in our story as Luke's brother Saul, who in fact died in 2019. We had been working on the book for a few years by then, with Saul as an active reader: our conversations with Saul were an influence on this project right from the start.

We would also like to acknowledge those others who loved Saul and are absent from our fiction, though they were there for Saul in life: Megan Barker, Maria Fernanda Calderón, Ewa Podolska and his friends at Goldsmiths.

* * *

Early chapters appeared in draft form in these publications, and with kind thanks to these editors:

(2021) 'نساء عليون', translated into Arabic by Nariman Youssef, Mophradat: Mai Abu ElDahab
(2021) 'Outside', *Triple Canopy* 21: Maya Binyam
(2018), 'Enn Gramaten', *Dialetcy* Bookworks and Common Guild: Maria Fusco
(2018) 'Emergency', *Animal Shelter* 5: Hedi El Kholti and Chris Kraus
(2017) 'G.', Starship 16: Gerry Bibby
(2016) The Swedish café. *EROS* 7: Sami Jallili
(2016) 'Individualism', *BOMB Magazine* 134: Mónica de la Torre
(2014) 'Debt', *The White Review* 12: Ben Eastman and Jacques Testard

With special thanks to Maya Binyam at Triple Canopy and Mónica de la Torre at BOMB for their particularly thoughtful, sensitive and rigorous edits and the stimulating conversations around this.

Additional thanks to Big Joanie and Eva Prinz, and also to Anna Webber and Seren Adams at United Agents for all their help.

Natasha Soobramanien, British-Mauritian, and Luke Williams, Scottish, are the authors of *Genie and Paul* (Myriad Editions, 2012) and *The Echo Chamber* (Hamish Hamilton, 2011), respectively. They used to live in Edinburgh but Natasha now lives in Brussels and Luke in Cove.